THE HENCHMAN TRAINING ACADEMY 3: EXTRACTION

L.K. URBAN

The Henchman Training Academy 3: Extraction

Copyright © 2022 by L.K. Urban

EBook ISBN: 979-8-9874402-0-9
Trade Paperback ISBN: 979-8-9874402-1-6

Edited by Kailey Urbaniak
Cover design by Angela Stevens

Published by WIP Publications LLC
Colorado Springs, CO 80907

WIP Publications eBook Edition 2022
WIP Publications Trade Paperback Edition 2022
Printed in the USA

Get your writing in progress: wippublications.com

CONTENTS

CHAPTER 1
FIRST CLASS

Rossi's private jet was a reflection of himself, first class in every detail. Rows of oversized black leather chairs filled the cabin, and highly polished chrome sparkled in the bright sunlight. The flight crew looked as though they had stepped out of *Italian Vogue*, all with matching well-tailored navy suits, ruby-red neck scarfs, black stilettos, and impeccable hair and make-up. This aircraft was larger than Fowler's, which blew Matt away. *This is fucking incredible.* Matt shook his head in disbelief because one, he had been kidnapped—yet again—and two, because if anyone was going to be kidnapped, this was one hundred percent the way to go—in this magnificent private jet on his way to an incredible Italian villa.

At least, he assumed that was where they were headed. Rossi and his team of Henchmen had only spoken Italian since they'd taken off. Matt's phone had been taken from him as quickly and gracefully as they had thrown him into the Range Rover outside of Pinky's. It had all gone down so quickly. Matt couldn't help but wonder what he could have done differently. Would a class at the HTA on *How Not to be Kidnapped* have helped? Maybe just being more aware of his surroundings was more like it.

Months ago, when the OT's Henchmen-for-hire had tried to kidnap or kill him in almost the same spot, neither Matt, Franco, nor David H. had been paying attention to their surroundings. This time, Matt's guard had been down again. The OT, who until recently had been the only person Matt feared wanted to kidnap him, was no longer a threat, and he just wasn't expecting this at all.

Matt knew Pinky had security cameras in the parking lot. Christ, he had helped install the newest version of digital security cameras just a few weeks prior. If by some small chance she hadn't seen him being thrown into Rossi's black Range Rover, Liz would figure something was hinky when he didn't arrive back to the DMF House for his favorite meal. It was Tuesday, Taco Tuesday. Matt's appetite was legendary, and missing his favorite night of dinner would draw attention, he hoped. Fuck, the first time he had been allowed to drive alone, he got nabbed. Life had sure gotten strange since he started his Henchman career with DMF.

Matt couldn't argue with the comparison Rossi gave when he pointed out how polite and non-violently his Italian Henchman worked compared to the DMF Team. His Team's nickname was M&M, short for meat and muscle, for Christ's sake. The Italians were smooth and just about flawless in their job. No meat and muscle needed. It was as if they set the tone for the rest of the kidnapping experience. He wondered if they were ever going to just kick the shit out of him for no reason like the last idiots who'd kidnapped him did. Was this suave, chill vibe to throw him off so he got comfortable and let his guard down? Was this a psychological game they were playing? *I'm confused as fuck right now*, Matt almost said aloud.

Matt noticed that none of the Henchmen were on their phones watching Netflix or drinking Starbucks like the last two assholes who kidnapped him. Matt's previous kidnapping, orchestrated by the infamous OT, had been a huge debacle; it was messy, unplanned, and unprofessional. If it wasn't for Amber, he probably would be dead now. *Amber, fuck. I could use her and her world-class Henchman skills right now.*

Matt observed the Italian Henchman from across the aisle. Their presence intrigued him with how invisible they made themselves but how powerful their presence was at the same time. Instead of slurping a Frappuccino from a straw in a plastic cup, they were drinking hot tea out a porcelain cup and saucer, holding their pinky finger up while sipping their tea.

From what he could piece together, Rossi was pissed because of the creation of the HTA, the Henchman Training Academy, the project Matt had been working on for the last several months. Rossi hadn't looked at him or paid him attention since they'd gotten into the jet, but it was almost as if he didn't need to explain himself more than he already had.

It was hard for Matt to stay on hyper alert, to return to the familiar fight-or-flight state he had lived in for so many months, in these comfortable chairs. He obviously wasn't going anywhere for the next ten hours, or so, so Matt thought he may as well go with the flow and live a good life until the plane landed.

Matt's often predictable stomach was rumbling, telling him it was time to fill it. He could smell food being prepared, which tantalized his senses. The smells floating through the cabin made his mouth water. He could hardly wait to see what amazing Italian cuisine would be placed in front of him. He suddenly snapped back to thinking logically about this meal, and not thinking it through with his empty belly. Oh, shit. What if they didn't offer to feed him? That would totally suck to sit and watch the rest of the men eat, but he was a prisoner after all. His mind began to race and go on the defense. He wondered if they might try to put some type of drugs into his meal? Would they try to poison him? How would he be able to tell if the food was safe?

Matt started to sweat, legs bouncing up and down. His breaths were short and uneven, and he felt like he was going to throw up, all signs that he was about to go over the edge. He had learned how to successfully navigate a stage-five panic attack after spending over a year living in the DMF Henchman House. Matt purposefully slid back in his seat, gripping the armrests to help ground him. He slowly closed his eyes and took deep breaths through his nose, counting one, two, three, four, five, holding it, and releasing for the same one to five count.

Matt was startled back into reality as the blonde flight attendant bent to set a glass of water and red wine, both in crystal stemware, in front of the tray she had adjusted to the right level.

In an enticing British accent, she said, "Excuse me, sir, are you feeling well? You looked as though you may need some water. Is there anything else I can do for you?"

Matt's eyes darted to the Henchmen who were sitting like sleek marble statues, to Rossi who had his nose buried in a magazine, back to Vanessa, the flight attendant, as her silver name tag read. Despite being in the predicament he was in, he had noticed Vanessa as he boarded. She was what some of the guys on the Team called a *real head turner*. She stood no less than a foot shorter than Matt. Even in her tailored flight attendant uniform, anyone could see she was in great shape. Her well-developed legs were what gave that away. Her short blonde bob framed her heart-shaped face, and the navy fabric of her uniform complimented her blue eyes.

"No. I'm fine, thank you. The water is perfect, Vanessa."

"Right then, sir. Please let me know if there is anything I

can do to make your flight more comfortable. Dinner will be served momentarily." She smiled sweetly.

She must not know what the situation is, Matt thought. *Or did she? Get a grip! You need to think as clearly as possible, being paranoid about everything won't help a bit.*

"No need to worry and have stress, just enjoy the ride," Rossi said from across the aisle.

"I plan on it. I'm certain my time with you will be short. Jimmie will have a team here waiting for you once we land. I can't wait to say I told you so," Matt said.

"Oh, my friend, we will see. I have been in contact with Jimmie. I asked him for permission to have you escort me back to my villa. He let me borrow you, I think that is what he said. No, it wasn't borrow, it was lend. Yes, he agreed to lend your services to me.

Matt crossed his arms. "Well, that's bullshit. Jimmie wouldn't do that. Maybe you forgot to mention that I had no choice but to go with you. You didn't ask me! Jimmie isn't one to agree to something like that without informing me."

"It is, how you say, false pretenses. It seems I didn't really give him a choice either. It was kind of last minute that I informed him you were coming with me. Please now Mat, make room for the beautiful meal. I picked the menu out myself, all five courses," Rossi said, moving his glass of red wine to accommodate the first course being set in front of him.

Vanessa and her counterpart, Edwina, made their way to Rossi and Matt with a beautiful Caprese salad. Matt watched as Rossi said a silent prayer, making the sign of the cross across his chest and kissing his thumb and pointer finger.

"Ahh, *mangiamo,*" Rossi said, taking his first bite of fresh mozzarella.

Matt checked in with his gut, not his belly, for what his

intuition was telling him about whether or not it was safe to eat the food.

"*Mangi*, Matt. If I wanted you dead, you would already be dead. The meal is prepared, it would be rude of you to not eat."

He was relieved when Vanessa placed the Caprese salad in front of him and filled his wineglass. Taking a quick bite and sip of wine, he said, "Can you tell me the fuck this is all about, then? What am I doing here?" Matt's tone was demanding, and he raised his voice enough that the inconspicuous Henchmen at the front of the plane stood, ready to pounce.

Rossi motioned to them to sit, nodding that it was *buono*, good.

They swapped a lovely plate of arancini out for the Caprese salad, and Matt's wine glass was re-filled.

"The HTA. I don't like the idea. I am going to have you, what you say, observe how my Team works, to show you that no changes should be made. You do not understand or have respect for history. It is a very American thing to do. Go make changes to suit your needs," spat Rossi.

"Whatever, dude. You really don't know what the HTA is all about. It isn't to change things, just train the Team to work at the top of their game. We train them in specialties like athletes are trained to do things the best they can be done," Matt replied.

"That is not how I understand it. I do not want to have this conversation now. I want to eat my *pasto delizioso*. You should do the same," Rossi said.

CHAPTER 2
TOUCH DOWN

THE ENTIRE MEAL took over an hour to consume. Swordfish grilled to perfection, risotto alla Milanese, plump cheese ravioli, with tiramisu as the grand finale. The carbs and many glasses of wine were a tough match for Matt, who was trying to stay awake the rest of the flight. He fought to not doze off, wondering it if was humanly possible to stay awake under such conditions. He briefly reminisced about times in college where he was stressed with school and football. Back then, he could drink copious amounts of alcohol and never get too shitfaced. That was probably attributed to the stress absorbing the alcohol in his system. He noticed that when he wasn't stressed, having two beers would leave him feeling loopy.

Matt awoke to the jet descending for landing. His ears needed to pop and clear themselves of the pressure built up over the last ten hours in the air. He glanced out the small window to see it was evening, the city lights twinkled like jewels waiting to be scooped up. Matt half expected Liz or Jimmie at the very least to be standing at the bottom on the jet stairs waiting for them to land. A familiar face would be comforting at this point.

No such luck. He took a step out of the plane, standing on the top stairs searching the airstrip for signs of them. *Maybe they are on their way*, Matt thought. He turned to one of the Henchman. "Excuse me, but since this apparently was all planned and approved, can I have my phone back now?" He stood, frustrated at getting no response from them.

"They do not speak any English. Probably best you ask Mr. Rossi about your phone," the flight attendant Vanessa told him.

"Ok, I wasn't sure if they were faking it or not."

Vanessa lingered on the steps out of the plane. "It was brilliant to meet you, Matt."

Matt hesitated slightly before he spoke, thinking about his Amber. Turning to Vanessa, he asked, "Are you staying in the area? Maybe we can meet up for a drink or something. I have no idea how long I will be here is the only issue," Matt said, surprised at his unusual boldness asking a woman out as smooth as that went. Laughing to himself, he thought, *So smooth, because you know you're a fucking prisoner! No shot you are going out with Vanessa, much less any other woman.* But the thought of having her on his side, perhaps being able to get her to help in his escape plan, was what any well-seasoned Henchman would do.

She flashed him a bright smile, and said, "I will be here until my next job, which I never really know when that will be. The other issue is that you don't have a phone." She winked. "Here is my number. I look forward to your call," she said, discreetly handing him an elegant business card with her name and phone number in raised black ink.

She's a classy chick to have her own business cards, Matt thought.

With that, Matt was gently ushered to the white Lamborghini Urus, the Italian brand of SUV. "Holy shit, I didn't even know Lamborghini made anything but sports cars. This is a sweet ride, I'll give you that, Rossi."

"What makes you say this is not also a sports car? *Andiamo, Tommaso!*" shouted Rossi.

The driver, Tommaso, punched the gas pedal with such force that both Matt and Rossi flew back against the seat. "That's more like it, right Tommaso? So much horsepower! Can you feel that, Matt?" Rossi roared.

Matt knew this ride back to the villa was how he was going to get a feel for the roads, villages, and other landmarks he would need as he planned his own escape. But playing Rossi like he was still a rookie Henchman was the impression he wanted to give. "Impressive, yes. Where are we headed now, the villa?" Matt asked.

"Which villa, Matt? I have more than one."

"I guess I'm referring to the one I have been to before. This area looks familiar. Last time I was here, I wasn't paying the same amount of attention to where we are. Probably something I should work on, being more aware of my surroundings."

Rossi smiled coyly. "Your surroundings, oh I see. But yes, Matt, that villa. The one you have visited. I heard you asking about your phone. You may not have it back yet. I want to see how long it will take your superpower HTA Henchmen to come to your rescue. Until then, you are under my house arrest. You know how that works. Just like when you first arrived at the DMF house, I believe." Rossi laughed.

"Are you serious? This is a game then? To prove that your Henchmen are better than ours? How does someone win or lose?" Matt asked.

"The only rules to winning this game is for them to rescue you unharmed. I believe my Team can prevent you from being rescued for an indefinite amount of time," Rossi explained.

Matt shook his head. "I really don't like being a pawn in

this little twisted game. I like the unharmed part. But other than that, this is bullshit." His mind raced to figure out what his next steps could be. He was trying to plan his way out and not get emotionally attached to the feelings he was having, which could quickly turn to panic and hysteria. Being that he was not a rookie, really, any longer, keeping his head on straight was crucial, keeping his emotions in check was even more so.

Rossi sighed like he was bored with this conversation. "I do not see you as a pawn, Matt."

"What am I supposed to do this whole time?" Matt asked.

Rossi pulled out his phone and didn't look up at Matt. "I have heard you like to watch Netflix. We have that here just for you. I am done talking to you now. It was a long flight, and it is late, no more words please."

Rossi snored the rest of the way to the villa and grumbled something in Italian while Matt sat shaking his head in frustration. Again, he found himself wanting to think his way out of this ridiculous situation like a true Henchman would. *What would Franco, Liz, or even Amber be looking for right now?* For the time being, it seemed like he would be safe and like no one was going to kick the shit out of him, which was a relief. But, just in case this was just another mind fuck, he was going to be on high alert. With the time spent working out at Pinky's, Matt had gotten into fantastic shape, so he had that on his side. But how to escape? He wanted more than anything to do that, to prove to Rossi that his Henchmen were soft. They acted so differently than his Team would have. For one thing, they were so quiet. Matt noticed that these guys took Henchman rule number one, never speak on the job, very seriously. When Matt was on the job, traveling to or from a job, they shot the shit the whole time. These guys never did more than grunt or give a slight head nod to each other. It was as if they had a whole separate code of conduct that was never broken. They were more like robots, giving off very little of their own personality. There had to be a happy medium between the loud personalities of his Team and the trancelike state the Italian's worked in. He decided to watch and observe and see if the softness and politeness was an act to throw him off.

The Urus made its way to the iron gates of the familiar villa Matt had been to under much different circumstances when he worked as security for Fowler. As the Urus came to a stop on the elegant stone driveway, Rossi yawned and said, "*Portami.*"

One Henchman rushed to his aid and delicately picked Rossi out of the SUV, lifting him as if he were a child. Rossi's head slumped against the chest of the Henchman, and Matt swore he heard him snoring once again. The Henchman carrying Rossi walked swiftly, but also softly, so as not to wake the man-child Rossi from his deep slumber.

Matt stood in awe. *Are you fucking kidding me?* Matt had only ever carried Fowler up to the DMF house once because he had been shot and was just about dead. This asshole was just tired. Wow. This is sure a different world. Matt tried not to laugh as he pictured David H. carrying Jimmie into the House, like that would ever happen.

The villa was as impressive as he had remembered. Rossi must have spent a small fortune on the outside lighting of the villa. It looked like a scene out of a movie. The door to the main entrance opened to a two-story vestibule. In addition to the main house, there were wings on either side. The sound of the Henchmen's shoes clicked on the white marble floors as they carried Rossi into the darkened main floor hallway. Two new Henchmen appeared and ushered Matt to the south wing of the villa. Matt kept his head on a swivel as he had learned to do when arriving in unknown places, the presidential swivel, as he termed it. He took in all he could, making mental notes about his possible escape plans. He would take his mental pictures with him for the night and sort through options he could come up with after some much-needed rest. Just as he turned for one last look, an ominous-looking Henchman dressed in a black Ninja-ish uniform with a leash attached to a gigantic Rottweiler dog in each hand. *Note to self, make friends with the pooches.*

CHAPTER 3
NOW WHAT?

As HE WALKED through the incredible mansion that was now his temporary home, Matt looked for signs of CCTV or any type of security cameras or equipment. He intentionally walked slower than usual so he could see and hear as much as possible. Matt wasn't sure when or if he could leave his room. He still wasn't sure of the rules of the game they had invited him to play were. Most likely because of the time of the night, there were few other people to greet them, which was disappointing. Matt wanted to know the numbers he was dealing with to include while plotting his escape. The good thing about arriving in the middle of the night was that it made it easier for him to detect the small red lights scattered along the ceilings and walls of the home. *I know what those are,* Matt thought. CCTV is all around me here. He recalled early on at the DMF House, they replaced the red lights to a low-light white light, so they weren't as noticeable as the red lights. *Only people who wanted you to know they were being watched would keep the red lights,* he thought.

Matt stood in the doorway of his new room briefly before entering. The Henchman who walked him there gave a rather violent, two-handed shove in his back to push him all the way into the room then slammed the door, leaving Matt alone to discover that there was an actual touch of violence in these soft Henchmen.

"Fuck you, asshole," Matt said through the closed door. He hoped those words were universal and the Henchman could understand them.

As beautiful as the house was, the room Matt was given was plain and underwhelming. The last time he visited the villa, they gave him and Liz a room that was elegant, with lush furnishings. This room wasn't bad, but it wouldn't make the list of five-star accommodations like the last one did. It was comfortable enough for his stay, but it did not reflect the uber classy, fancy Italian vibe the rest of the house threw off. Without a phone, he wasn't sure what time it was, except that it was way past baby Rossi's bedtime. Matt toured the room to find that he had his own bathroom, which was stocked with personal care items, thank God. The closet was empty, the bed was soft, and when he turned the TV on, his name appeared as a user on a Netflix account. His adrenaline was running on fumes now, what a day. Could it be real that this day started with him having a coffee with Liz and Amber in the DMF kitchen? Jesus, a lot could happen and change in the blink of an eye.

He had come up with a couple of options for him to escape but knew he needed to have a definite, well thought out plan in place. There would be no reactionary escaping. No, in the moment, *I'm outta here,* escapes, unless there was a very clear path out. On the drive up to the villa, Matt had paid close attention to how far they were from a main road and town. His best guess would be a good fifteen-to-twenty-minute run to get off the property and back out to a main road. The town was about double that distance away. Since there was no intense security around the perimeter of the villa, Matt wondered how hard it would be to simply walk out of the villa, explore where they hung the keys for the fleet of cars, grab a set, and go. If the front door wasn't a viable option, maybe he could climb out a window. Satisfied with his initial planning, and with nothing else to see or do, Matt sat on the edge of the large, king-sized bed, pulled back the plush, thick, light gray comforter, took his shoes and socks off, and crawled into bed. He was asleep before he could even turn off the small bedside lamp.

———

Matt woke from his jet-lagged slumber with a start, not remembering where he was at first or how he got there. He sat bolt upright, confused, looking for a sign of anything resembling his own room at the DMF house and finding nothing. With a deep breath in, the realization hit him, and he fell back onto the oversized down-filled pillows. *Fuck, those stupid assholes took me from my life. I was on a roll!*

Deciding it best to shower and rinse off the last day of flying and being kidnapped, Matt rolled out of bed and headed to do just that. He often used time in the shower to escape and go to a fantasy world where life was good, easy, and not this complicated. As he was deep in thought, he heard the door to the room shut. His first thought was of Liz. He smiled and thought of how many times she had peeked her head into the bathroom to tell him to hurry the hell up. But no, he was snapped back into reality. He definitely wasn't in the DMF House.

He immediately turned the water off, grabbing a towel to wrap around his waist, ready to fight off any unwelcome Henchman in his room.

Carefully opening the door from the bathroom, not

knowing what to expect, but ready to rumble, what he saw was not what he expected. The bed was covered in new clothes, shoes, socks, underwear, piles upon piles, all in store bags, still wrapped in the tissue from those upscale stores.

Matt stood in awe of the amount of clothes and the price of them. They left the tags on. Some of the bags had hundreds of euros' worth of clothes. He chose a new outfit to wear for the day and hung the rest in the closet. After he dressed, he went to check the door. It wasn't locked, so he could leave if he wanted. And he did want to. His stomach was speaking to him, asking for it to be fed.

The villa was pulsing with activity as Matt made his way down to the first floor. There were Henchmen everywhere, walking like they had some place to be. Matt tried to follow his nose to find the kitchen, but he wasn't able to find a smell to lead him in that direction. Since no one had stopped him or even looked at him, he felt like it was acceptable to wander around and get a feel for the place.

Matt wished he could understand a fraction of what he was hearing. He felt like a tourist in the villa. He thought to stop and literally ask directions for where he could find food. Just as he was about to, he saw one of the Henchman with a mug of coffee. Matt headed down that long hallway in hopes of at least finding a coffee. He felt kind of shitty after all the red wine he drank on the flight.

Taking a couple of rights and then left turns, the hallway became less grand. Feeling like he was getting off the beaten path, Matt figured the kitchen must be hidden away down these less austere hallways. *Thank Christ.* There, in all its glory, was the kitchen. But are you shitting me? The kitchen was not set up like the DMF kitchen, where the food was laid out and you served yourself. No, this place had an actual wait staff taking orders, refilling coffee, bringing out more food, whatever was requested. First class meals, who would ever want to leave this place?

With some hesitancy, Matt saw an open table for him to sit at. Hoping it wasn't too much of a social faux pas to sit at that table, he looked around to see if anyone took issue with it. Again, no one looked at him. It was an interesting feeling to be invisible. Without asking, an older gentleman brought not only a coffee cup and saucer to him, but after he filled the cup, he left the sterling silver coffeepot on the table. *Good man*, Matt thought. Nothing like the first sip feeling, but what about food? There were no menus, and he didn't know the language to get the waiter's attention.

The first cup or two of caffeine brought a new sense of awareness. It was time to observe his surroundings once again. *You aren't on vacation, you idiot, pay attention!*

Just then, the same waiter appeared with a plate of assorted breads and rolls, cheese, and a few berries scattered across the picture-perfect plate. The waiter turned and left before Matt could try to mumble a thank you to him. The meal was just enough to satisfy his belly and give him energy to go explore more of the villa. After he switched gears out of vacation mode, he was making mental notes of who else was having breakfast. There were only two tables with one or two Henchmen, nothing out of the ordinary, except for the Henchman in the far corner table. No one spoke to him or paid him any attention. He was the only Henchmen that brought work with him; he had a stack of papers he was shuffling through, while he kept his gaze in Matt's general direction. This guy was not a hands-on Henchman. Matt got the distinct feeling that he was only there to watch and intimidate him. *I want to remember this guy; he gives off the wrong sort of vibe*, he thought.

His goals for the day were to get his bearings and a phone. Slowly walking back to the main part of the home, he spotted the front door they had arrived at last night. There was no Henchman standing guard.

Curiosity got the best of him. Matt wanted to see how far he could get. Would it be this easy to walk right out of the front door? He had a vision of the first time he met Jimmie; it was in similar circumstances. That first night in the DMF House, he felt the same urge to escape.

Looking over his shoulder, more than once, he tried to be as nonchalant as he knew how to be but rushed at the same time. Putting his hand on the doorknob, he braced himself, expecting to be tackled, beaten, or at least thrown up against the wall in the patented DMF Henchman hold—face smashed against the wall, arm twisted behind his back to the breaking point, windpipe crushed—but nothing of the sort occurred. Maybe the cameras weren't on during the day? He was willing to give it a shot. He was prepared to take a beating. Hell, he'd had his ass kicked more than once and survived.

Heart racing, he was outside. It was that easy. Now, all he had to do was either climb the gate or wait hidden in a bush or behind one of the large trees until someone left or arrived. Perfect, he would just walk right out. *Dumb, soft Henchmen,* Matt laughed to himself. What idiots. They sure could use a couple of classes at the HTA. They didn't even know how to monitor a prisoner.

He made his way down the long, perfectly manicured driveway toward the large iron gates. *Joke's on them,* he thought. He could make it to the village and find a phone to call Liz or Jimmie. They would come get him in no time. A thirty-to-forty-minute run would be a piece of cake. This was too easy, Rossi must be a real prankster.

When he arrived within six feet of the iron gate, the worst

pain he had ever felt pulsed through his body; it was excruciat-
ing. It was as if he was going to explode from the inside. His
body crumpled instantly, and he convulsed. His last thought
before the world turned black was that his trip to the kitchen
hadn't such a good idea; they'd poisoned him.

CHAPTER 4
THAT REALLY FUCKING HURT

Matt's eyes fluttered open. His whole body ached, and his head throbbed. His first thought was that he was dead. How could someone survive that amount of pain and not be permanently fucked? As his brain fog lifted, he realized he was in the unfamiliar bed of the Rossi villa and not actually dead. Taking a deep breath was almost impossible, but he knew that was important as a coping mechanism for this type of situation. He replayed what he could remember. *I was walking down the drive after breakfast, and then something zapped me.* Matt hadn't noticed that there were two Henchmen sitting in his room and a third man who was obviously not a Henchman, as he looked to be Fowler's age.

"Good evening, Matt. I am Doctor Moretti, Signore Rossi's private physician. May I ask how you are feeling?"

The two Henchmen stood as Matt answered, "Like shit. That's how I feel. I'm glad you speak English so I can tell you what I think of this place. Is it common practice to poison people who eat here, or am I just the lucky one?"

"Poison? Why would you determine that is what happened to you? You were not poisoned," Dr. Moretti said.

"Oh, is that right? Then what in the hell happened to me?

Cause something out of the ordinary sure as shit took me down hard and fast," Matt said, trying to sit more upright in his bed.

Dr. Moretti smiled and said, "Yes, I can understand why you thought you were poisoned. That is not the case. I forgot you are new to being a Henchman, yes?"

"What does that have to do with anything? But yes, I'm sort of new. I guess you could say that," Matt replied.

"You did not notice the small antenna along the gates and walls that surround the property then? I assume a more experienced Henchman would look for that straightaway."

Matt shot him a quizzical look. "Antenna? No, I didn't think to look for anything like that. What are they for?"

Dr. Moretti turned to the Henchmen in the room, and translated what Matt said for them. The two Henchmen in the room laughed to themselves then looked down, trying to be respectful as the doctor looked to them before answering. "The antennas are there to create an electric fence of sorts. We cannot have security there all day and night. Most larger compounds use this system. There's an electric force field that surrounds the property, and it keeps us safe during off hours when we can't have Henchmen on duty. You were electrocuted, not poisoned."

Matt felt panic set in, wondering what other secrets this house would reveal to him. "What the fuck. Seriously? But I saw men closer to the fence that I was. How come they didn't get fucked like I did?"

"They are chipped, you are not," Moretti said.

"Chipped, excuse me, but what does that fucking mean?" Matt asked.

"The people who serve in this house are implanted with a chip. This chip allows them to bypass the electric current that flows on the perimeter of the property and the parts of the villa that are on a stricter lockdown," Dr. Moretti said.

How was he supposed to know about the stupid little antenna on the outside wall? No one had ever mentioned that to him. Is that a European thing, to put microchips into their Henchmen? DMF didn't have that. They had the viewing room, which needed to be manned 24/7, not turning the Henchmen into mutants. Maybe the little antenna was a good idea, but the thought of having to be chipped cringed Matt out in a big way. "Good to know," Matt said bitterly. "Maybe someone could have told me sooner. Since I've never been electrocuted before, can you tell me if I'll have any permanent damage? And when I will feel better?"

"Your shock may have been painful to experience but there will be no lasting effects to you. Stay here and sleep the rest of the night. You will feel fine in the morning," Dr. Moretti said as one of the Henchmen handed Matt the remote for the TV.

"Netflix," was all the Henchman said as the three exited the room.

Matt sighed as he tried to lift himself out of bed. He felt weak and needed to brace himself on the nightstand to steady himself. He needed some water and to see if his body still worked properly. On the edge of the nightstand on the other side of the bed, he noticed that there was a meal neatly set out. Two bottles of water, pasta with meatballs, steamed vegetables, and some cookies. *This place is a mind fuck, that's for sure.*

As Matt finished eating his meal, he felt despair about his escape plans. They needed to evolve and be more well thought through, no doubt. He at least knew now that walking out the front door wasn't his best bet. Tomorrow, when he was feeling better, he would search for where they kept the car keys. Assuming he could hit the gas and fly past the zap zone without having as detrimental effects as this time, but he also knew a zap was a zap, and that was not a pleasant experience to go through.

CHAPTER 5
DEAD ENDS

Dr. Moretti was right. Spending the rest of the evening in bed suited him just fine. The meal left behind didn't sit too long before Matt cleaned the plates. He reached for the remote and figured Netflix was as good a place as any to get lost in. Once again, he was asleep before he could turn the lights and TV off. He wasn't sure if it was the jet lag, and time zone difference, or being electrocuted, but the morning light came too quickly for him. He would have just as soon sat in bed that day too, but the allure of learning more about the house grabbed him, plus the craving for another round of coffee in the kitchen/five-star restaurant got him motivated to change and take a stroll.

Matt surprised himself by not getting lost on his way for his caffeine fix. He had his wits about him enough to focus on the CCTV cameras. It was hard to see if the lights were actually on during the day. There were not as many Henchmen milling about the house this morning, which made it easier for him to wander the halls of the villa, embracing as many details as he could. He encountered more closed doors than open. The open doors were a mix of offices and larger conference-type rooms. He hadn't seen Rossi since they'd arrived. Matt had been wondering if Rossi's story about letting Jimmie know he was being taken here as a pawn in some weird fucked up game was bullshit or not. He was leaning toward it being a load of shit. Matt knew Jimmie well enough to know that Jimmie was a meticulous planner, not a fly-by-the-seat-of-his-pants kind of guy.

As Matt passed one of the open-door offices, he noticed there was an old-fashioned conference desk phone. That was on his list of things to find in the scavenger hunt that his life had turned in to. He walked past the room a couple of times, thinking of his plan. How long could a call to them take? A few seconds, less than a minute, he guessed. He should be able to get that done before the CCTV showed everyone who was watching what he was doing, if they even were even bothering to monitor their cameras right now. On his third trip past, he quickly darted into the room, gently closing the door behind him. His heart was racing, and his hands shook as he lifted the receiver to his ear.

Sweet, a dial tone, but shit. How do you make an international call?

Matt had never called anyone out of the country. He dialed o for the operator, as he'd seen that once in a movie. Silence, nothing. Panic. *How about just dialing the main number at the DMF house,* he thought. Closing his eyes, he knew exactly where the phone would ring in the back office where the errand board hung. Feeling sick, he wanted to get back there more than anything. He was desperate to hear anyone's voice but silently wished Liz would pick up on the other end. Instead, all he heard was a pre-recorded message in Italian that he could not understand. Slamming the received down, and silently screamed to himself, *fuck, fuck, fuck. Note to self, figure the fuck out how to make an international call.*

The shot of adrenaline from trying to make the call, partnered with the caffeine, was wreaking havoc with Matt's heart rate. He supposed large amounts of electricity dumped into a body could also do that to a guy. His heart rate elevated to such a speed that he felt like he had just ran a hundred-meter dash. Not wanting to get caught in this office, his shaky, sweaty hand reached for the door handle. Pushing the handle down to open proved difficult. *Christ, am I having a fucking heart attack?*

He was sweating through his clothes but was determined to make it back to his room. *Stairs are going to kick my ass,* Matt thought. The stair railing was a lifesaver, as he needed it to hold on to as stumbled back to his room.

The stair railing wasn't the only help Matt got going up the marble staircase. Two familiar-faced Henchmen rushed up to him. Matt quickly assumed this was it. The predictable ass kicking was finally going to happen. *What a shit time for this to happen. I won't be able to defend myself at all!* He braced himself for what he assumed would happen next. His body tensed for the blows he was about to receive, but that didn't happen. What happened shocked the hell out of him. The two Henchmen, grabbed his arms on each side, helping him navigate the staircase. *They are helping me? What the fuck is that all about?* Instead of being put in an arm bar, he was being gently guided back to his room.

The two Henchmen didn't say a word as they opened the door to his room. Still bracing for a blow or two, they sat Matt on his bed. Again, the Henchman picked up the TV remote handing it to him, and said, "Netflix."

Collapsing on his bed for the rest of the day, he was disappointed by the dead ends he found on the other end of the phone but confused by his accompaniment to his room.

As the sun set, Matt finally could get out of his bed to move about his room. He stood by the window, never having looked out it. In the twilight, the view was beautiful. The plush rolling hills of northern Italy were silhouetted in the distance. He could find no flaw with the perfection his window captured. If he was here on a vacation, he would have to pay big money to have this view. *This sure as shit ain't no vacation*, Matt grumbled as he walked to the shower.

After his shower, there were no clothes littering his bed this time, but someone had delivered a cart from the dining room. Matt counted six stainless steel cloche domes on three different shelves of the cart with a couple of bottles of water and, of course, red wine that was already open. No need to give him a wine opener as a possible weapon. One plate was as delicious as the next. His belly was pleased. *Eating like this is great, but since I can't work out at Pinky's, my jeans may not fit when I get out of here*, Matt thought. *Take it easy on the food, don't have to eat it all!*

After a pause to shower and eat, Matt wanted to get back to planning his escape. One of the first thoughts he had was that perhaps he could befriend some Henchmen and ask to learn how they worked, just like the old days at DMF. Go on some ride-alongs and observe. Then, when the time was right, he would run away from them and disappear into the cityscape. Matt was pleased with himself. This seemed like a perfect solution. It may take some time, but it was going to work. An added bonus for him could be he may actually learn something from these soft Henchmen. That truly was the direction the HTA was headed, although he would never tell Liz that.

CHAPTER 6
FOLLOW ME

MATT WAS FEELING BETTER and too restless to sleep again. He needed to walk off some of the dinner and wine. Leaving his room, he was never sure where he could go, especially since Dr. Moretti said there were places in the villa where you needed to be chipped to move about. To be safe, he decided to try a couple of the hallways he'd already been in.

As he approached the last step at the bottom of the long staircase, he heard Rossi's familiar, high-pitched voice. Matt's first instinct was to run. He felt the fight-or-flight response kick in, then he quickly remembered this man had asked to be carried into his home like a child. Instead of running, Matt summed up all the bravado he could muster.

"Well, good evening, Mr. Rossi," Matt said, sounding more like James Bond than himself.

Rossi smiled. "Ah, nice to see you this evening, Matt. I was just going to ask that you be brought to me. What do they call this a, uhm, coincidence?"

"There are no coincidences, only fate," Matt replied. Those pillow talks with Jimmie were fresh in his mind.

"Whatever you say. Will you please follow me to my office where we can talk?" Though it was a question, Rossi's tone made it sound like a command as he started walking away. The indirect command was reinforced as, out of the shadows, two Henchmen appeared to accompany him.

"Wait," Matt said, standing firm. "Before I follow you, I want to know if something will zap me again. Dr. Moretti said there were places in the house that are more secure than others. I would imagine your office would be in one of those off-limit areas. I am not going to be zapped again."

"Oh yes, that is right. You are the rookie Henchman who didn't see the obvious antenna at my home," Rossi said, laughing. "We have, how do you say, shut down the system momentarily for you to follow. Unless you would like to be chipped?"

"Fuck that. No, I'm not being chipped and tuned into a mutant like these guys."

Rossi shrugged and turned to walk down a hallway that Matt had yet to notice. His hesitancy to follow was met with the same two-handed shove in the back that he got the first night in the villa.

Rossi's office was opulent with lavish furnishings, just what Matt had pictured. Glossy marble floors, highly polished wood trimming, beautiful expensive wall art, and small sculptures. Rossi took a seat on the floral print sofa near the lit fireplace. Matt took a seat across from him in a teal accent chair. The two Henchmen stood behind Rossi, while two additional Henchmen stood facing them standing behind the teal chair. As soon as he sat, he noticed another man standing by the curtains trying to look inconspicuous. It was the guy he saw in the dining room, the one with the creepy vibe. He gave the same stony stare to Matt.

"I want to know who this asshole is," Matt said, pointing to the man standing at the curtains. "Is he here to stalk me or what?"

Rossi turned around to see the man and chuckled. "Oh,

him? Don't mind him. He is my, what do you call it, personal assistant. Don't pay him attention. He likes to hear my meetings, that is all."

Matt sat back, satisfied with the answer, but not ready to ignore the shadow in the corner.

"I see you are nervous about having this conversation," Rossi said with a smirk. "It is never good to show how you are feeling."

Matt hadn't noticed his leg begin to bounce, as often happens when his anxiety takes its place front and center in his nervous system. His teeth clenched and a quick shake of his head indicated that he agreed, although begrudgingly with Rossi.

"What is this meeting about? Are you intending to let me go?" Matt asked.

Rossi's smile widened, which made Matt want to punch him in the mouth. Was this kidnapping a joke to Rossi? "Not yet. I want you to learn more about how we do business in my home and in my company," Rossi said.

"I don't know what your problem is with the HTA. If you would let me explain more about it, you may not feel the same way. I think we could all work together and learn from each other. It doesn't have to be one way or the other," Matt said.

"That is where I disagree with you. You didn't learn the right things while you *trained* at DMF. Here, you will learn the right things."

"What are the right things? Learning how to carry your boss like a baby and tucking him in at night? Or are you referring to not being reactive, not hurting innocent people?" Matt said.

Rossi ignored the jab and leaned forward in his chair. "Ahh, so much more than that. There is much to learn without even using words. I don't hear you speaking of loyalty. That concept is not part of your program, and you would not know how to even teach it. Loyalty is all there is. If there is no loyalty, then it makes no difference how one shoots a gun or drives a car."

Matt didn't want to admit it, but perhaps Rossi was onto something. They hadn't planned a class on loyalty at the HTA. He wasn't about to let Rossi know he was a bit intrigued by the idea. He was going to push back on this outdated concept. "But isn't loyalty more of a concept than a skill? We're teaching skills, which would lead to more loyalty. You know loyalty is a foreign concept to some of these millennials and I am one, so I would know," Matt replied in more of a question than a statement.

"That's what I thought. Who is there to teach to you the important history of Henchmen? I think that should be your priority."

"We do have a course on the history of Henchmen," Matt bluffed. "But you have to agree that improving their skill sets is a good idea too."

"Perhaps. I may be a stubborn man, but I can assure you, change as you are requiring is not the change I want to see happen in my lifetime," Rossi said in a sharp tone that Matt took notice of.

Taking a long breath before he answered, Matt said, "Well, I'm sorry to hear that. We're excited about it. And you better get over it, because our ultimate goal is to take the HTA global," Matt said.

"I am trying to be reasonable!" Rossi said, slamming his hand on the table next to him. He hit the table with such force that the lamp on it wavered back and forth until the Henchmen reached out to steady it.

This was the first time Matt had really seen Rossi lose his cool. Matt sat up straighter, wondering what Rossi's next move would be. He was still expecting to get into it with these guys at some point.

Rossi straightened his jacket and relaxed slightly. "I think tomorrow we will have you go out with my men to see how different things can be. They will come get you in the morning." Rossi rose to leave.

Matt stood as Rossi made his way to the door with a Henchman on each arm. He was sure this little field trip with the Italian Henchmen would prove enlightening. How much better could they really be than the DMF Team? *Thanks for the talk, you crazy old man, and fuck off too*, he thought, closing the door behind Rossi and his Henchmen.

CHAPTER 7
FIELD TRIP

Matt didn't sleep, tossing and turning with visions of what his day was going to look like riding along with the Henchmen of the Rossi villa. He knew he would stand out like a sore thumb. He didn't have a suit to wear, and of course he didn't speak the language.

In the morning, he rummaged through his closet, trying to find the most Henchman-like outfit he could find. The best he came up with is a black pair of trousers and a plain white button-down shirt. He looked himself over in the mirror and decided that was as good as it was going to get. Matt wasn't sure what time they were leaving. He hoped he had time to run down to grab coffee.

There was a delicate knock on the door which Matt was not expecting. Outside the door, there were two large, well-dressed Henchmen, both wearing aviator-style sunglasses. The blond Henchman reminded Matt of Franco. Ever since Matt had known him, Franco had kept his naturally dark hair bleached blond. *Jesus, I wish he were here right now.* The dark-haired Henchman handed Matt a to-go coffee and a bag that contained two chocolate croissants.

"Thanks, man. You read my mind," Matt said, offering the men a smile.

Both Henchmen looked Matt up and down, shrugging their shoulders as if to say, *I guess that will be a presentable outfit to wear for the day.*

"Come," the blond said. Pointing to his chest, he said, "Enzo." Enzo then grabbed the dark-haired Henchman's arm and said, "Carmine."

Nice, we are finally communicating. Love it. Matt smirked. He followed them to the back of the villa, where he had yet to travel. The Henchman walked at the same pace as the DMF Henchmen, which was still not Matt's preferred pace. Keeping up with them meant he needed to step it up into a slight jog. They walked swiftly to the Urus. The engine purred to a start, and they headed straight out the front toward the gate where Matt had been zapped only days ago.

They relegated Matt to the backseat once again. He had earned his way up to riding in the front with the DMF Team. *C Squad again,* he thought. Enzo shut the door as he slid across the black leather seat. *What's with the no door handles in their vehicles? Are they always in the business of kidnapping?* With the door handles permanently removed, he deduced he must not be the only "prisoner" transported in the vehicle. Matt's trauma response kicked in as they got to the very place the invisible electric gate sent unexpectedly him to the ground. Matt took a deep breath, waiting to see if the pain would return. The Urus slowed down, slower and slower, to where it was close to stopping. Matt struggled to breathe. "What are you doing? Just go past the force field, please!"

At the very point, the Urus stopped and reversed back and forth several times. The Henchmen laughed, both saying "Zuuussss zuuusss," mimicking the sound of electricity flowing.

"Fuck you both. It's not funny. Assholes," Matt spewed.

The first errand the three went on was to pay a visit to what looked like a factory from the parking lot. It was in a rural setting, isolated off the road. There were three armed guards at the entrance who waved the Urus in without question. They parked and immediately exited the vehicle.

Matt followed, taking in all that his senses would allow—sights, sounds. It was a typical northern Italian countryside, peaceful, with hills and the color green as far as you could see. The sounds he heard were faint, more birds calling out to one another than traffic. He noted nothing out of the usual, so far.

The large, garage-like doors were open, which Matt thought was strange. Wouldn't they want to keep whatever this was under wraps? He noticed the workers paid no attention to the Henchmen but gave them plenty of side-eye glances, accompanied by whispers to one other.

They walked to the back of the factory through a semi-hidden door into a warehouse. The warehouse didn't appear to look unique in any way until they reached another heavy metal door, which took them to a dimly lit staircase leading to a base-ment level. Matt was so curious that he forgot to be anxious or to panic. He shook his head in disbelief when they reached the bottom of the stairs.

It was an enormous room with row after row of long tables, each with at least half a dozen men sitting in front of three monitors each, headsets on, all eyes trained on their computers. It was eerily quiet. The only sounds were the clicking from the keyboards, and the occasional cough from one of the men behind the monitors.

What are they fucking doing? Matt squinted to see what was on the screens. It reminded him of the CM, Cyber Minds Team at the DMF House, but on a much grander scale. Carmine took out his phone and took photos of the men and the work being done. None of the computer geeks looked up.

Enzo stood behind the chairs of several of the geeks, taking notes on a clipboard.

None of the keyboard warriors missed a beat of their non-stop clicking.

After twenty minutes, and multiple pictures taken, the Henchmen turned to leave, never having said a word. No throwing things around, no shouting and threatening. Matt's patented one-arm clearing of the desk would not fly here.

"That's it? You aren't even going to talk to them?" Matt asked, trying to catch up with them at the top of the stairs.

"*Non piu*, ahh, no more," Carmine said.

That was unreal. It astounded Matt how easy it had been. They hadn't even opened their mouths.

On the way back to the villa, Matt felt the energy in the Urus shift, becoming more tense. Looking out the back window, there it was, the reason for the Urus picking up speed. A shiny red sports car too close for anyone's comfort. The Henchmen's conversation sounded panicked and faster. Enzo adjusted the rear-view mirror, briefly making eye contact with Matt in the mirror. Carmine was doing the presidential swivel, back and forth, even up to the sky, using frequent hand motions as exclamation. Matt wondered what could possibly be happening. The visit to the warehouse-turned-IT-coding-den had been uneventful as far as Matt could tell.

The shooting began in rapid succession. Matt instinctively ducked as far down into the backseat as he physically could. The Urus reached top speed in seconds. Constant gun fire peppered the entire SUV, but the bullets were not penetrating the vehicle.

Bulletproof, nice touch, Matt thought. Matt felt safe enough to peek his head back out the window. He watched as the sports car came so close that he could see the passengers inside. It was two slick-looking Henchmen in black suits.

Enzo expertly navigated the winding terrain, weaving in and out of any traffic he encountered. The red sports car was not having any of it. As it got closer, the sounds of the bullets hitting the Urus became louder. It was a strange feeling hearing the bullets ricochet off the Urus and not be able to penetrate and injure him.

"Dude! Are you going to shoot back? Do something!" Matt yelled from the floor of the backseat. "How many rounds can this thing take before the bullets make their way into the car!"

Carmine ignored Matt's plea to fire back, continuing to look to the sky. "Ah, *magnifico, guardare*," he shrieked. Enzo's eyes darted to the sky, and he smiled.

The Urus slowed as if to make a right turn off the main road.

"What the fuck! Don't slow down! Jesus, why are you going off the road? Oh my God, you two are idiots!" shouted Matt.

The red car, still in pursuit, followed obediently onto the small, rural, barely-paved road. Matt followed the Italian Henchmen's gaze upward, out the skylight overhead.

"No fucking way." He saw what had caused Carmine to cheer. It was a helicopter.

The sleek black chopper flew low to the ground, with the side door wide open. It was so close that Matt could see the helicopter was heavily armed. A passenger in the helicopter stationed himself behind the impressive heavy machine gun mount with a hand on either side, waiting to get the ok to fire.

It was like a scene from a movie, for Christ's sake.

Just then, the Urus made a violent, hard left turn so that it was now facing the red sports car. The force of the Urus changing direction on a dime sent Matt faceplanting into the window. Matt scrambled back sit upright, so as not to miss the action. He gently touched the left side of his cheek and felt a lump beginning to form. The helicopter sniper unloaded its ammunition into the red sports car before they came to a complete stop. The sound of the helicopter gun mount, unloading its cartridges into the red sports car was terrifying, but watching the car be completely destroyed only feet away was something else.

Matt pulled himself up to his seat to watch the carnage. The helicopter flew off, and they began their drive back to the villa in silence. There was no debriefing here, just drop it, stuff it, and don't deal with it.

Matt was the first to speak. "You guys, wow. That was fucking intense. Who were those guys? The guy in the chopper took care of business. Does he work in the house with you?" Neither man responded. Matt sat back in his seat and did some deep breathing until his nervous system realigned itself.

At least there was some similarity. These Italian Henchmen also buried their trauma and stress just like the guys on his Team. At least the DMF Henchman had a debrief, these guys just zipped it up real quick. The gentle, classical music playing in the car helped him relax. It wasn't like he could understand what they were saying, his Italian was at the pre-school level at this point in his stay.

Matt thanked the nonresponsive Henchman before heading up the stairs to his room.

He was halfway up the stairs when a woman walking in the main hallway near the front entrance caught his eye. Matt doubled back and hurried down the stairs. *I swear that woman looked exactly like Vanessa, the flight attendant from the other night.* He chased after her, having to run to catch her. Calling her name didn't get her to stop either. Finally able to reach her, Matt grabbed her arm to spin her around, confirming, yes, it was Vanessa.

"Vanessa, what the hell? What are you doing here?" Matt said in a lowered voice.

Her response startled him. If he didn't know better, he would say that she just gave him the patented DMF death stare. It was such an effective death stare that he immediately dropped her arm and took a step back.

"Christ, ok. I guess I didn't see you here then. My mistake, ma'am," Matt said, walking away backwards, afraid to turn his back on her.

He had no clue what that was about, but he wasn't that much of a rookie to not understand the death stare meant to leave her the hell alone.

CHAPTER 8
BOREDOM

OVER THE NEXT FEW DAYS, Matt again continued to tag along with Enzo and Carmine to observe how this team did their errands. The errands were more of the same, going to visit other semi-hidden coding dens, an art studio, and a small women's clothing boutique. It was the same at each: few words spoken, lots of photos and videos taken, no trashing the place or threatening words shouted. Not that he wanted to be involved in a high-speed chase and an aerial assault regularly, but a little excitement would be nice. Matt was growing so freaking bored and homesick. He wished he could be home in the DMF kitchen for taco night. He wished he could put on a movie and have pizza and beer with Liz. He wished Franco and David H. could razz him at Pinky's. The thing he longed for the most was spending time with Amber. He had realized even more since being here that life is short. *There are so many things I want to say to her. When I get back, I'm going to lay it out to her, tell her how I really feel,* he thought. He didn't know why he had even asked Vanessa out. There was no one he wanted to see other than Amber.

He hadn't seen Vanessa again since that random appearance in the villa, not that the thought of her hadn't crossed his mind. He had replayed their encounter over in his mind several times, trying to grasp clues as to why she'd reacted the way she did, and what the hell she was even doing there in the first place. Why was a flight attendant hanging out at the villa, anyway? Matt pondered this question over his morning coffee, staring off into no place in particular. He used to do that a lot when he sat in that shitty little desk at Tailgater's Insurance. He used to look out his window and daydream about places like this. Maybe he had dreamed too hard, since he was living a dream right now. Some would call it a nightmare, but the last year or so had opened Matt's eyes to a world he never knew existed. It was all a matter of perspective, he thought. He could be angry he was being held captive, or he could learn from it and be grateful for the experience. Jimmie's philosophy on life had taken hold as part of his own evolving life philosophy.

Returning to his room, Matt saw his bed was made up as usual, but today, folded neatly on his bed, were the clothes he was wearing the day he arrived at the villa. They had been laundered and returned. Sitting next to the pile of clothes was the business card Vanessa had given him. *Christ, they even check the pockets before they wash our clothes.* Matt wished he could call Vanessa and see how she fit into the puzzle that was his life. *Note to self: add 'how to make international calls from obsolete desk phones' to the curriculum at the HTA.*

With nothing on the morning schedule, Matt continued pondering his life circumstances with a walk around the villa. He had been here a few weeks now and had started to feel some disappointment in the fact that he hadn't been able to figure out a way to escape. His plan of running off while on an errand proved to not be feasible, and the fact that no one from the DMF Team had come to his rescue was heavy on his mind. Maybe they were all sick and tired of him needing help. He supposed they could consider this latest kidnapping to be another fuck up, although he technically didn't break any of the Henchmen rules. Never speak on the job, never do an errand on your own, never argue with an order, never hesitate, know your role, stay in your lane. Those five rules had been drilled into his head so many times over the last year, Matt knew them by heart and felt a connection to them. He remembered back to the meeting with he'd had with Jimmie when he'd typed those rules into his phone. *God, I wish I had my phone!*

But, he had one last ditch effort to try to basically steal one of their vehicles. He thought this was a better time to try this since he had been out several times with Enzo and Carmine and knew his way around better than when he first got there. While sitting in the back seat, he paid strict attention to the roads and villages they passed through. It took some time for him to see where they stored the keys to the fleet of vehicles, and when he did, he saw how impossible it would be to casually take a set. In fact, it made him cringe.

On one morning he was to go out with Enzo and Carmine, instead of them coming to get him, he waited downstairs for them. Pretending to be enthusiastic about the day's errands, he followed them to the 'key station' to see just how they were distributed. The Henchman who gave out the keys sat behind a glass window in the small closet-like room. When anyone would come for keys, they were scanned for their chip. They had a handheld scanner to swipe across the Henchmen's collar-bone region. Once the light on the scanner blinked green, they were given a set of keys. *Jesus, that's completely fucked up,* Matt thought, but also wondered if it may not be worth it to get himself chipped, just to check out a vehicle and get the fuck out of there. Better put this one on the back burner for now.

Although Matt enjoyed watching the Henchmen come and go from the kitchen, he didn't feel much like eating and being social most days. He routinely spent time in the dining room, observing comings and goings of the Henchmen. By now he could recognize their faces, and who partnered with each other, and was even picking up some Italian.

Matt sat in the kitchen with an untouched pastry in front of him, stirring his coffee absentmindedly. One of the Henchmen Matt was watching finished his meal and got up to leave. That's when Matt noticed it, the cell phone left on the table. He didn't react immediately. But took a more cautious approach, waiting for the Henchman's possible return. That didn't last long, however, when he saw the waiter coming to clear the table. Matt sprang into action with one thought in mind, to swipe that fucking phone off the table. The word nonchalant drifting through his mind, he swaggered to the empty table and scooped the phone into his pocket in one swift movement.

It took all the self-control he could muster to walk and not run to his room. Excitement spilled over, and he did race up the stairs. Shutting the door behind him, he thought to take the phone into the bathroom. Even at DMF, the bathroom was a CCTV-free zone.

Matt could feel his heart pounding in his chest and sweat forming along his brow. He gently slid the phone out of his pocket, setting it on the sink. It was on the lock screen, and he had no way of being able to open it. Calling the Italian police didn't feel like the right move at this point, who knew if they weren't bought and paid for by Rossi? He figured his best shot was to wait for it to ring, then he could answer it. His thoughts were racing. Was that the way it worked? But what if they called it while trying to find it? Worse yet, what if they had the find my phone feature on? They would come break down the door the moment they located it? Was this a piss poor idea?

After taking some of his patented deep breaths, he got himself together enough to realize this was a pretty dumb and desperate idea. Even the Henchmen who weren't the brightest bulbs on the tree always had the find my phone feature enabled on their phones. He had to ditch the phone someplace, and quickly. He had so far avoided a royal ass kicking since he'd been in the villa, but stealing a phone could change that. Stuffing the phone back in his pocket, he left his room and headed out the one side door of the villa that he knew was a safe place to wander the grounds. Walking at a true Henchman pace, he headed to the row of olive trees and flung the phone as far as he could into the grove. *Well shit, now what do I do to get out of here?*

Matt decided to walk the perimeter of the grounds and enjoy the day and keep positive. He would not let this failed plan crush his hopes. He had been through too much to think that this was the end. The navy-and-white-striped hammock was waving in the breeze, calling his name. What the fuck else did he have to do except take a nap in the afternoon sun?

Matt jolted awake to the sound of voices nearby. He recognized one of the Henchmen as the one who left his phone on the table. His partner was standing and calling the phone to try to find it. He had to admit, he loved watching the Italians talk with their hands. They were so animated. Once they picked up the phone, Matt didn't need to understand their words. He knew by the waving of hands that they were both relieved to have found the phone. *They, too, use find my phone. Better they found it there than in my pocket.*

He woke from his afternoon nap feeling depressed. He was not just missing the DMF Team, but his own family. He hadn't spent much time with them since he started working as a Henchman, but this latest predicament made him long for some family time. After a long yawn and stretch, he knew himself well enough that his predictable belly would keep nagging him if he didn't go fill it. He slowly made his way to the kitchen. His depression lifted some when a beautifully prepared plate of food was set in front of him. It was hard to stay depressed with food this delicious. Matt noticed that he always felt more relaxed and almost high after the meals.

After filling up on lasagna, cheesecake, and of course more red wine, Matt was ready for another fun-filled night watching Netflix in his room by himself. He strolled with his hands in his pockets, feeling not only depressed, but homesick. DMF had become his home, and he missed the atmosphere, the interactions, the friends he made, all of it.

Crawling into bed, his heart hurt, an emotional pain he'd never really felt before. *I just want to go home*, were his last thoughts before falling into a red-wine-induced slumber.

CHAPTER 9
FREEDOM

A HAND GRIPPED TIGHTLY around his mouth shocked Matt out of a dead sleep. The force of someone trying to smother him, or so he assumed, kept him from sitting upright to fight off whoever was in his room.

When his eyes focused, Matt could make out who was now straddling him on the bed, pressing her hand over his mouth with all her might to keep him quiet. Vanessa.

"I know how this must look, but please, I am not here to hurt you. Do you understand that? I work for Pinky. She sent me here to get you out. If I take my hand off your mouth, you need to promise you will not be loud. Do you promise me? Nod if you do," Vanessa said in a stern but quiet voice.

Pinky? Did she really say Pinky? Still confused by the circumstances, Matt hesitated, then nodded. Vanessa slowly removed her hand from his mouth. Matt didn't yell but quickly grabbed Vanessa's wrist, trying to gain some control over the situation.

Before Matt could react, Vanessa turned the wrist grip Matt had on her and flipped him over onto his belly, his face shoved into the pillow and arms twisted behind him in an unnatural shape.

"I told you to bloody chill out! Don't fuck this up and make it harder than it needs to be. Did you hear me the first time? Pinky sent me to get you out of here, why are you trying to fuck this up? Now, can you calm down and stop?" Vanessa whispered.

Matt tried to stop squirming in this highly embarrassing position.

"I'm going to release you now, but don't try me again. You won't like what comes next when I get pissed."

Little by little, she lightened the grip on his arms and lessened the weight pressed against the back of his head until she released her grip completely. "Good boy," Vanessa said.

Matt slowly rolled over and sat up in his bed. "Jesus, were you actually going to break my fucking arms? Give me a fucking break already, I was asleep! It took me a second to focus." *How the fuck does she know Pinky? Jesus, of all people, I didn't expect her to be my savior.* Matt gasped, still trying to clear his throat.

"We don't have time to chitchat about that. We will have time to address those questions on the plane ride home. Now, are you ready? Will you follow my lead?" Vanessa asked.

"Sure, I guess so. I'm going to need to debrief this escape once we get in the air. I will behave, I promise," Matt said.

"Get dressed as fast as you can, right now," she commanded.

Matt whisked himself into the bathroom, peed quickly, threw on one of the nicer outfits he hadn't worn yet, splashed some water on his face, and followed Vanessa out of the room without a look back.

"What about the chips? Are you chipped? Because I'm not chipped, and I don't" Matt stammered.

Vanessa turned and grabbed Matt's broad shoulders. "Calm down. You won't be hurt. Jackson is here in the van, and he has disabled the force field. At least, I'm pretty sure he did," Vanessa said, winking.

"Christ, Jackson is here? And is it disabled or not? It isn't fucking funny," Matt shouted in a whisper.

"It's fine. I'm fucking with you. Let's go, no more scaredy-cat bullshit."

Vanessa headed down yet another hallway Matt hadn't explored. It was eerie and dark. He noticed there were no red lights littering the hall and ceilings, meaning they had disabled the CCTV feed. Vanessa walked as fast as the other Henchmen, which left Matt jogging to keep up. She was navigating the dark hallways like she'd been here a million times before. They arrived at the end of a hall where there was a small bathroom with a window. Vanessa swiftly pushed it open. It looked like the seal on this window had already been broken, making it easier to open a window in a one-hundred-year-old villa.

"Go on," she said, gesturing to the window. "And be careful. We're still on the second floor in case you forgot. I'll be out right behind you."

Matt obeyed her command and climbed out onto the ledge. His left foot was not on anything steady, and he gripped the edge of the window for support. He squinted to see where he could set it when he saw lights from a vehicle pull up near the fence.

"What are you waiting for? Oh my God. How new are you?" Vanessa huffed.

"I'm trying. Is that our ride that just pulled up, or are we getting caught?" Matt asked.

Vanessa ignored him and took the lead, hopping from one ledge to the other with no fear or hesitation. It was dark out, and Matt was larger and not as agile as her. His large frame was not built to jump around like a petite gymnast like Vanessa. He tried to follow her lead and to make the final leap, but slipped and slid for the most part. When he finally landed on the ground, Matt had missed the mark of her last jump and ended up sliding down the rest of the way on his ass. As gracefully as Vanessa stuck her landing, Matt was the complete opposite. It wasn't that far to fall, but it was awkward as fuck.

He landed with a thud, as Vanessa tried not to laugh. "Let's go, we are almost out of here!"

Matt had to trust that Jackson had disabled the force field just as he did with the CCTV as he ran past the six-foot zap line. Vanessa had already given the black iron gate a forceful shove, moving it just enough for them to slide through. Matt squeezed himself enough to be free.

He was free. Matt jumped into the van, pulled the door closed, and turned to see two of the people he had missed more than anything.

CHAPTER 10
LET'S GET OUTTA HERE

Liz and Franco sat smiling in the back seats of the van, Skippy was in the driver's seat, with Jackson navigating. "Nice landing, Sport. Good to see you still in one piece," Liz said, reaching over to give Matt a big side hug.

Matt looked to Liz and Franco, hardly believing his eyes. "You don't know how great it is to see you both. I'm sorry you had to come here to get me. I was trying to figure it out on my own," Matt said, putting his head down. It was humbling for him to see his friends hadn't forgotten him and had risked their own safety to come to him. Relief wasn't a big enough word to describe how he was feeling, happiness was.

"Don't be too hard on yourself. This was super weird for us too. We were just glad, again, that Pinky had her eyes on Rossi this whole time. She's known him for years and knew he was up to something," Franco said.

"Rossi told me Jimmie had agreed to this and that it was a game for you to rescue me. He was confident that it would never happen. He's so pissed about the HTA, because he thinks we won't teach respect, or whatever. God, I am so glad to be out of there. Thank you, Vanessa, I owe you one," Matt said.

"No problem. Just doing my job," she said.

"Hey, Skippy, Jackson. Thanks for coming," Matt called to the front of the car.

"Like the lady said, just doing my job," Skippy replied.

"We heard you didn't notice the antenna. That must have sucked for you," laughed Jackson.

"How did you not know about that? It's, like, Henchman 101. Little antenna around the perimeter, proceed with caution," Liz said.

Vanessa laughed. "I thought it was kind of funny myself. You should have heard all the jokes they were making about you. Making zapping noises throughout the villa."

"Well, I'm glad you all think it was so fucking funny. I thought I was going to die. If you haven't ever had the pleasure of being electrocuted, consider yourself lucky."

"Here they come. We got farther than I thought we would, we should be good," Skippy said.

Matt spun his head to see who was coming. He couldn't see who it was from the seat he was in but heard the purr of what he thought was another Urus. "I thought we were fine!" shouted Matt.

Liz placed a hand on Matt's arm. "Calm down, Sport. We got this covered. This is what we do, remember?"

Matt noticed that all three of them, Liz, Franco, and Vanessa, had pulled weapons from under their jackets, preparing to play their own game of how to elude capture. It was the black Urus that was hot in pursuit of their van, since they had traded in the white one after the helicopter incident. The speed of the Lamborghini was no match for the family van they had rented, yet no one except Matt seemed to care.

"Did you check for the helicopter? They have one, I saw them use it. The aftermath is not pretty," Matt said.

Liz positioned herself to face the back window of the van, both hands steadying her weapon. She offered a quick glance to

Matt and said, "Their chopper is out of commission. We took care of that. Give us some credit, Sport. Why do you think it took this long to get here?"

Matt ran his fingers through his hair and said, "I thought you were pissed at me, for one. But wait, you took their chopper out? That's impressive. I want to hear that story."

Vanessa had moved to cover the left side of the van, "This guy just oozes with self-confidence, doesn't he? He's kind of cute though, I can see why Amber's got it for him."

"Amen, the chopper story will go down in DMF history as one of our best take downs. But give me a break right now and don't bring up their romance. This isn't the time for him to get all googly eyed. Hold it steady, Skippy. These assholes don't know what a good shot I am," Franco said from the opposite side of the van from Vanessa.

Amid the chaos, Matt felt a twinge of disappointment that Amber wasn't part of the rescue mission. Maybe he had been misreading her intentions once again. He was quickly snapped back into reality by Skippy, who was weaving in and out of traffic like the expert he was. This van wasn't made to be in a high pursuit chase and win, that was for sure.

"What is it with these guys? Why aren't they taking any shots? If it was the other way around, I would have unloaded on these assholes. How much farther to the airfield?" Franco asked Jackson.

Looking up from his tablet, he said, "Two minutes. You guys ready to roll once we arrive?"

"Roger that. Matt, just follow me. We have a plan, so no going off script. Do what I say, and nothing else. Got it?" Liz said.

With a tilted head and an eye roll, Matt replied, "Yes, Liz. I got it. I won't mess this up."

"You're probably going to need to move a little quicker than you did jumping off the side of the villa, just saying," Vanessa added.

"Ok, jeez. I got it. Run after Liz, I can do that. Don't let me get in your way," Matt said.

Skippy was driving with focus and intent. His eyes were trained on the road ahead, with brief glances at his phone that was locked into an iPhone holder on the dash.

"Better hold on to something, Sport, he's about to do his *Top Gun* move," Liz said.

Matt looked for something to grab. Just in time, he wrapped both his arms around the seat in front of him.

"Three, two, one, here we go!" Skippy yelled as he slammed the brakes on, pushing on the pedal with both feet. The force of the abrupt stop and Skippy turning the van slightly to the left sent the van in a full three-sixty, now facing the Urus head on. The Urus maneuvered to avoid crashing into the van.

Skippy drove the van down a darkened path, barely visible to Matt. The road, if you could call it that, was filled with bumps, almost as if it was newly created just for this rescue attempt. Skippy had the newly groomed road memorized, as there were numerous tree stumps that had been left a little too high for a smaller car to clear without causing damage to the vehicle.

The Urus was again in pursuit, but the driver was struggling with the undefined road, hitting many of the tree stumps. The obstacle course the Urus was on was enough to slow them so the van could make it to the clearing where a sleek black helicopter, not unlike the one Matt had seen serve up carnage, was humming and ready for lift off.

As the van came to its final stop, Franco threw open the doors, jumped out, and sprinted to the waiting chopper. Vanessa, Liz, Matt, Skippy, and Jackson all scrambled out of the van and ran as quick as they could, heads down, as they approached the whirring blades of the chopper. Matt thought he saw someone out of the corner of his eye, near the edge of the woods they had just driven through. Liz raced past him, grabbing his arm to keep him moving forward.

The six made a successful run to the chopper. Vanessa slammed the door shut as the aircraft lifted off into the night sky.

Matt stretched to look out the window and was stunned by what he saw. It was Amber. She had emerged from the woods and had laid a spike strip across the entrance to the clearing. This was the last piece of the escape puzzle. He watched as she disappeared into the woods.

"Was that Amber? How will she get out? Can we go back?" Matt shouted over the noise of the helicopter.

"Oh my God. Yes, let's go back and get her, brilliant idea. I'm so glad you are here to think of that," Vanessa said with sarcasm.

"I told you it was bad," Liz said to Vanessa.

"What do you mean? What's bad?" Matt asked.

"They're talking about your gigantic crush on Little Miss Red Head," Franco said.

"Do you really think she needs us to come get her? Do you know who she is?" Vanessa scoffed. "Amber is a complete badass. She could have done this whole rescue herself. This is child's play for her."

"She will probably beat us to the jet," Liz said in a slightly more reassuring voice to Matt. "Want to take that bet, Franco?"

"Hell no. I'm not taking that. I want to keep my money," Franco said.

"Alright, I guess I was being a softy. All bullshit aside, I really missed you guys. Thank you again for coming," Matt said.

"Did you like my Top Gun move? Did you get the reference to the movie?" Skippy asked.

"If I say no, don't get pissed. I haven't seen the movie in a long time," Matt said.

"Dude, you're so lame. Never mind then, just remember, 'I'll slam on the brakes, and they will fly right by,'" Skippy said.

The helicopter flight was longer than Matt expected it to be. He wondered how it would be possible for Amber to beat them to the jet. Though after his experience with her, he wouldn't put it past her. The flight was long enough that he relaxed into the rhythmic humming of the engine. The adrenaline rush was wearing off, which felt good to get his body back into homeostasis.

"The stay in the villa did you some good. I thought I was going to have to wake you up. You didn't even fall asleep. Good job. We're landing," Franco said.

"Thanks, man. I really tried to live like a true Henchman while I was there. Not going to lie, I got sleepy. Jesus, I'm really out of it. The stress just drained out of my body. I tried to find my own way out. I really did, had a couple of plans that just didn't pan out. Hopefully, this is the last time you guys have to come get me."

Franco yawned and said, "It's what we do."

The landing was soft, and as the blades of the chopper slowed, an eerie quiet settled over the airstrip. Day was breaking, with soft pastel colors taking over the sky. The landscape was more mountainous than it was around the villa and brought with it cooler temperatures.

"How far did we fly? Where are we?" Matt asked.

"Is he always this anxious and full of questions?" Vanessa asked Liz.

"Give me a break. I'm just trying to put all the pieces together," Matt said.

"Really? Who cares where we are? It doesn't matter. Just hurry and get on the jet so we can leave this place," Vanessa said.

"God, is she always this grumpy?" Matt mumbled as he stepped aboard the jet.

"Just an FYI, we flew for a couple of hours, and we landed in Switzerland," Franco explained to Matt. He paused for a moment and a smile spread over his face. "Shit, I was right. Glad I didn't take that bet."

Matt looked up to see Amber leaning against the jet, arms crossed. His stomach flipped, his knees became wobbly, and he couldn't contain the wide grin.

"What did you expect? I'm no rookie," Amber said, smiling and looking directly at Matt.

"Holy crap. You made it. You're here. I won't ask you how, cause Grumpy over here was just busting my balls about asking too many questions," Matt said, nodding to Vanessa.

"When you look like I do, well, let's just say, it opens many doors for you," Amber said, flipping her dark red hair over her shoulder.

"Amen to that. I had no doubt you would be here," Liz said, placing a hand on Amber's shoulder. Matt was glad to see Liz and Amber seemed to be on the same friendly terms as when he'd left them.

The DMF crew gathered their gear from the chopper and one by one entered the sleek private jet. Matt recognized the jet as being Fowler's, the same one Matt had traveled on with him on his first trip to the villa. Franco was the last one on the plane. Matt could see him paying the chopper pilot, in cash. The flight crew helped the weary passengers stow their gear and get settled. Matt laid his head back and thought it was going to suck if he ever had to fly commercial again.

"Hey, Vanessa, can you get me a drink? You did such a good job last time we traveled together," Matt joked.

Vanessa gave Matt the death stare while buckling her seat belt. The jet taxied to the open field runway. Minutes after the doors to the jet were closed, they were in the air over the beautiful mountains of Switzerland. Although he assumed they were headed back home, Matt wasn't going to ask any more questions. The rest of the crew had all grabbed blankets and pillows, reclined their seats to the sleeper setting, and were asleep soon after take-off. Matt wanted to debrief, but looking at how totally exhausted his friends were, he decided the debrief could wait, and he joined them in a much-needed slumber.

CHAPTER 11
WHO KNEW?

Matt woke to the smell of freshly brewed coffee and sunlight streaming through the jet windows. The mood was relaxed in the main cabin. Franco lay awake on the sofa on the opposite side of the aircraft scrolling through his phone. Liz and Amber had taken seats next to each other and were chatting in whispered voices. Vanessa was up and about chatting with the flight crew. Jackson and Skippy were reclined in the seats facing Matt and were still out of it, not ready to face the day.

"Here you go. I remember how you like your coffee, almond milk right?" Vanessa said.

Matt sat forward in his chair to accept the hot coffee. "Thank you. You didn't have to get that for me. It's been a good flight so far, seems like we all caught up on sleep."

"These guys needed it too. They have been working nonstop for the past three days. They work well together, and they did a good job. It went down without flaws. That doesn't happen by accident," Vanessa said, sitting next to him.

"No, I suppose not. They are good friends, too." Matt paused to take a sip. "I'm curious. You said you were working for Pinky. How do you know her?"

"Pinky. We have her in common. I'm not sure how much

you know about her, and I'm not going to get into all that. What I will say is that she is a rather well-connected woman. She has many facets to her. I can't wait to see who she is now. Working at a gym? That's a new one for me," Vanessa said, chuckling.

"I've heard only a small part of her story. I only know her as a ditzy blonde who has a crush on my boss, Fowler. She pulls that off like a pro," Matt said.

"She is a pro at whatever she dips her toe into. I met her when I was a teenager. I had a rough start, probably not unlike her, I assume. She took me in, treated me like I was family. She trained me to be a survivor and to take my life back, and she taught me that I had the power and control to not be a victim of my circumstances. I think I believed her because she walked the talk. Because of her, I have done things, seen things, met people I never would have, and traveled the world. I owe her a lot," Vanessa said.

"Shit, that's not who I would have ever imagined Pinky was. Another question for you. Until now, you seem to be annoyed with me. What's up with the chit chat now?" Matt asked.

"Annoyed? That's a matter of perception. I get a little wound up while on the job. I like things to go at a certain pace, and when they don't, I get annoyed, I guess. A little sleep and some coffee always do the trick. Let's start over? I promise I won't be so irritated with your questions too," Vanessa said.

Her British accent was charming, and Mat enjoyed listening to her talk. It made the conversations more dynamic. Her blonde hair was clipped up in the back, and her blue eyes sparkled in the sunlight peeking through the windows. Matt leaned in a little closer to her while she spoke.

Matt nearly jumped as he felt a hand on his shoulder. "Aren't we the chatty ones this morning? I didn't know you two were so close. Maybe we weren't briefed on all the ongoings between you two," Amber said.

Matt looked from Amber to Vanessa and back to Amber. If he didn't know better, he would say Amber sounded a bit territorial, and he kind of liked it. "We were just getting reacquainted. I guess you two know each other, then?"

"We know *of* each other. I had only heard of the heroics she's performed across the globe," Vanessa said.

"Aren't you sweet? Heroics. Would you mind if Matt and I had a word in private? We haven't been able to reconnect. You know, we have a complicated relationship." Amber smiled.

Vanessa stood, placing her hand on Matt's shoulder, and said, "A relationship, is that what you are calling it? But sure, I will let you two have some space. Enjoy your coffee, Matt. I'm looking forward to you showing me around the DMF House. I hear it's rather large."

"Reconnect, what was that all about?" Matt asked.

Amber frowned and watched Vanessa take a seat next to Liz and turned to Matt to answer. "She's just a complication. Now, how are you doing? Everything ok? You came out of this kidnapping in a lot better shape than last time."

"No blindfolds for you either. No medical suite stays for me, it's a win-win for us," Matt said.

"Nothing wrong with a little blindfolding once in a while," Amber replied as she stood to take her seat across from Liz and Vanessa.

"Is it finally my turn to talk to the wonder boy now? What the fuck, I should have taken a number," Franco said, taking the seat next to Matt. "Better watch out for that one," he said, nodding to Vanessa. "You may be in over your head with her. Are you ready to get back to business?"

"Thanks for the warning, but I know what she can do to me

if I'm not careful. Did anything worthwhile happen while I was away?" Matt asked.

"Actually, yes. It's done. The whole thing is done! The contractors finished up, we are good to go, ready to open. There wasn't that much to finish when you left, but I have to say it looks fantastic," Franco said.

"Seriously? How did you manage that? Those contractors were ridiculous when I was there trying to get them to move faster," Matt said. "The last time I saw it, I thought it would never get done. You will have to share your secrets to get their asses moving."

"Let's just say we used some old school Henchmen techniques to get them to comply with the completion date," Franco said.

"I love it! I wish I wouldn't have wasted my time trying to be nice and sympathetic to them. That didn't get me anywhere. Dude, I am so excited to see it," Matt said.

Matt noticed Liz was finished with the girl talk. She was standing in the back of the cabin doing some light stretching of her back and hamstrings. He took this as an invitation for him to meet her there.

"I need to go check in with Liz. I can't tell what her mood is. Is she ok?" Matt asked Franco.

"She's fine, *I think*. She did get a little rattled when we first heard about you and Rossi flying off into the sunset with each other. Once she saw the security video of you being escorted into Rossi's Range Rover, she was a little less concerned. They were so gentle with you, we all laughed a little about that to be honest," Franco said.

"They were gentle. It was weird, I kept waiting for them to kick my ass, and it never happened. Thank you for the update though. I'm getting pumped to see the HTA get off the ground," Matt said. "You should have seen what they did for him once we got back to the villa! It was insane. Rossi was asleep when we got there. Get this, he asked them to carry him inside! A grown ass man being carried in like he was an invalid or some shit. Shocked the hell out of me."

Franco laughed at the thought of either Fowler or Jimmie being carried up to bed.

Liz saw Franco get up to lay back on the sofa and quickly filled the empty seat next to Matt.

"I didn't realize I was going to have to wait my turn to talk with you. You are popular with the ladies, I see. Vanessa seems to have succumbed to your charm as well. Do you have time for me now?" Liz said.

"I'll always have time for you. The Vanessa thing is super strange. On my flight over, she was a flight attendant, then I saw her in the villa, and the rest is history, I guess. Is she staying with us or what?" Matt asked.

"I think she is staying for a couple of days, catching up with Pinky. I'm not sure Amber wants her poking around her territory, if you know what I mean," Liz said.

"You mean with me?" Matt asked.

"Yes, you, silly. Amber is not thrilled she is here. She'll get over herself in time," Liz said, smiling. "So, Franco told you the good news? The HTA is ready! We can set a grand opening date. I was thinking about the first of next month, that gives us about three weeks to get organized. Does that work for you?"

"Yes, that will be perfect. I'll have to go by my school supplies when we get back." Matt laughed.

"It's good to have you back in one piece. Knowing that they didn't hurt you made this a lot less stressful to plan. We'll be landing soon. My dad and Jimmie are looking forward to having you back in the House," Liz said.

"They are? That's nice to hear. And I'll keep my distance from the ex-flight attendant, for now," Matt said.

CHAPTER 12
HOME SWEET HOME

It was a quiet afternoon when they arrived back at the DMF House. Secretly, Matt had hoped that someone would have said something nice to him or would acknowledge him in some way. A 'happy you're back,' or 'nice to see you, bro' would have been nice. But there was nothing of the sort. There were only a couple of Henchmen in the kitchen having a late day coffee. *A head nod would have been nice*, Matt thought.

"Don't forget we're meeting with my dad and Jimmie in an hour. Just enough time for you to unpack and watch some Netflix." Liz laughed.

"I've had way more than enough Netflix in the past few weeks, I'm good, thanks. How did you know about that? Vanessa?"

Vanessa, who was fumbling with her wheely suitcase in the doorway, asked, "Did you say my name? This is a nice place, Matt, can you show me to my room?"

"Sport, you just go unpack," Liz interrupted then turned to Vanessa. "I'll take you to her room. He may get lost on his way back."

Matt watched them go toward the opposite wing of the House before heading up to his room. He stood briefly in the door. This, this is what he missed. His own space. He felt safe here, life was good once again. On his bed sat a brand new iPhone in the box with a note in Liz's handwriting. *Keep track of this one, Sport. What are you on, iPhone number three in the past year?* Matt laughed. He'd lost his phone when he'd first come to the DMF House and again when he was kidnapped the time before. Hopefully, there wouldn't be any more traumatic events that would result in him needing a new phone anytime soon.

After unpacking and setting up his phone, he laid down on his bed, spending a moment reflecting on his time at the Rossi villa. Strangely, the only time he'd felt like he was in danger was in the Urus while it was being riddled with bullets. In the first few days of his kidnapping, Matt wondered if they were leading him to believe in a false sense of security, so he would let his guard down, then they would attack and be violent, but no, nothing of the sort. What takeaways could the HTA use from that model of Henchmen?

―――

Matt and Liz both received texts to meet in Fowler's office. They met in the hall in front of the office door. "Just like old times, huh Sport?" Liz smiled, punching him in the arm.

"Ouch, yes, just like old times. I feel like I never left," Matt said, opening the office door.

"Good to see you back, Matt. Looking better than ever," Fowler said. "Have a seat, I can't wait to hear what that asshole's problem is this time."

"It's good to be back. Thank you for putting out the resources to come get me. Just so you know, I was working to devise some plans for me to get out on my own," Matt said.

Jimmie laughed. "We heard about that. Would have been

tricky without being chipped. We knew Jackson could disable that crap for you guys."

"Yes, everyone laughed about that but me. That shit hurt. That leads me to say, we need to make sure we include a 'What to look out for in your new surroundings during a kidnapping' section to the HTA curriculum. Also, how to dial internationally. I found an old desk phone, but I didn't know how to make an international call," Matt said.

"Good ideas. Feel free to add whatever you think needs to be included to the HTA. But can you explain to us what Rossi's deal is, why's he pissed this time?" Jimmie asked.

"Right, about that. Rossi brought me to his office to say he's mad about the HTA. He thinks it's wrong to train Henchmen, and that we are not training to what is a core value to the profession, which is loyalty," Matt said.

Fowler shook his head. "He's angry about that? Jesus, he must be bored out of his mind. He pulls a stunt like this all because we want to train Henchmen? What a piece of work this guy is."

"I tried to explain our concept to him, but Rossi was obsessed with the loyalty part of it. He believes that there is nothing without that and that you can't teach loyalty," Matt replied.

"Actions bring about loyalty as well. Investing in long-term employees, treating them with respect breeds loyalty. Maybe this whole 'loyalty can't be trained' idea is a European thing," Jimmie said.

"I think you could be right about that," Fowler said to Jimmie. "Rossi sure was pissed when he called here."

"He called here? What, when he found out I was gone?" Matt asked.

Fowler nodded. "He thought we would never be able to get past his 'state-of-the-art' security system," Fowler said with air quotes, scoffing. "The dumbshit hires enough cyber guys. You would think it wouldn't be that easy to hack into his system and dismantle the helicopter."

"How was your time in Italy?" Jimmie asked.

"The vibe in the villa is pretty chill. The only time we ran into some shit was when I was out running errands with a couple of them. I think Rossi must have pissed someone off. The guys chasing us showed no mercy when it came down to it," Matt said.

"I talked to Pinky about him. It seems Rossi is going around and looking to pick fights, sort of. He has been going to all the larger organizations and finding shit to complain about. I think he's a bored old man who needs to find a hobby," Liz said. "I'd like to show him what a real fight looks like. What a huge fucking waste of time and resources. No offense, Sport, but really?"

"So, it wasn't just me and the HTA then? I guess that's a relief. Maybe he's looking to take more on. I wonder if he's stepping on other people's territory," Matt wondered.

"Pinky is working on finding out more, like who all he's pissed off. She thinks the guys trailing us in the red sports car were from an organization that is run by a bunch of millennials. They're German, and they think they're the shit and are super sassy about it," Liz said.

Jimmie bobbed his head. "I have heard of them as well. They are known as the Cyber Verbrecher, which translates to Cyber Criminals in English, or the CVs for short. They make their own rules about this business as they go along. They are not following in the grand tradition of the organizations of times gone by. They are causing havoc in Europe and across the dark web."

Fowler took off his glasses and sighed. "I hate to ask, but what are we talking about here? What kind of havoc, Jim?"

Jimmie stood up from his chair and took a couple of steps before he answered, "From what I can understand, they have been jumping into very wealthy people's personal accounts. The amount of money they have been siphoning is staggering, or at least it would be to you and I, but to these folks it's just enough to piss them off. The intel I've gotten is just nuts. They do all this shit on the dark web, wave it under their noses that they took a few million, and then they completely fuck with them and send them pictures."

"Pictures of what?" Fowler asked.

"Let me guess, of them partying it up and what they are buying with their stolen money," Liz scoffed.

"That's it. Yes. What balls these guys have. They send videos waving and blowing kisses at the camera. It's real bad," Jimmie said.

Matt got up to grab another beer and said, "I would not want to be around when they get caught. That'd be really fucking ugly."

"So what you're saying is that they are snot-nosed little punks who think they know everything. If they know what's good for them, they won't come around here trying to show off," Fowler said.

Liz snorted. "Ok, tough guy. I'll let Pinky know to pass the word onto the CVs. Glad she speaks German so nothing will be missed the in the translation."

Matt took a long drink from the glass bottle and wondered just how many languages and lives did Pinky actually lead?

"We have them on our radar. Max and Jackson are monitoring them," Jimmie said.

Liz was beaming like Matt had never seen before, it was almost confusing to see her so animated. She said, "Let's leave it at that for now. We can talk about some good news now. The

HTA is ready to go. We have set a grand opening date for the first of next month. It's going to be epic."

There were times when he still couldn't believe this life he'd fallen into. He hadn't always felt lucky, but right now he was. He was out of the nine-to-five grind, not bored, and was the lead in getting the soon to be world renowned HTA up and running.

"Congratulations, you two. I know how much work has gone into this. We are both very proud of what you have accomplished," Fowler said, smiling.

"Thank you, but we haven't had any success just yet. Let's see how the first class goes. I'm nervous excited about it," Matt said.

CHAPTER 13
THE GRAND OPENING

THE GRAND OPENING was scheduled for a couple of weeks after Matt's return. The construction was done, just a few finishing touches like hanging the blinds and filling the snack bar. Spending most of his time with Liz, running around finalizing details, was exactly what he needed to get back into the swing of things, it was just like old times. Being busy with mundane things like running real errands was a nice safe way to be busy and get out of the house. He had planned on taking his romance with Amber up a notch or two once he got back and settled. But Vanessa, she had put a kink in his plans. It seemed that every time he turned around, she was there, smiling and looking pretty fantastic. Amber had noticed Vanessa was always around too and brought it up to Matt at Pinky's.

"I wanted to ask you about Vanessa, if that's ok."

Matt tensed and tried to play it off like it wasn't bothering him too, and said, "Sure, what did you want to ask?"

"It's just that she's around a lot. I like her and all, but I just want to understand what your intentions are with her. I guess I'm asking if you are welcoming her advances. That's fine if you are. I just wanted to know, what are your intentions are with me?"

He was caught off guard and wasn't too sure himself about his intentions toward her. He often wondered if he could truly get past how they first became acquainted. Reflecting back on how he met Vanessa, it wasn't exactly on the up and up either. Maybe he would be better off dating someone who wasn't in the same line of work as him.

"I don't think I've been encouraging her. But you're right, she is hanging around a lot. I chalked it up to her not really knowing anyone else here, maybe she was lonely or something."

Amber raised her eyebrow and said, "I would suggest you sort things out, for all three of our sakes."

———

The celebration was kept on the down low. Only members of the current DMF Team were invited, and it was more of a traditional open house. The Henchmen were instructed to come by at scheduled intervals throughout the day. The big reveal was met with positive reviews, lots of eyebrow raises, and slight head tilts. For Henchmen, this translated to, *good work. I'm giving this thumbs up.* David H. spent most of the day giving tours to the groups of Henchmen. He was embracing the role of being the bridge between the "regular" Henchmen and the Top Five who were now instructors.

———

Matt was at post sitting behind the front desk watching as the groups of Henchman came to tour the HTA. As he predicted, none of them left without stopping at the snack table. That was one thing they always had in common, eating. It was a mixed bag of comments about the HTA and the new requirements for the Henchmen. Some were unsure, some were insulted, and some were up for the challenge. Pinky was stationed at the table to one, to keep it filled, and to listen to what comments were worth noting.

Matt always enjoyed watching Pinky work, especially now that he knew more about her. She was mysterious but gave no clue to anyone about her complicated past. He often wondered how she balanced life at her gym with being an internationally known leader of her own set of Henchmen.

Matt went to refill his plate, and without even thinking about it, walked to Pinky and gave her a hug, "Thanks for being such a huge part of the success here. None of this would have happened without you."

"You've come a long way since the first time we met. Do you remember that? You looked so overwhelmed. Did you ever imagine being part of a day like this? Anyway, thank you for including me," Pinky said. She had closed her gym for the day in order to better accommodate the Henchmen's tours, followed by their registration into the HTA. As the tour ended for each of the groups of Henchmen, they were directed to the front desk. Franco spoke briefly with each Henchman to establish what track they would eventually enroll in then directed them to meet with their new instructors. Matt and Liz were on standby in case there were any questions that Franco couldn't answer. They tried not to hover, as they wanted Franco to embrace his role of being the advisor to the new students.

"Franco is really taking to being the guy in charge, isn't he? I think he kind of digs it," Liz said.

"I do too. The HTA has brought out benefits that we never saw coming, you know? It has just added another dimension to being Henchmen," Matt said.

"That's true. I hope we can get them all onboard. There are still some stragglers."

Matt smiled and said, "Pinky is getting that list of names together. We can make them our special project."

Henchmen who wanted to become experts in driving met with Skippy. Henchmen who wanted to learn to make things go boom met with William. Gabe was the go-to guy to instruct Henchmen in beating the shit out of people. The experts in firearms was Ricky, and the expert in bullshitting, the male version of being a Honeypot, was left to David M.

Each Henchman left with a packet of information about what their lives would look like for the next few weeks, along with the new HTA uniform. The new HTA students were given an assortment of T-shirts, sweats, and hoodies to wear throughout their enrollment at the HTA.

As Matt and Liz were monitoring the sign-up tables, they overheard two Henchmen waiting in line to talk with Skippy say, "What are we in the police academy? My cousin went through that, and they all wore something like this." Andreas, his nametag said. The newest Henchman to enroll with Skippy.

"Or like we are in Army basic training. But really, it's kinda cool. I like the logo," said Paolo.

The CM Team had created the new HTA logo, which was in the shape of a shield that was divided into four sections in blocks of alternating red and black. On the top of the shield in bold block script was the word 'Henchman,' with 'Training Academy,' below it. Simple but effective.

The news of the opening the doors to the HTA spread across the dark web quicker than Four could whine about the speed of the servers. The CM Team made the call to anonymously start posting on the dark web about the HTA. They had no idea that it was going to go viral, at all, but it did.

Jackson called for a meeting to give everyone an update the activity they'd seen floating around on the message boards.

Matt and Liz were just leaving his room to head to the conference room for the CM Team meeting when Vanessa appeared at his door. Liz sighed, and said, "Can we help you?" Matt always appreciated Liz running interference for him. He just hadn't found the mental energy to figure out how, if at all, Vanessa would be part of his life. At the moment, Amber was still the person he wanted to pursue.

"Hey Liz, nothing to help with. I was just bringing Matt some sweets. My mum sent me a care package from home. Too much for just me, so I thought I'd share."

Matt walked to take the small box filled with the sweet treats, and said, "Thank you Vanessa. You know I have the worst sweet tooth, ever. What is all this?"

"Well, what we have here is some of Britain's finest. This is a Lion bar, to die for. These are Jelly Babies, super yummy, and these are Galaxy Caramels, which I personally love."

"I can't wait to try all of it. Thank you," Matt said, setting the box down on his bed.

"We have to get going now, Sport. We have a meeting to get to," Liz said.

"Don't let me keep you, but I do expect a full report of which is your favorite," Vanessa said.

In the conference room, Liz turned to Matt and said, "You better figure that one out. I can't believe I'm defending her, but you need to be straight with Amber if she's not the one for you."

"I agree. I'll talk to her soon, I promise."

The CM Team was being inundated with requests, questions, comments, and some major shit talking from the Rossi gang. They had planned for some activity but did not prepare for the volume. It became more than they could take on. With much dread, Jackson had to go against his better judgment and ask Four to help with the logging, response, and coordination of the HTA fanfare. Matt and Liz set weekly meetings with Jackson from the CM Team to keep them in the loop. Today Max, Jackson's father, was joining them.

Matt and Liz looked at each other as Jackson and Max sat across from them. They both looked rough, rougher than usual. Especially for Jackon, who was never one big into personal hygiene anyway, it had gotten bad. He needed a shower and shave, big time.

"What's with the beard, Jackson? Not much time for personal care, huh?" Liz asked.

"No, Liz, there really isn't. I'm fucking working twenty-four-seven. I suppose you're going to tell me I smell too?"

"Do you really want me to answer that?" Liz asked.

"Never mind that. We appreciate your hard work on this. There's going to be plenty of time for showers when this is all done," Matt added, trying to meditate the conversation.

Leaning back in his chair, Jackson said, "Thanks for having my back, dude. I don't have time to explain my showering schedule. You know, the only situation I would want to include Four in any of our projects is if it was specific and whine-proof. So far, he is doing an incredible job."

"Really? That's good news, though not exactly what I was expecting to hear. I suppose responding to messages on the dark web fits into his skill set," Matt said.

"It really does. He can be an asshole and talk shit to anyone, especially if he remains faceless," Liz said.

"Are we all cool with him having an open mic? I mean, who knows what he is saying to people? Is this making more work for you to monitor?" Matt asked.

"Way ahead of you there. I have friends, work friends, who

do that for me. They let me know if they see something that is way off base and that I need to follow up on. It's been great, actually. Keeping Four busy with this keeps him out of our way, and we really needed someone who can expertly navigate the volume," Max said.

"Miracles can happen. The OT working for us? Who wasn't surprised when we actually captured him only to find out he was a whiny little jerk," Liz said.

"Whiny little jerk is too long of a name," Jackson laughed. "He seriously thinks we call him Four because we like him, that it's a term of affection. He loves that we call him Four now, he loves that we gave him a nickname. Feeding his ego keeps his annoying chatter to a minimum."

"I'd still go with whiny little jerk if we could! I can't believe Amber went and bought him some goldfish and left it on his desk. What's her deal?" Liz said.

"He's a jerk, but I guess maybe she knows what it's like to not have any friends," Matt said. "Or she's just playing him. She's good at that, right?"

"She knows how to read people, that's for sure," Liz said.

"Well, I hope he likes his fish. But I'm more interested in hearing how the HTA is being perceived online. Has it been good, bad? What's the word? Has there been anything concerning come up?" Matt said.

Jackson and Max made eye contact. "We want to keep you in the loop about this. It may be nothing, but it's something that I have seen pop up more than once on the chats. It's about Rossi. I feel like there could be some nasty shit about to go down," Max said.

"What do you mean? You think he's going to do something, or someone is going to do something to him?" Liz asked.

"From what we can tell, there's a bounty on his head. At first, we thought it was a joke, because who really cares about the old man in Italy, you know? But then we heard more specifics about what would happen to him if he set foot on US soil," Jackson said.

The thought of being on someone's hit list again triggered Matt, he stood and said, "He's coming here? Why? Not for me, I hope. I've seen enough of him."

Affectionately reaching for his arm, Liz said, "Don't worry, Sport, we have your back. But if he is planning a trip here, we should keep an eye on him. Right, Jackson?"

"Of course, we are monitoring his whereabouts. We will keep you posted. There are so many people who want him dead, he will be lucky to make it back home if he is stupid enough to show up," Jackson said.

"Please do. I'm not interested in an unplanned trip to Italy any time soon," Matt said.

CHAPTER 14
FIRST DAY - AGIN

MATT DRESSED for his first day at the HTA with some hesitation and anxiety. It was his idea, his creation, his contribution to not only the DMF Team, but to the rest of the world, and yet he had to start from the bottom, again. Sighing, Matt knew why. He had disobeyed orders, on several occasions. It was a consequence of his insubordination, or was it stupidity? Although he was trying to not have a poor attitude, this demotion felt like a kick in the teeth. Throwing on a new pair of black HTA joggers and a matching T-shirt, taking one last look at himself in the mirror before heading downstairs. Hoping he didn't he didn't look like a dork, he prepared himself for any razzing and jokes that would come his way. Taking Liz's class was the one he was looking forward to the most. With the time they spent preparing her, he wanted to be there to encourage her in a way that only best friends could do. He knew what she needed to hear to be most confident going into a totally new role as an instructor at the HTA.

Matt entered the kitchen and immediately felt more like he was part of the Team than he ever had. All the Henchmen he had passed in the hallway and in the kitchen had the same combination of HTA gear on. It was nice to not feel like an outsider. None of the Henchmen laughed or poked fun at him. The mood was lighter, and the overall energy was filled with enthusiasm and pride. Matt could sense that the Henchmen also felt an even stronger bond to each other. They were laughing and holding their heads higher, as if they knew they were part of something special.

"Do you want to ride with me over to Pinky's, shit, I mean, the HTA?" David H. asked.

"That would be great, thanks. Can I ask if this is mandatory? I mean, are you assigned to be my bodyguard again? Did you guys hear something? I know Rossi may pay another surprise visit," Matt said.

"Look at you, bro, being so smart. It is mandatory, but I also thought I could use the company today. I'm a little fucking nervous. It's like I'm back in high school again. That's not a place I want to re-visit. Terrible memories. Weird how some experiences sit in your mind and pop up when you don't expect them to," David H. said.

"Mandatory. Well, shit. After I graduate from the HTA, maybe I will be the one giving rides and won't need to have a chaperone. But I know how you're feeling. Re-visiting parts of your life you thought were over kind of sucks," Matt said.

———

Pulling into the parking lot, David H. said, "Fuck, I have to remember to park in the back now. Old habits die hard, you know?"

Since being back from the villa, Matt was being more intentional about paying attention to his surroundings. He wasn't just going to jump out of a car again without doing a quick head swivel.

"I'll let you do the honors," Matt said, moving aside so

David H. could push in the numbers to the digital lock on the back door of the HTA, aka Pinky's back door.

Liz and Amber arrived earlier to make sure everything was set up just right and were waiting by the door as Matt and David H. entered.

"Well, don't you two look cute," Amber said.

"You know you're the only one to say something about how we look. We're all a little on edge. I hope you aren't being sarcastic," Matt said, walking by.

"Of course not! Sorry! But I meant it. I wasn't being sarcastic. Good luck today," Amber shouted.

Matt could see Pinky waving at them from the gym's front desk. "This must kill her to not be included in this," Matt said.

"She's included more than you think, Sport. Don't feel sorry for her," Liz said locking elbows with Matt.

"I'm sure she is. Are you walking me to class? That's so cute," Matt teased.

"Yes, I am indeed walking you to class, of which I am your instructor for today. Show some respect," Liz said.

"Pardon me, Ms. Fowler. I wasn't sure how you figured everything out for the first day since they kicked me off the planning committee," Matt said.

"Oh yeah, that's right. I forgot you had something to do with this, didn't you? Wink, wink, yes. For this introduction class, I'm taking one third of the class at a time, Franco one third, and my dad and Jimmie the other third. We will all speak for about forty-five minutes, then everyone will take a break and move to their next classroom," Liz said.

"That should be enough for the first day. I'm sure it will be a lot of information to take in," Matt said.

"I'm glad that you will be in my class first, the support with your being there makes me feel better. It's going to be fine, but I've never done anything like this before. Standing up in front of a room of people isn't something I do frequently, probably not since high school," Liz said.

He noticed Liz had a dry mouth and was eagerly sipping water out of her new HTA water bottle. He'd never seen her anything be cool, calm, and collected when faced with new situations. "Of course, lead the way," Matt said.

He was there as a requirement for his entry back onto the administrative side of the HTA, but also to be there for Liz. He sat in the middle row, not in the front. No self-respecting Henchman would sit in the front row by choice. The Henchmen who sat in the front row only did so because those were the only empty seats. Matt had chosen a seat next to Sal. He hadn't ever worked with him, but he was friendly with him.

"This shit's crazy, am I right? I never thought I would be back in school again," Sal whispered to Matt.

Matt nodded his head in agreement with Sal and turned front facing. Liz's pacing was making him nervous too. He stared intently at Liz until she met his glance. Raising his chin slightly, he took a deep breath in, hoping that she would mimic him and do the same.

Matt leaned in when Liz began class. He thought back to the night she took him back to his condo and wasted those two idiots. Now, they looked at life very differently. Her topic for the opening day class was about organization and finding that to be key to being a successful Henchman. He had helped her pick that topic, since it was one of her favorite things to talk about. They figured it would be easier for her first talk to be about something she had a passion for. The Henchmen listened intently to her explaining that over the next few weeks, she would give tips and tricks on how to always stay on top of things and how to be prepared for any job in minutes.

"I am going to require you to bring laptops to each class. If you have any problems, either Matt or I can help with that."

Matt could see that none of the Henchmen could figure out why having a laptop in class was necessary. They were confused, shaking their heads, and shuffling in their seats.

"Listen, I would describe none of us as computer literate. My anxiety level is getting pretty high now, I'm not gonna lie. The thought of having to work on a laptop to be organized freaks me out," Sal said.

"What's that all about, Liz? Can't we just remember stuff? Why a laptop?" Mario asked.

Matt remembered Mario from the first night at the house. He was hanging around with Snoop while Snoop was on door duty. He'd seen them lifting at Pinky's a few times. Mario's claim to fame at the DMF House was that he was the fattest Henchmen in there. Matt used to wonder if it bothered him at all to be called fat by the other guys. He seemed to embrace it and was comfortable with his size, never telling them to shut up or walking away when the razzing got too bad.

"Being able to use a computer or laptop is important. I'm going to teach you how to make an Excel spreadsheet. You all know what a spreadsheet is correct?" Liz said.

Matt felt the tension in the room go up when she mentioned Excel. He was ready to jump in and defend her if he needed to about the reasons for her request.

"Yes, I'm pretty sure we all do. Are we supposed to carry the laptop around with us on jobs? I don't understand," Mario said.

"You don't have to get it now. That's why we are having this class. You won't be asked to take them with you on jobs unless they are required for that job," Liz said.

"If I wanted to be on the CM Team, I would be there now," Mario said, as the room chuckled.

"If I didn't know better Fats, I'd say you were trying to be sassy with me. Trust me on this, ok? There is more to come on this. Before we end for today, I just want you to know that we will go slowly, with this, no need to worry about it," Liz said.

Amber had been assigned to knock on the doors of the three classrooms to let them know it was time to move to the next class. Pinky's job was to not only field questions from gym members about who the new tenants were, but to supply coffee, drinks, and food for the Henchmen to grab in between classes. Food was always an excellent motivator when it came to thirty or so three-hundred-pound men. The swarm around the food table indicated that having food each day was important and a great way for them to have a quick debrief about what they learned. In a traditional office setting, it was the same as meeting at the water cooler to take a break from the daily grind.

Matt's next stop was to Franco's classroom. He was designated to teach the Henchman how to talk about their jobs with family and friends. No one really believed that being a Henchman was a 'real' job, so what did they say when people asked? Matt had often wondered that since he first came to the House. Personally, he had come up with telling people he worked for a security firm called Twilight Security. He still fumbled over his words when asked what exactly he did for Twilight Security. He learned it had been hard for the other Henchmen as well to come up with something to say when asked how they could afford such nice cars and homes, being as uneducated as they were. They were often mistaken for being drug dealers and working with the mob. Not having another story to tell, they just went with it, which led to trouble for their kids since they were known around the neighborhood as having a dad who sold drugs for a living. Throughout the course, Franco would give them the tools they'd need to be comfortable sharing with people where they worked and what they did. In addition to teaching them to each have a backstory, Franco would offer ways for them to save and invest their money. All the Henchmen were making over six figures, most never having extra money to invest in anything but their rent and car payments.

"This class will give you practical information and life skills. It's just a very different lifestyle than we came from, and there are things I can teach you that will help understand it better," Franco said.

"My kids get picked on all the time because they assume I work for the mob. I had to scare the shit out of a bunch of them one time to get them off my son's ass. I didn't know what else to do. I gave them all the death stare and then flashed them my piece. They went nuts and ran off. Probably could have handled that better," Tyler said.

Matt was enjoying getting to know a more personal side to these guys that he had seen on almost a daily basis, but never saw them as dads or even husbands. The only thing Matt had ever heard about Tyler before this class was that he had the most kills out of all the Henchmen at DMF. If he heard correctly, the number of kills he had was in the triple digits.

The room laughed, but also understood the predicament since they had similar stories about how their wives were mistreated in social settings as well. Matt thought at least he didn't have to come home every day and explain to his family what he'd done at work that day. It was hard enough to make shit up to feed his mom and sisters when they spoke on the phone every so often. Franco assured them that after this class was done, they would all have a better grasp on what to share with people about their jobs, more information about their finances. He often wondered if these guys ever dreamed of having money like this roll in. Franco was the perfect person to teach this class, since he had come from a similar background as they had, but also went to some college. Franco was really in his element and showed no signs of nerves like Liz had.

The sandwich wraps they ordered for the snack table were a big hit and were gone after the first break. The pizza always was a hit, and Fat Sully's offered to be an unofficial sponsor. They donated the first dozen pies to the HTA's first day. Matt made a final round at the snack table, and he was off to Fowler and Jimmie's classroom. He could feel the atmosphere had downshifted to a more relaxed feel. When the day started, there was a lot of defensiveness and uncertainty in the air. The first two rounds of classes seemed to have put most people at ease.

Jimmie and Fowler would take turns teaching as Fowler could not commit to the full term. It had been determined the full term for the core classes would include four weeks, meeting three times a week in the mornings. Once they got to the specialty classes, it would be up to the individual instructors on how long they needed. Each teacher had come up with a different length give or take a couple of days.

For this first class, Fowler would talk to the class about what bosses really need from Henchmen, from his perspective. He wanted to share with them how to be the best asset while working on a job. Jimmie would share some of what he learned over the years in so many countries while in the Army and the art of Zen. He wanted to take his time with the class to help the Henchmen learn how to calm their minds, have a self-care routine, and how to relax.

"I know some of you must think this kind of stuff is for sissies, but let me tell you, I know firsthand it isn't. I have seen Jim go from being a high-strung, arrogant—sorry Jim—but an asshole, to the serene, well-grounded guy he is today. So, I would take it seriously," Fowler said.

"I'm glad you brought that up. I was an asshole. I hope to share some of my insights with you. And what Ed has to say applies to you now, and if you were to ever move on and have a new company to work for. Just a lot of common-sense informa-tion." Jimmie spoke in a sharper tone than Matt had heard before. Even when he was in trouble, Jimmie still had the Zen flow about him, not what he was hearing today.

"Can't imagine what our homework will be in this class, go home and meditate?" laughed Tony.

"I can handle that better than trying to make a spread-sheet," said Mario to the class.

"There you go. This won't be so bad then. Listen, before you go, I want to say that I am proud. I am proud of you guys, and I am proud of our organization for taking on a project like this. I hope you realize that this, the HTA, will change the way Henchmen work and how they are respected in the world. You are making history, right here, right now," Fowler said.

"Class dismissed. Go enjoy the rest of your day. For those of you staying to get a lift in at Pinky's, it's ok to leave your cars parked in the back," Jimmie said.

Matt was looking forward to meeting up with Liz and Franco to hear what their experience was. They had planned to meet in his room after dinner for a debrief. All he knew was that he felt lighter, and like a tremendous weight had been lifted. The first class was done, thank God.

CHAPTER 15

WORD ON THE STREET

Jackson called a meeting with Matt, Fowler, Jimmie, Garrett, and Liz to give them updated information about Rossi's impending trip to the US. Matt was anxious about what the news was but grateful that Rossi's next visit would not be a surprise. How many times could one guy be kidnapped, anyway? Twice in a lifetime is two times more than most people.

"Thank you for meeting on such short notice. I think this is worth sharing with you and getting a plan in place," Jackson said.

"Of course, what's the crazy old man up to now?" Fowler said, taking a long drink from his new HTA logo mug.

"Like I said, he's really trying to piss people off. I don't get it. But what we saw today on the message boards was crazy," Jackson said, pushing his dark hair out of his bright blue eyes.

"Go on, please," Matt said eagerly. He wanted to know how this may affect him, and as a result, the rest of the Team.

Garrett reached to grab one of the chocolate frosted dough-nuts left over from the earlier meeting, eating it in two bites. "Sorry, I'm starving. Even a stale doughnut helps. I've been doing some digging of my own. Here's the thing, I don't think it will. Over the last few weeks, Rossi has been poking around into other US companies' data, almost on purpose, so he would get caught. It's very easy to pin down who's been digging around where they aren't supposed to."

"Rossi's company, called Rossi Internazionale Moderno, RIM, have been planting viruses, messing with stuff. Nothing big, but almost like hey, please pay attention to me. Very amateurish," Jackson said.

"It's like he swatted at a hornet's nest, just to fuck with them," Jimmie said.

"Exactly. Rossi pisses people off to get their attention, then this is the kicker. He wrote this in his latest message, and I quote, 'I will come to your country very soon. I am putting a bounty on my head. Because you all know who I am now, I dare you to come find me, and to take me as your prisoner. I will pay anyone who can actually get to me five million US dollars. I am risking my personal safety to show you that Henchmen do not need to change, they do not need to go to school to learn. DMF, this is a special invite to you, but all offers are welcome. I am adding an additional five million US dollars to any of the HTA Henchman graduates who find me.'"

Jesus, what a freak. Who would put a bounty out on his own head? He's not right in his head, Matt thought.

"This guy. What is our world coming to? Asking to be fucking kidnapped? What intel do we have on his influence on the rest of the Henchmen organizations? I wonder if he's been able to persuade any of them to follow him." Fowler said.

"Are you fucking kidding me? He's asking to be kidnapped? He is a crazy bored old man. I say let's go get him. I know that he is a whack job, but we could almost look at this as a test case. Like how we can pull our Team together, you know, the new look of DMF," Liz said.

"I knew you would say that. We need to think this through.

Jackson, has he said anything else that would make you think it really is just this? Not a trap for us to be exposed?" Jimmie said.

"I really think it is what he says it is, a game of cat and mouse. But to go back to Fowler's question, from what we can tell, he is building a following. We have been tracking some of the chatter, and to be honest, some of it is beginning to turn against DMF in particular," Jackson said.

"Well, shit. How are we going to play this game then? Ideas, anyone?" Liz asked, looking in Jimmie's direction. "We knew that there would be some opposition to us being the 'experts' and training people. Not everyone thinks it's a good idea. But if he is taking the lead in getting the troops rallied against us, then we really do need to rethink our response."

"I say we wait. If we amp this up, and pay more overt attention to him, then he will have more to use against us. Does that make sense to everyone? Let someone else go grab the crazy guy, then we aren't the bad guys again. We just did that with Four, we don't need another one to deal with," Jimmie said.

"Are you sure we don't want to grab him first? This is pissing me off, I would like to tell him where to shove it. We can sit and watch, but in the meanwhile, I am going to prepare our offensive. Let's be prepared for if or when we need to make our presence known. We can show the critics what we know and how the old-school way of sloppy, unprepared, and reactive is out of touch with the rest of the Henchmen," Liz said.

"Me too! But I'm not sure this is the right time to do that. I'm leaning toward Jimmie's idea. But I'd also like to have a backup plan. I'm thinking we just follow the turd and see who nabs him first, let them get all the glory," Fowler said.

"So, we're assuming he will get caught then?" Matt said.

All five sets of eyes rolled with that comment. "Did you not see how easy it was for us to come get you? That asshole is going to be out five million dollars. I'm taking bets on how long it will take," Liz said.

"With everyone involved in the HTA on some level now, it may be challenging to free the Team up to monitor his whereabouts. I can bring in some of the guys from the long-term Team. They are used to the monotony of waiting and watching," Jimmie said.

Matt looked confused with his eyebrows scrunched together, "Wait, hold on, I don't know who or what the long-term Team is."

Liz patted Matt's shoulder and said, "Yes you do. They are the Team that was put on security detail of your family and friends when you first came to the House. That is how we kept them safe until we got the OT, aka Four."

Matt was nodding, "Oh yes, now I remember. It's been a minute since I thought about that. They did an amazing job, no one even knew they were being watched."

"I like that, Jim. Can you get things moving on your end? Jackson, good work on keeping up with this mess on top of everything else you have going on. The next few weeks should prove interesting," Fowler said.

"Last thing, let's keep this story among friends. No need to share with the entire Team just yet. I'd say the Top Five, Amber, and David H. will be enough right now. It doesn't hurt to have extra sets of eyes out there. I have the rest of the necessary legal team in the loop. If he's not careful, he could end up in one of our prisons. He could learn the hard way, you can't just shoot your mouth off and say whatever you want about companies. Consequences my friend, consequences," Garrett said.

CHAPTER 16
WATCHING AND WAITING

News of Rossi's self-bounty spread quickly across the dark web message boards. Since Matt was not on the errand board any longer, he spent his free time sitting in the CM suite of the House. The messages from Rossi and his team were pretty shitty and disrespectful. The theme he was on this week was how American Henchmen were lazy idiots with no class. They were monitoring his ridiculous messages per Garrett's request. He wanted to have all of his communication documented if needed for future negotiations. No one was sure how his rants would affect the enrollment of the HTA, and business in general with DMF.

"Look, I know this all may sound like a waste of time and resources, but I'm taking direction on the higher ups. They want this shit to keep as files. If there is a decline in revenue, then they want to be able to directly correlate this to Rossi. You know as well as I do that when you hear something enough times, it can become the truth," Garrett said.

"He is poking the hornet's nest again, I see. Do people actually take this stuff seriously? He is just spewing lies about people. That's such bullshit," Matt said.

"Part of what he said is true, right? I mean, these guys, the

Henchmen he's targeting, aren't that bright, which is why he's saying it. It's for them to see and get pissed. He's baiting the really dumb ones. I don't think the above average ones will, but who knows," Jackson said.

"He will get the overreactive Henchmen, which is exactly who we want to train. The Henchmen that walk in and blast people first, for no reason. Those guys are the worst, so wasteful. They're the ones who give all Henchmen a bad rep," Matt said.

Matt left the CM suite feeling melancholy with a touch of homesickness. He was walking up the stairs with his head down, not paying attention to anyone else in the world, when he walked straight into Amber's path.

"Hey, Matt. Are you ok? You seem pretty checked out."

Matt grabbed onto the railing and said, "Yeah, I was in the midst of throwing myself a little pity party. I think I'm over it now."

"I've thrown myself a few of those over the years. Want to talk about it? I'm free the rest of the day," she said.

He had already opened the door to his room, gesturing for her to come in. "That would be great. There are a couple of things I wanted to talk to you about, anyway. Now's as good a time as any."

Unlike Liz, Amber boldly crawled on his bed, propping pillows against the headboard. Liz most times sat on the dresser. Having Amber on his bed made his heart skip a beat, despite her throwing off a friendly vibe, as opposed to an 'I want your body' vibe.

He didn't hop right up on the bed next to her, instead he paced the room, careful to leave the door open. He thought it better to be transparent at this point. "I guess I was reminiscing about my life before being here. Some days it hits harder than others. It's weird because it's not like I miss much of it, it's maybe more the familiarity part."

"This isn't familiar to you yet? I would think it would be. Maybe it's different for me. I've been travelling for years now. Home is where I lay my head, you know?

Now it was Matt's turn to sit on the dresser. "I acclimated to life in the DMF House. You're right, I call this home now. But, I miss parts of my previous life. Not working as an insurance sales agent isn't what's giving me pangs of sadness, but the many hours and nights I used to spend gaming with my friends at The Basement haunts me."

Amber leaned forward on the bed, and asked him, "Don't you keep in touch with them now? I thought it was ok for you to talk to whomever you wanted to now."

Matt put his head down with some shame and didn't make eye contact with her. "I haven't kept in touch with my friends as much as I intended to. It was just too complicated to have them as friends for the first year or so. We texted back and forth, but that has dwindled down to barely anything now. Liz has asked me on different occasions if I wanted to bring any of them on to DMF."

Amber moved closer to him and said, "That was generous of her. Have you taken her up on the offer? I think it would be great to work with a familiar face."

"I'm conflicted about it. As you well know, this can be a dangerous and an unpredictable life. How could I ever forgive myself if one of them got hurt, again, because I had encouraged them to be part of the DMF Team?"

"Would they come on as Henchmen, or what? I thought your pals were more along the lines of the CM Team? That wouldn't be too dangerous," Amber said.

"Yeah, it would be the CM Team, so way less chance to get hurt with them. But I still carry the guilt of Paul getting wounded during the shootout at The Basement. They would like it here. I am sure of it. Maybe I should reach out."

"I think that's a good idea. You said you had something else to talk to me about?" Amber asked is a rather sultry tone.

Matt's heart rate just went up and his belly did some flip flops. "Ok, yeah, I just wanted to talk to you about . . . us. Seems there is a lot that needs to be talked out. I guess Vanessa being here made me think more about it."

"Vanessa? How so? Are you interested in her now?" Amber asked.

Matt hoped off the dresser to take a seat next to Amber. "I was. Then I thought about it more and decided that I would rather get to know you better. I want to understand more about what this is between us. I'm just not sure how to do that."

"You want us to date, like *normal* people?

Matt blushed a little, and said, "Yes, I think that is what you would call it. I'm not too sure how normal dating can be here, but I would like to find out."

Amber leaned over and got so close that Matt could smell her peppermint gun on her breath, he knew this was it! Their first kiss. She leaned in even close so their noses were touching and said, "Well, let's fucking figure it out."

It had become a daily routine for Matt, Liz, and Amber to congregate at the front desk of Pinky's after class at the HTA. They would spend most of their afternoon taking turns working the front desk while doing either paperwork or, in Matt's case, homework. Secretly, Matt loved being with the three women. He felt safe with them around, plus the large windows in the front gave him a clear view of the parking lot and anyone who might linger longer than necessary. He had the talk with

Vanessa about him and Amber being exclusive. Matt was surprised to find out that Vanessa's attention had turned toward an old fling she'd had back in the day. She told Matt that he was fun while it lasted, but she was otherwise occupied with her blast from the past.

"Does David H. like the break he gets when you hang out with us? He's really getting into his new *leadership* role. It's sort of cute, don't you think?" Amber said.

"I think he appreciates the break from being with me 24/7. I like the company as well," Matt said, grinning.

Liz gestured like she was putting her finger down her throat to make her throw up. "Aren't you two sweet? Yuck."

Amber and Matt smiled at each other until Pinky bounced up and gave them all a high five.

"How are the three musketeers doing today? It makes me so happy to see you all getting along and becoming such good friends," Pinky said.

"Don't encourage him. We don't need any more googly eyes today," Liz said.

"Pinky, have you been able to find anything out? I have never gotten such shit intel as I have now," Amber said.

While the Henchman world was eagerly waiting for Rossi to begin his game of cat and mouse, Amber, who was the most well-connected of anyone in the House, had called in too many of her contacts to find out Rossi's next move. Strangely, the information being filtered down to her was useless.

Pinky motioned the three into her office. "Let's go in here, not everyone needs to hear this."

There were not enough chairs for them to sit in, so Pinky took the seat at her desk. "I have run into dead ends. It's super confusing since I actually know this guy, you know? I suppose it leads to the allure of his little game. I have to wonder how deep his little plot goes. I have been around too long to think that his request to be kidnapped is all there is to it," Pinky said.

"What do you mean? Isn't that enough?" Matt said.

"I think I know where you are going with this. Can I take a guess?" Amber said.

"Let's hear it," Liz said.

"So, Rossi gets everyone at a company all riled up. These companies get more and more mad, which is exactly what RIM wants. They really want these companies focusing on that, only. This will inevitably leave gaps in their usual routine. Gaps that open up for RIM to dig into. Being able to take over, or at least have the upper hand in other people's business dealings," Amber said. "It's all very middle school. Somehow, he's able to find dirt on these companies. Dirt that no one was supposed to find out about."

"Everyone has dark stories that they don't want people to know about. He must have been planning this for some time now. He's throwing people off their game by dropping these little gems on them and threatening to share them with the world," Pinky said.

Liz and Amber nodded in agreement.

"Exactly. There are several layers to his crazy ass plan," Liz said.

"What? That seems too complex and well thought out for that guy. I've seen him being carried in his villa like he was a child. Seems like a stretch to me," Matt said.

"Dude, do you really think this is all about the HTA? Seriously, do you think he is going to do all this crap just to prevent that from opening?" Liz said.

"Take it from three well-traveled chicks, this is way more than the obvious," Pinky said.

CHAPTER 17
VANESSA

Pinky had come by that morning for an impromptu meeting with Fowler. Every so often she was summoned to his office. No one ever had the guts to ask why she was there, but the general consensus was that they were having a passionate fling. Matt and Liz noticed Fowler was always in a much better mood after she left.

"Hey Pinky, why don't you sit and have coffee with us? No need to rush back to the gym," Amber said.

"Only if Vanessa stays too," Pinky said, motioning her to come to the large round table.

Vanessa had laid low since her talk with Matt. There was not much else she could do. Her previous Henchmen posting with Rossi had come to an abrupt end when she was on the team that brought Matt home.

"Sure, we'd love to have her join us, right guys?" Amber said, looking to Matt and Liz for approval.

Amber rose. "Let me go grab a full pot and bring it to the table. Five cups to fill this morning, it's a little coffee party. Maybe some pastries too."

Vanessa took a seat and eyed Matt. "Now that I'm not busy chasing after you, I'm going to need a proper job here. You know I was posted with Rossi for several months prior to coming here."

Pinky returned with a coffee pot and started refilling mugs. "That's true, she needs some work. I had not cleared her to return to her European Henchman home since I have not deemed it safe for her."

Liz offered a coy smile at Vanessa. "I heard rumors you had, however, made acquaintances with some of the Italian Henchmen while at the Villa."

"Vanessa, why don't we start by having you join the weekly meeting? We meet here to share some of our perspectives on Rossi's plan," Matt said.

"Or any other information we think would be helpful as far as the timeline. This is an informal morning meeting, so don't worry about getting all dolled up," Liz said with a slight eye roll.

"The only requirement is to keep the coffee flowing for those of us who need it," Amber laughed, setting the mugs, coffee and pastries on the table.

"Ah, that first sip feeling. What would we do without this shit?" Matt asked. "Can you guys catch me up on what the CM Team has been working on? It's so hard to not get caught up in all the shit going on there. Those guys are badasses. I don't think you all realize how much they do for DMF. I think they need more recognition."

"Maybe. But those guys on the CM Team don't see what they do as work. They think it's incredible that they get paid to basically play games all day and night," Liz said.

"It's like that everywhere. All the places I've been, those guys don't like special attention, just like Liz said," Amber said.

"The CM Team is still busy collecting all the slanderous things Rossi is saying. Garrett said he wants them to catalog the other shit they are saying, the blackmail stuff. He said since we are tracking ours, why not keep tabs on who else he is trying to tie up in knots?" Liz said.

"I guess you have a better perspective than I do. I haven't had much time to catch up with Garrett. Everyone have a full cup? Are we ready to start our meeting?" Matt said.

All five held up their mugs and toasted each other. "Cheers to us," Amber said leaning closer to Matt. The whole table noticed they were sitting so close their thighs touched.

Matt noticed Vanessa raised her eyebrow as she absent-mindedly glanced at how close he was sitting next to Amber.

Liz cleared her throat, and said, "Vanessa, what can you tell us that we don't already know about this whacko Rossi? Is he losing his shit, or is he scheming it up?"

Vanessa held her mug under her nose and closed her eyes as she inhaled. "He's bloody nuts if you ask me. He's also brilliant and bored. The combination of that and the fact that he has literally no one to answer to, well, that is just a recipe for a mess like the one we have on our hands. I have contacted my *special* connections back at the villa."

"The connections being the Henchmen you befriended in the villa?" Matt asked.

Vanessa nodded her head and smiled, "Yes, Matt those connections."

"And? What did they have to say?" Matt asked.

"From them, it's been bloody crickets. Nothing. It's the strangest thing ever. Rossi must know something about loyalty that we don't. Between all of us, and we can't get a bloody bit of information!" Vanessa said.

"Maybe those chips he's embedded in his Henchmen are more than he's letting on. They walked around like zombies. Didn't you notice that too? I thought it was just a cultural thing, being super chill Italians," Matt asked.

"They were kind of stand-offish with me, something I have

never experienced. I thought I was losing my touch," Vanessa said with a wink.

Amber sat up straight and put her hand over Matt's, patting it gently, and said, "Well, shit. For me personally, I've never had that happen either. I wonder if we shouldn't take a trip over there and see what the three of us Honeypots can find out. If we run into dead ends, then there is something more than extreme loyalty going on in that villa."

"I think we may be onto something here. How does a little girl's trip to Italy sound? What do you say we get this thing planned out right now? I am going to *tell* my dad and Jimmie, not even ask. This isn't open for discussion. If none of you have been able to get information from here, then we go there," Liz said.

Another HTA coffee mug salute by the five, and then planning began.

Pinky stood to leave, "Thank you for the coffee, but I need to get back to my baby, the gym. I know you three can conquer the world if you have to. I'm not worried about you lovely women going alone. No one else should be either. That includes you, Matt. I'm headed back to my gym. You ladies let me know if there is anything I can do from here. You know I have your backs."

He knew Pinky was right, but still. His best friend, girlfriend, and Vanessa. It frightened him to think about any of them getting injured or worse. He also knew they could handle their business, and there was absolutely nothing he could say to change their minds.

All three women had never worked with other women on the job. They were always either alone or *one of the guys*. Matt enjoyed watching the lively conversation but was wondering how he was going to be part of this well-thought-out plan.

"Hey, you guys are on a roll with this whole thing, and I

don't mean to sound like an asshole, but I came up with the idea, sort of. I know I can't be a Honeypot, well, I suppose I could if we needed that, but how can I help?"

The three women looked at each other and started to laugh. "What's so funny?" Matt asked.

"OMG, how many times were *we* the ones who came up with the plan, but were not included in it? We have worked with idiots most of our careers. This is like a dream. Right, girls?" Amber said.

"We've got to get Pinky involved in this too. We would be foolish not to take her up on her offer to at least be part of the plan, or ground support. She would be gutted if we left her out of it," Vanessa said.

"Hold on, she implied she didn't want to go. Bringing her with you would just enrich the adventure no doubt. Why don't I go over and talk to her. She trusts me with her *baby*." Matt said.

The women stopped giving each other a glance, with no words spoken, and a shoulder shrug, as if to say, *why the hell not?*

Amber was the first to speak, "That is awfully sweet of you to offer. I just hope you want her to tag along because she will have a positive impact on our mission, and not to babysit us."

"Or to keep an eye on us so she can report back to you," Vanessa added, "Because if that's the case, you got her all wrong. She is bloody queen and would never be disloyal."

Matt smiled before he answered, "You earned a trip to the villa for a little girls' time, that's all. I mean come on, when's the last time Pinky wasn't at the gym all day?"

Liz set down her HTA mug with a determined grin, and said, "Right. Well get over there and work your magic. She's super well connected and knows jobs like this better than most."

The three women absentmindedly got up to leave, still plotting and throwing ideas out, while Liz took notes on her phone. Matt got up to leave, noting that he would not be part of the planning, and said, "Don't mind me, I'll just run over to Pinky's have a little chat and do my homework for the HTA, no worries," Matt shouted to the three. Those Italian Henchmen better watch out. They had no idea what was coming their way.

CHAPTER 18
BORED IN CLASS

To soften her up, Matt stopped at the Bean and picked up a hot green tea for Pinky. He knew it was her favorite, and for good measure, he thought to take the last chocolate muffin with him too. He watched Pinky for a moment before he went inside and marveled at how she danced around her gym chatting with folks all day long. She had amazing people skills and remembered everyone's name she spoke with. Not many people can say they are good with names, but she was. She saw Matt coming towards her with the treats and smiled, "Is this all for me!? How did you know I was needing my tea? And the muffin, well that is just a perfect little pick me up."

They walked to the desk and sat on the tall chairs behind the desk. Pinky set her tea down and peeled the baking paper from the muffin, offering Matt the first bite. "I know you have something to say Matt, spill it, what do you want do you have to say for yourself?"

"Am I that obvious? You're right, I do have an agenda. Before we jump into that, I wanted to ask you what you think about Rossi, and his crap, I mean, if you were the one making the decisions, what direction would you have taken with him?"

Pinky studied Matt before answering him. It was as if she

was calculating how much to share with him. "You know, to me, there are just so many variables with this. I think I would have started off differently. Perhaps being a little more proactive. He didn't just turn into a psycho, he's been on my radar for a few years. Rossi has a lot of strange habits, and none of have been dangerous up until now. This *chipping* of people, well to me that's just crossed the line. You know that he is trying to build his own army, just like what Eddie is working on now."

"Building an army? Is that how you see what the HTA is all about? I guess it could be perceived that way, maybe I was being naïve," he said

"Maybe just a little," Pinky winked. "You see, the life experience I've had teaches me to think in reverse of what typically happens with people. I struggle from time to time wondering if all I think about is worst case, and how things could fall apart before they even have a chance to gain momentum."

"Maybe that is how you survived and thrived really in a very scary place. I don't know your whole story, but from what I heard, you are a true survivor, that has every reason to doubt peoples motives."

Pinky's eyes were staring down at her lap, looking up she asked, "What exactly have you heard about me? We've never had the chance to sit and get to know each other on that level."

"No, I guess you are right, we haven't. Well, in a nutshell, what I've heard about you is that you had a shitty family, and you ran away when you were young. You joined the circus in some random Polish city, and toured around Europe, learning languages, and meeting lots of people, some of them with very tangled pasts. I ever heard a little gossip that you were responsible for a couple of *coups d'etat* too."

"Oh those little government skirmishes! What you've heard about me is sufficient, for now. Let's just say I met some very powerful people while on the road. One of the things that I was really good at, which is what I credit my success with, is being able to see gaps. I saw gaps, and I filled them. Pretty simple equation."

Matt had a curious look on his face, "Gaps, what gaps? Kind of like what I saw, and created the HTA, those kinds of gaps?"

Pinky smiled towards the door as Amber, Liz, and Vanessa walked in. "Those gaps. You don't realize how stupid and weak powerful men can be at the sight of a beautiful woman. Especially when that beautiful woman is trained to charm and disarm."

Matt sat back in his chair, "The Honeypots, that was all your idea. You created that whole network throughout Europe."

"You would be surprised what you can find out with softness and femininity versus muscle and might. I got amazing results, and people noticed. It got a little too hot to handle, so I scaled my operation way back."

"Sounds like you are ready to get back in the game. Pinky, you need to go with them. They need to learn from you," Matt said with pleading eyes.

Pinky didn't look back at Matt when she spoke to the three women, "You know what, after my little chat with Matt, I've decided to come with you. It's time I turned up the heat."

———

Matt was glad that he had the HTA classes and the homework to occupy his time since Liz, Amber, and Vanessa were deep in planning operation Honeypot. Even Pinky was not at her usual post at her front desk. Matt had to fill in for her there and give up some of his time in the CM Team's control room. He didn't mind so much, since he could still see the girls at their meetings in Pinky's office. Matt had never witnessed such precise planning and attention to details. After one of his shifts at the front desk, he went into Classroom A to empty the trash bins, when he interrupted a meeting the Honeypot crew was having. They were in deep conversation about what was hanging on the whiteboard. It was the blueprints which he recognized as the floor plan of the villa. The detail was incredible, all the CCTV cameras, the doors that remained closed, the hallways where a chip was needed, where each of the tables sat in the dinner room. These were not your average Henchmen hatching a snatch and grab. This sort of planning and detail was exactly what Matt was trying to bring to the HTA. Less reactivity, more preparation, when time allowed for it. *We could use this as a case study one day,* he thought.

Matt had successfully completed the four-week-long intro courses required when entering the HTA. The best part had been watching his best friend, Liz, get up in front of the class and teach. After the first-day jitters wore off, you would never know that she hadn't done it hundreds of times before. Jimmie and Fowler's classes were nothing new to him. He had already heard most of what they had to say during Matt's 'onboarding.' It wasn't until these HTA-specific classes did he realize that none of the other Henchmen were given the same inside information. He always knew his circumstances were different upon his arrival there, but seeing how the rest of the guys had never really had any meaningful conversations made him feel a tad bit special and more connected than he previously felt.

Franco's class ended up being more therapy than anything else. Franco originally wanted it to be life-skills-based. Ultimately, it turned into the Henchmen speaking about how their lives led them down the path to becoming part of a Henchmen Team. David H. was not exactly eager to share his story about the event that led him down the Henchman path, but he had promised Franco he would speak up the first class since they weren't sure anyone else would.

"We are going to get started with class for today. David H. has asked to go first. It seems he is rather nervous about sharing his story, so no ball busting for him today. I mean it. If you can't say something nice, say nothing at all," Franco said, motioning David H. to the front of Classroom B.

The anxious David H. made his way to the front of the room. It was interesting for Matt to see these oversized men that killed for a living looking like they were mere children who were expected to tell a well-kept secret. Matt didn't want to make a big deal out of it, but if he didn't know better, he would say they were being vulnerable.

With his eyes trained on the tops of his shoes, David H. recounted an event that happened to him while he was in elementary school around the age of eight. Reading off the written prompt, he read to the class, "Please describe an event in your life that led you to want to become a Henchman. For me, it happened on the last day of third grade. It was a small school, called Ludington. There was a kid, Schmidt. Well, good old Schmidt was in the highest grade, grade six, and he was the school bully. I mean, he was a real piece of shit. He had picked on nearly everyone at some point. The whole school was afraid of him and hated him. God, I just remember what an asshole he was all the time. Well, on this last day, two boys, who were older brothers of some kids in my class, came to the playground just as we were dismissed. These two older boys jumped Schmidt and began to kick the shit out of him. We pretty much watched and cheered. Then, this is some twisted shit right here. The two older boys stopped beating his ass and threw him up against the brick wall of the school, near the bubbler. They held him steady against the wall on either side so he wouldn't break free. They told us to form a line. As each kid got to the front of the line, the older two instructed us to either punch him in various parts of his body, telling us to keep one of our knuckles out so it hurt more, or if we didn't want to hit him, we could spit on him. That's where the bubbler came in handy. It was one punch or spit per kid. Up until that moment in my life, that was the most amazing thing I ever did. I've never forgotten that feeling of being in control. We felt so righteous walking away knowing that we got to feel some control over that piece of shit Schmidt. Looking back now, it was pretty fucked up since the adults in the school must have known what was happening and turned a blind eye."

"Wait, what part of that story made you want to be a Henchman? I mean, we aren't always the good guys, the heroes," Matt asked.

"David H., can you give us more explanation? And tell us what a bubbler is," Franco said.

"Ok, yeah, I can. So, first a bubbler is a drinking fountain. We just call them a bubbler. But I thought it would be obvious to you. I have never been a bully, and maybe not a hero either. But as a Henchman, I use my physical size to protect and to take care of my boss for *good*. I have a reason for me tossing people around, or getting rid of them, just like the brothers that set up the whole last day of the school scheme. I have a purpose," David H. said.

"Well said, David, you have a purpose. I like that. We all have a purpose, and that day you found yours. Do you guys want to hear how anyone else got here?" Franco said.

The class of Henchmen gave a slight nod of approval. Matt now knew that a slight nod was considered an enthusiastic yes amongst Henchmen. The slight nod was one of the many behavioral cues he learned during his time at DMF. He glanced over at David H., who was looking less stressed and anxious about life now that he had shared his backstory. Trying to picture him as a little confused boy made Matt smile, we are all confused in life, but to gain clarity about your future that way he did wasn't the way he would have ever imagined. His future had always been sports related, on a basketball court or a football field. That's where he felt purpose and passion. That was gone now, he was training to be a Henchman for Christ sake. At least David H. knew his future and followed it.

Franco scanned the room for volunteers, stopping at Matt, and said, "Why don't you share your version of how you ended up here?"

He really didn't want to tell his story again, but there were a few newer Henchmen who weren't in the House on that night. He would much rather hear about the other guys and how they ended up here, but since Franco asked, he would be a team player and give it his best shot.

Tyler let out a distasteful grunt and said, "Isn't he going to be a teacher here? Why is he even in this class?"

David H. spun around and gave Tyler the DMF death stare, and said, "Give him a fucking chance to speak, alright?"

The room settled as Matt began to tell his story. He wanted to emphasize how far he'd come since that night. "I'll start off with the job I had before I came here. I sold insurance. It was my first job out of college, which is where I got my nickname, College Boy."

The class sniggered, and stopped after Franco said sternly, "Remember what I said about ball busting guys."

Matt took a deep breath and continued, "I used to spend a lot of time at a place called, The Basement. I had a group of friends, and we played video games there almost every night. One night Fowler came in for a meeting, and well, long story short, he was shot and injured. I ended up taking care of business, taking out the guy who wanted him dead, and bringing him back to the DMF House."

"Wait, you wasted a dude? You don't seem the type," Mario said.

Again, David H. turned around death stare intact, and said, "He fucking did. And he wasted three assholes right in this parking lot," he said, pointing toward the front lot of Pinky's. "Franco and I would be dead if he didn't have rule number four down like a motherfucker."

"No shit? Well, never mind, dude. You got what it takes despite the rumors I've heard about you being a fuck up," Mario said, looking between David H. and Matt.

Franco laughed before he spoke and said, "Well, Matt's had more than anyone's share of fuck ups. But the thing is, that is why we created the HTA. He's had his share, but who here hasn't? It was through making those fuck ups, that he was honest and said, 'This isn't for me.' For you guys, it is more about it is being for you, but making you the best at what you chose to do. He is in this class because he created it, and if this makes sense, needs to learn it too."

"Thanks Franco and David. I think I should mention that I also hold the House record for being kidnapped, twice in less than a year," Matt said.

The fellas chuckled, and Matt said, "Franco, maybe you can share your story as well?"

Franco took a seat on the front table and said, "No better time than now. I don't know how many of you know, but I was in college once upon a time. Several universities recruited me to play basketball for them," Franco said.

"You were a college boy too? Maybe you should have kept that a secret," laughed Tyler.

"I thought we were over that by now," Matt grunted.

"I ended up loving being at college. It was a big transition for me, but I found the guys on the basketball team to be a substitute family for me. I was a good student and kicked ass on the court. Christ, I had never been on an airplane before going to college. When the team traveled to away games, I felt like a fucking rock star. Free plane rides, free gear, free food before and after games. It was like a dream come true. In the past, getting a new pair of basketball shoes came with sacrifices with four boys and one parent. In college, I had several extra pairs of shoes sitting inside my locker each week. During my second year at college, I met a girl. Her name was Sydney.

"Oh, you met her in college? I had no idea," Matt said.

Franco smiled. "We became inseparable, and I was happy. The end of my sophomore season, we found out we were going to be parents. I always vowed to never leave my kids like my dipstick of a dad did to us. I quit school and got a job to take care of my growing family."

"Bet no one was happy about that," Tyler said.

"No one was happy about it, but I wanted to be responsible. We had trouble making ends meet in the crap jobs we both had. Paying for daycare was a tremendous burden. I had many sleepless nights trying to figure out how I could make enough money so that Sydney could stay home with our daughter."

"Crap jobs is right. If you want to be on the up and up work wise, without an education, it's tough, man. Paying bills doesn't come easy," Tyler said.

"Right, so you get it. I was offered a deal to help coach a youth basketball team, which gave me a free gym membership. One day, I was at the gym and ran into an old friend from high school. This guy invited me to apply for a security job at the same company as him. I was skeptical at first, as it was a huge salary. Where I came from, if it sounded too good to be true, it was too good to be true. I went home and talked to Sydney about this strange offer of employment. Perhaps out of desperation, we agreed I should take it. I started at DMF as a rookie, never hearing about the type of work they did. Being a Henchman, well, early on it came sort of natural to me, and the money made it worthwhile. My dream of having Sydney stay home with our daughter and live a comfortable life had come true."

"The fucking money we make in this job blows my mind sometimes. For real, I could make this easy if I was selling drugs, but that shit is way too stressful," Tyler said.

"Exactly. My priority was to make my family comfortable. But let me tell you, I quickly learned that I could not come home and have a 'Gee honey, how was your day?' conversation. Well, I guess I could, but mostly it would be made up, or a PG rating version of what really went down. I tried to always keep my daily activities vague and not specific. It seemed to work, but it left me feeling guilty about not telling her the truth. Sydney was so happy staying at home, and I didn't want to take that away by telling her the truth," Franco said.

"So, you took this job to be a responsible father. As Jimmie would say, that is your *why*. You were a hero to your family. See, we can all be heroes, it's just the way we look at it," Matt said.

"Ask all the dead guys if we are heroes, and you'll probably get a very different answer," Franco said gravely.

Matt knew right away that his attempt at humor was not in good taste. He was trying to be one of the guys, and again, he just missed the mark.

CHAPTER 19
OPERATION HONEYPOT

OPERATION HONEYPOT, aka, OHP, was the topic of conversation for most of the guys on both the CM and the M&M Teams. None of them had ever heard of chicks plotting and putting together a job like this all on their own. The DMF Henchmen had witnessed Liz in action over the years and knew she was more than capable of taking care of business. It was still a new concept that some were slower to embrace than others. They all had seen what Amber had done to Matt and knew that her feminine charms were tough to ignore, especially when she was using them properly. Since Vanessa was new to the House, it was generally assumed she could hold her own with the Honeypot crew. Until OHP, the DMF Henchmen knew Pinky as the ditzy blonde who had a huge crush on Fowler, and who owned the gym they all worked out at. With Pinky's involvement in the OHP, the story of her past spread like wildfire throughout the Henchman gossip channels.

Matt was working late at the front desk finishing up an assignment from Franco's intro class, a monthly budget on an excel spreadsheet, when the OHP Team emerged from Pinky's office. A few months ago, he wouldn't have placed any bets on the future of Liz's and Amber's relationship status. Liz was so angry with Amber when they first brought her back to the House. He often had flashbacks of the van ride home after they rescued him. Amber blindfolded, with Liz kicking her in the shins as they made their way back to the House. The two women quickly found they had more in common than not, and with the many similarities and life experiences, they formed a bond. Matt could see the trust for each other continued to build when he saw them laughing at their own inside jokes.

The tension that was so apparent when Vanessa first arrived at the House was gone now. Once Matt made it clear that his choice was Amber, and not Vanessa, things shifted, and she was accepted into the group. If it wasn't for her relationship with Pinky, things may have been different, but the consensus with that if she passed muster with Pinky, then she had to be ok. Vanessa's latest boy toy was a pleasant distraction for her and welcomed by both Liz and Amber, since they knew she had abandoned her intentions of getting with Matt. No one was exactly sure who he was, but it was obvious she was smitten with someone. Her once tidy blonde bun was now worn as a messy bun, with a sly grin.

Liz walked up to Matt having not said a word and hugged him.

That was very unlike Liz. "What's going on? Did the meeting not go well?" he asked.

Liz whispered in his ear, "Can we just go out, the two of us? I feel like I need to talk."

Without a question, Matt closed his laptop grabbed keys and said goodbyes to the rest of the crew. They walked with their elbows locked until they reached his car. It was rare that he drove when Liz was in the car.

He asked, "Where do you want to go? Back to the House, or out?"

"Can you just drive around a while?"

He looked over to answer her, and that's when he saw the tears rolling down her cheeks. The last time he was a witness to her tears, it had something to do with her on-and-off-again romance with Mo. Over the last year, there had been a few times Liz went to her, never the other way around. He secretly wanted to meet her and see the two interact, but he'd have to wait for that.

"Is it about Mo? Or the girls?" he asked.

She took short, uneven breaths while she searched for spare napkins to use as tissues. "God damn it. I hate when I lose my shit like this. The girls and I are fine. It's Mo."

Matt reached into the side pouch of the car and grabbed some extra napkins and handed them to her. "I figured it was her. What happened this time?"

Liz was trying to catch her breath and gasped, "She stood me up. You know how she never comes here? She was supposed to be here tomorrow. I didn't tell you because I had a feeling she wouldn't show. I fucking hate getting played. I'm not a naïve little eighteen-year-old anymore. I can see her games now. I read an article about it. I think she is what you call emotionally unavailable. I mean, don't get me wrong, I have my own issues, but at least my word is my word. I don't go back on that."

"Maybe who you were attracted to when you were eighteen isn't what you want now?" Matt said.

"Well, no shit," Liz laughed, blowing her nose. "There's got to be more to life and relationships than this. Maybe this time next year, we won't have to have my annual sob-fest."

"You know I would rather see you happy, so if we skip it, that would be fine with me," Matt said, gently patting her arm.

"It's just so dumb. I'm sick of feeling dumb and like I'm wasting my time. I think I'm done this time."

"Great, then be done! We can find you someone that doesn't make you cry, how's that?"

"When you say it like that, yes, I'm done crying about it. Fuck her. But you know what? I'm really fucking hungry now, let's go grab some food," she said.

"Whatever you say, and it's my treat."

"Oh, well, it that's the case, then you should know it was my turn to bring dinner back to the girls. They are already texting me to hurry back. I'll call Fat Sully's and tell them we are on our way," Liz said, blowing her nose one last time.

"Since we have a few minutes, I would love to hear what the plans are with the OHP. I saw those blueprints up on the wall, you guys are no joke," he said.

Liz smiled and said, "You got that right. I can't help but smile when it dawns on me that I am actually working with a team of other women. I just can't get over it sometimes. Working with them is such a different experience than how things used to go."

"What's so different?"

"I guess the biggest thing is that we don't have to lead with muscle and intimidation like you dudes do. We can be soft and mushy and get way further ahead that way. It's almost like a surprise attack, you know? It's more intuitive than the way you guys are. We have really taken our lead from Pinky. She has that whole cloak and veil act down," Liz said.

Matt was wide eyed and shaking his head, tapping on the steering wheel. "This brings back great memories for me. Jesus, I fell headfirst into Amber's honeypot. I almost feel sorry for those assholes with the three of you headed in that villa."

"I wouldn't worry about them. All you need to know about our plan is that it involves a lot of flirting and wearing clothes I would only wear in a nightmare," Liz said, getting out of the car to grab the pizzas.

Matt watched her walk away wondering how he got so lucky to have a friend like her.

———

Matt and Liz returned to Pinky's with no less than six large pizzas to share with anyone who was still there.

"It's about bloody time you got back. Let me take a couple of those off your hands," Vanessa said.

Matt set out the rest of the pizzas on the front desk and was interested in what Pinky was saying.

"You know, I'm not so sure it was a good idea to let the guys know my past. They all look at me differently now. I liked being the version of Pinky that they thought I was. I should have left it alone and still been my carefree, loosey-goosey self," Pinky said.

Matt had a mouth full of pizza and was still chewing when he said, "The guys aren't sure how to take you now, that's for sure."

Liz and Amber rolled their eyes and laughed. "Mouth closed when it's full please," Amber said.

Matt gulped to clear his mouth. "Sorry ladies."

"They may look at you differently now, but so what? You got their attention, and now they will respect you in a different way. Embrace it, sister!" Vanessa said.

"I guess you're right. I enjoyed being anonymous, to a point," Pinky said with a wink.

"After we pull this off, none of us will ever be able to be anonymous," Liz said.

Pinky smiled. "You got that right. These silly boys cannot keep up with us!"

"I can't wait to get this job rolling. I'm grateful we have Jackson on board to help with the cyber stuff, but I really wish we could have done the whole thing A–Z, just us girls," Amber said.

"Maybe you can find someone to fill that spot for future jobs. This one came up so quickly, and I think you did an awesome job in the short time you had to get this going. I can't believe you leave in the morning," Matt said.

Pinky looked to the girls. "Do you think we need to go over it one more time?"

"Hell no!" Liz exclaimed. "We are as prepared as we can be. Let's all get a good night's sleep and be ready to go. Tonight may be the last rest we get for at least a couple of days."

"Grab your gear, and let's get out of here. We can go out the back door, and I'll go lock up out front," Vanessa said.

"I'll meet you at the back as well. I'll shut things down on the HTA side," Pinky said.

Liz, Amber, and Matt, stood by the back door of the HTA, waiting for Pinky and Vanessa to make their way to the back door and head home for the evening.

"Shit, what is taking so long? I'm going to check on them," Matt said.

Matt walked around the corner to see that Pinky had turned off all the lights to the HTA and was next to Vanessa, standing off to the side of the glass doors behind one of the tall, full-sized plants.

"I knew something wasn't right. What do you see, Pinky?" Matt asked.

Pinky gave her head a quick tilt to the parking lot. Raising her eyebrows to Liz, who had walked back in with Amber, Pinky said, "Do you see what I see?"

"What the fuck? What is he doing here? God damn it!" Liz said in a loud whisper.

Matt turned to see Rossi in the parking lot standing near a black Range Rover. His emotions went straight to anger, and not fear. His first thought was to go out to the parking lot and beat the shit out of the old man, which was a switch from the *I don't know what to do* thoughts that used to come first. "What the fuck? Why is he here? I'd recognize that black Range Rover anywhere. Christ, glad we didn't go out the front door."

"What are you looking at? Who's out there?" Amber said, walking up to the small gathering behind the plant.

"Are you shitting me? Well, there goes OHP. Back to the drawing board," Vanessa said as Rossi tipped his hat to the crew inside Pinky's.

CHAPTER 20
NOW WHAT?

Liz was already on the phone before Matt could turn around. She had walked away from the window and was pacing the gym nodding as she listened to the voice on the other end.

"She doesn't miss a beat, does she?" Vanessa remarked.

"Nope, she's all business. Bet she's talking to Jimmie," Matt said.

Pinky was still standing behind the tall plant, eyes trained on the parking lot. She was also on the phone, speaking in another language, one of the many she was fluent in.

"Who's she talking to? And is she speaking Russian?" Amber asked.

"That's Russian, and she's talking to one of her contacts there, trying to get some information that would be helpful. She isn't having much luck. The person, who I think is Anton, said their intel was that he was still in Italy. Old man Rossi is sticky," Vanessa said.

"You speak Russian too? I feel like a schmuck. I only speak English," Matt said.

Vanessa shrugged. "Typical American thing, I guess. I speak a couple of other languages as well. But what do we do with Rossi? Can he really be so bold as to show up and show off with only a few Henchmen?”

Matt got close to the front window to see if he knew the Henchmen with him. “I know those assholes. That’s who they paired me with. It’s Enzo and Carmine in the front, I’m not sure about the other two. Are they supposed to spook us? They are just standing there like they have nothing to do.”

“We could totally take him, but he’s making this way too easy. It feels more like a trap,” Amber said.

As if Rossi could hear the conversation, he laughed out loud and nodded. One of his Henchmen got out of the Range Rover and came around the side to open the back passenger side door for Rossi. Before Pinky and Liz got off the phone, he was gone. The group waited to see if anyone else would magically appear, but no one did. The parking lot was empty and quiet.

“I want to go chase him, but I think that’s exactly what he thinks we would do, right? Be reactive and not think this through. We can’t do that. You’re right, has to be a trap,” Matt said.

Liz walked up to the windows, now off the phone. “We got this covered. Jimmie couldn’t get someone from the House over here quick enough, so he called the CUC. They are going to track him. He’s not gone, yet.”

“What is the CUC? Sorry, don’t know the acronym for that,” Vanessa said.

“Clean Up Crew. They take care of situations big and small for us. They are experts in getting to places and people,” Liz said.

“*Do svidaniya, spasibo*. That asshole,” Pinky said, putting her phone back into her sports bra.

“I take it you got some information?” Amber asked.

"I did, finally. I think we should share this information with Eddie and Jimmie. Liz, are they on their way here?" Pinky said.

"Yup, they are. This must be good if you want to wait to tell everyone at once. I'll go put on a pot of coffee. This could be a long night," Liz said.

Fowler and Jimmie arrived in separate cars, each with two Henchmen in the front seats. The four Henchmen flanked Fowler and Jimmie, walking them into the HTA. They posted two of the Henchmen at the front door and two at the back door, watching on the video monitor for any unwelcome activity. The rest of the group made themselves comfortable in Classroom C, the one with the conference room set up. Pinky sat at the head of the long conference room table. Just as they were about to get started with the extremely important debrief, the door opened. Matt felt like another bolt of electricity shot through his body, returning to the flight or fight response. Everyone but him and Fowler had a gun pointed at the door before it closed behind the intruder.

Garrett held his hands up. "Whoa, calm down everyone. Sorry I'm late. Didn't they tell you I was on my way?"

A collective sigh of relief filled the room. "You are such an idiot. You were so close to being pumped full of lead. Fucking knock or something next time," Liz said.

"Well shit, that would've sucked for me! Just doing my job! DMF in-house counsel should be at a debrief of this magnitude," Garrett said.

"Sit the fuck down now, Garrett. I want to hear what the crazy Italian has going on now," Fowler said.

"I don't think we will have any more interruptions. Pinky, you have the floor," Jimmie said.

"Glad you made it, Garrett. You may need to take notes on this one," Pinky said.

The room became still with anticipation about what intel

Pinky was about the share. The allure of not being able to pinpoint what Rossi was trying to pull made this even more exciting to hear.

"This is a lot more complicated than we planned on. The man we just saw in the parking lot isn't Rossi. At least, I don't think it was. It could be, but no one knows for sure," Pinky said.

"It was him. We all saw him," Matt said.

The OHP team glanced at each other briefly.

"What is it? What do you know?" Matt asked.

"His game of cat and mouse just went global. My Russian friend confirmed there have been Rossi sightings in no less than five other cities across the globe, all at the same time as our Rossi appeared in the parking lot. It's anyone's guess as to which is the real one, or if any of them were actually him," Pinky said.

"Oh, this guy is a fucker," Fowler said.

"Who has time for this shit? He *is* a bored old man," Liz said.

"Why would you make time for this? What's the point?" Matt said.

"Don't you see? He's getting the whole global cyber-criminal organizations to pay attention to this little game. The more they pay attention to him, the more time he has to infiltrate their data, their schemes, their business. The poorly managed ones, the reactive ones, will go down first. He will take over their company and slowly become powerful enough to take over all the cybercriminal activities in the world," Amber said.

"Holy shit, I think you're right. We need to get Max involved in this. We need to step it up. Do we have enough manpower to keep him out? Please tell me Four wasn't assigned to monitor anything but the message boards," Fowler said.

Garrett shifted uncomfortably in his seat, and said, "Well, here's the thing. Four started with the whiney shit and said he was bored with monitoring the message boards. So, it was with regards to keeping his co-workers sane that I gave approval for him to step it up and create new firewalls and security around our data."

Fowler sat forward with the death stare, and said, "I'm sure you ran it past Max, or at the very least Jackson?"

Garrett pulled his collar away from his neck, cleared his throat. "See, that may have been an oversight on my part. Four caught me in the kitchen as I was leaving, and I fucking hate talking to him, so I just said ok. I may have forgotten to share this with Max."

The mood in the room shifted from thinking Rossi was a complete asshole to thinking Garrett may have made a pretty big mistake. All eyes were on him, and he nervously fidgeted with his phone. Fowler looked agitated, tapping his thumb on the table, while Jimmie was on the phone with Max. Matt felt a sense of relief in watching when it was someone else's fuck up being dealt with.

"I'm glad to be on the other side of this one," he said to Amber.

She smiled and patted his thigh under the table. "I am too."

Jimmie ended his call with Max and shared with the room that Four's log in had now been restricted until they could determine what damage or breaches may have taken place.

"Ok, with that taken care of, where were we?" Fowler asked.

Garrett snapped back into reality, putting his phone down. "We were discussing having the manpower to handle Rossi's possible data breach."

"We do for now. He isn't going after our type of organization first, which gives us a little time to build up more defenses. Matt, what about reaching out to some of your friends from

The Basement? You've said they have some talents in the area," Jimmie said.

"Hold on here, I need a little clarification on which type he is going for first, please," Fowler said.

Garrett said, "He's going for the smaller, less developed organizations, ones that don't have the same infrastructure that larger, more established organizations do, like ours."

"Good to hear we can stay in the clear for the time being," Fowler said.

"The guys at The Basement. Oh, shit, yeah. I can touch base with them. I can bring them in and have Jackson talk to them and see if it is something they would be interested in doing," Matt said.

"The OHP will continue to work our angles. Seems we will have to tweak our original plans, but we will work on getting more information. If one of his Henchmen is talking, there will be others," Liz said.

CHAPTER 21
REUNITED WITH OLD FRIENDS

"IT's great to see you both. Thank you for coming on such short notice," Matt said, sitting down at his favorite table at the Vanilla Bean coffee shop that was in the same strip mall as the HTA.

"It's been a while, man. Great to see you too. I didn't even know there was a gym in this part of town," Paul said.

"We thought you were too good for us now with your fancy job and all. When The Basement reopened, we thought you would at least show up for the grand opening, you know, for old time's sake," Jonesy said.

"Things in my life got super complicated after that night. I apologize for that. I didn't mean to be a prick. Part of why I asked you here is to give a better explanation of my absence. I hope after you hear, it will put things into perspective," Matt said.

"We'll take what we can get, right Jonesy?" Paul said.

Matt spent the next ninety minutes getting the men up to speed on the inner workings of DMF, the OT, Rossi, the HTA, and some of the characters at play. It felt like someone had lifted a weight as Matt divulged his past interactions with

DMF. He wasn't aware how heavily it had weighed on him, not having proper contact with people who were in his life pre-DMF.

"Uhm, I'm sort of speechless right now. I'm not sure what to say. I didn't even know there were places like that in real life. I mean, Henchmen? What's that all about? You used to sell insurance," Paul said.

"I know, it's a lot to digest. Try living it, that was a kick in the ass," Matt said.

"So, let me get this straight. You want us to come work with you on what you said is called the CM Team? I'm not too sure about that. It seems dangerous. We aren't physically qualified. You're the perfect size, six-foot-four, over two hundred and fifty pounds, that's not us," Jonesy growled.

"That's a good point. But the guys on the CM Team, well, they look just like you. We insulate them from having to be physically engaged in the job. They have a really nice set up in the House. I'd like you to come meet with Jackson. You guys will be safe there, I promise. Wait until you see the whole setup. It's impressive," Matt said.

"Can we have some time to think about it? It's quite a story we just heard," Paul said.

"Sure, but I'm afraid I will need to know today. I can give you a moment to discuss with each other. I would really like you to come work with me at DMF. I think it would be a good fit for you both. Before I forget, I want to tell you about some of the benefits that come with the position. I think they may help with your decision making," Matt said.

"There are benefits? Yeah, sure, let us know what those are. I don't have any now!" Jonesy said.

"You will be able to live in the House, rent free. Living in the DMF House is something we encourage. It's a great place to learn more about how the whole organization runs. All meals are included, a maid, and a masseuse. The salary starts at $100,000, and because of me, you have insurance, medical, dental, vision, and life. I'll be over here when you are ready to give me your answer," Matt said.

Matt watched as his two old friends' mouths closed after hearing what the benefits included. He could tell from their body language that they were excited about the opportunity. They were whispering and smiling at the same time. After a couple of hand slaps on the table, they said in unison, "When do we start?"

Matt smiled. "Follow me back to the House, and I will introduce you to Jackson. I'm glad you guys are coming on board."

As the black iron gates of the DMF shut, Matt flashed back to the first time he'd heard them close. He had a bloody Fowler in the front seat of his old truck. Back then, he never would have imagined where his life would have taken him, and that he would work with two of his friends from a lifetime ago.

"Dude, this house looks like shit. Are you sure about the salary? This makes me a little uncomfortable," Paul said, looking around the outside of the House that clearly needed some TLC.

"Don't worry, I thought the same thing. Wait until you see the inside," Matt said.

Paul and Jonesy were awestruck as they followed Matt in silence until they reached the door to the CM Team's workspace. Matt opened the door to the hum of the servers, monitors, and fans.

Jackson was nose deep in monitors when they walked into the room. He had black headphones on with his head bobbing to whatever music he was listening to.

"Holy shit. This is *so* not what I expected," Jonesy said.

"I told you, crazy, isn't it?" Matt said.

"This must be them. If he didn't already tell you this, I'm Jackson, and I run this place. I have a spot here for you two. Let's see what you got," Jackson said.

CHAPTER 22
THE RETURN OF FOUR

Jackson gave Paul and Jonesy the thumbs up after they spent a long night doing battle on the dark web with some mysterious, faceless, cyber crooks. The battles included writing and rewriting code to change the data platform, and combating the bullshit lies that Rossi and his Team were spewing, and planting messages to detour hackers from anything DMF related.

The panic on the message boards made the CM Team laugh and feel like they were way ahead of the game.

During the last briefing with Jackson, he shared that since Rossi's scheme had hit the dark web, not only were companies who were less cyber savvy working round the clock to increase their own cyber security, but they were dedicating hours to digging up as much intel as they could to find Rossi and to put an end to this ridiculous waste of everyone's time. For the smaller, less sophisticated organizations, keeping up with the extra demands on their workload was sure to cripple them, which was what Rossi had planned on. If a solid organization like DMF was having to hire out and were struggling with the volume of work, then everyone knew that the face of cybercrime was about to change into a monopoly if someone wasn't able to stop the madness.

Matt was already finishing his second cup of coffee when Jackson brought beleaguered-looking Paul and Jonesy to the kitchen to grab coffee and breakfast. If Paul and Jonesy could have been invisible, they would have been more comfortable. Matt watched as they walked with their heads down, eyes trained on the floor, not wanting any attention to be drawn to them. The kitchen was nearly full with Henchmen from the M&M Team. It was the first time the two new CM Team members had seen that many tons of men in one place.

Matt waved them over to sit at the table with him. They looked relieved to see a familiar face in the crowd of oversized, grumpy-looking Henchmen.

"Hey guys, don't let them scare you off. Not many of them are morning people. They look less scary as the day goes on. How did it go last night? Did you like it?" Matt asked.

"Dude, this is still really fucking weird. I'm still trying to wrap my head around this whole setup. But yeah, it went well, right Jonesy?" Paul said.

"I think so too. They have a sweet system in the CM room," Jonesy said, taking a long sip of his heavily creamed and sugared coffee.

Jackson walked by their table, nearly crashing into it. Pulling off his headphones, he said, "Sorry, my bad. Mind if I have a seat? You guys are catching on really fast, so that's cool. I know you're new and all, and I hate to do this to you, but I'm going to have you work with Four. He's been working on this project day and night, and whether he admits it or not, he needs some help. I hope he doesn't kill the deal for you guys."

"Really?" Matt groaned. "You're tagging them with him? Ouch."

"What's to hate about it? Who is this Four guy?" Jonesy asked.

"He's just a guy on our Team who is, well, a little abrasive," Jackson said.

"Actually, he's straight up an asshole. But we need him for a couple of reasons that I won't get into now," Matt said.

"He's the best we have now, so I would just prepare yourselves for him," Jackson said.

"Can we meet him first? I tend to get a little anxious with new people," Paul said.

"Probably a good idea. I'll walk you over to his cube," Jackson said with a sigh.

"After we caffeinate, please. I need some food too. How does this work? Do we just go grab what we want?" Paul said.

"Yes, anything and as much as you like," Matt said.

Paul turned to Matt and asked, "Will you go meet this Four guy with us? We'd appreciate it."

"Sure thing. Wait until you see him, quite a character, right Jack?" Matt said.

"I'll agree with you on that," Jackson said.

The side eye glances followed the four men as they left the kitchen and headed down a rarely used hallway. Four had continued to be so annoying to everyone that he was in the same room with that they moved him to a space designated just for him. It made everyone happy to not have to deal with his constant whining and complaining, which became his trademark.

Jackson held the door handle, closed his eyes, put his head down, and slowly opened the door just a crack. The shriek that came out of the room startled the four of them.

"Dude, what the fuck was that? It sounded like a wounded animal," Jonesy said.

"He's such a little fucking anti-social freak. Don't mind

him, he doesn't like when people *let the light of day into his turf,*" Jackson said, rolling his eyes.

The howling and shrieking became louder as the door came fully open.

"Who's here to bother me today? I wish you would let me know you are coming to disrupt my entire life! You know I hate to be disturbed! Ahhhhh! Can you go away or is there any real reason for you to be here?" shrieked Four.

"Dude, chill out. What the fuck is your problem?" Matt said, walking up to Four, who stood about one foot shorter than Matt.

Four used his middle finger to push his glasses back to the proper palace on his nose and looked up. "Oh, it's you, the Precious Prince of DMF. What are you doing here?"

"I'm here to introduce you to some new guys. Your one-man team just got expanded to a team of three. And please keep your fucking mouth shut. I still have permission to whip your ass whenever I feel like it. So, keep it shut, and try to be polite, not such a whiny little toddler," Matt said, bending down to meet Four's eyes.

"I can tell you want to say something, but just don't," Jackson said to Four. He turned to the other guys, who looked like this was the absolute last place they wanted to be. "This is Paul and Jonesy. They just spent the night working in the main room. They know what they're doing, so let them. Got it? They will come in here with you, beginning next week."

Four opened his mouth, but as Matt took steps closer to him, he stopped as if to check with himself about how to be socially acceptable. "Welcome to my world, you two. I will see you tomorrow," Four said in a loud, robotic voice. Turning to Matt, Four squinted and whispered loudly, "How's that? Is that appropriate?"

"Yup, that's good. Just one more thing. These two are my

best friends, so you better be on your best behavior. We go way back, and if I hear you aren't being a Team player, well then, there's going to be problems," Matt said.

"Whatever. I will try to treat these two snitches like they are part of the family. But let me tell you a little something too. If they don't cut it, I won't keep my promise to you, and everyone will hear about their lack of performance," Four said, turning his back to the group. "Please leave now! Unlike you, I have actual work to do! Adios!" Four screamed.

"Fuck off, Four," Matt said, slamming the door behind him.

CHAPTER 23
THE INVITE

With Paul and Jonesy accepting their offer to become part of the DMF Team, their first order of business was to quickly to close up the parts of their lives that would not be accessible during their time with DMF.

Matt accompanied them to see Franco who was assigned to work with them individually and instruct them on next steps—things like what to say to friends and family about them not being as available, where they were going, helping them get out of their leases, and giving them a brief rundown of key players on their Team.

"I know Matt told you a little about the HTA. We are requiring all new Henchmen to enroll. But because of the fucked-up situation we are in now, we will defer your enrollment until we have your time to spare," Franco said.

"I thought Matt said we aren't really Henchmen, so why do we have to go to the HTA? I really don't want to ever have to kick the shit out of someone, or at least try to. And I think I'm speaking for both of us," Paul said, nodding toward Jonesy, who bobbed his head and shot Matt an accusing look.

Matt felt some pangs of guilt since there were a couple of issues he hadn't exactly addressed with Paul and Jonesy. He had hoped that none of it would come up. How would he be able to explain that Four was the one who put a bounty on his head, who wanted him dead?

"I get that, and you won't have to take anything but the core classes. That way, you will get a nice overview of the larger system involved. Once you complete those, then you will move into the track designed specifically for the CM Team," Franco said.

"Ok, that makes sense then. I'm good with just staying in the main room and doing what I know best," Paul said.

"And that's exactly what we want. People working at the top of their skill set. I'd like to walk you around, give you a tour of the House, and make some introductions. How about we do that, and then you two head home to begin to transition back here?" Franco said.

When the tour of the DMF living quarters arrived in Matt's room, Liz was perched in her usual spot, sitting atop his dresser. "Here we go, the gang's all here. Welcome gentlemen, I'm Liz. Matt told me all about you. I bet you are wondering where your rooms are. I can take over from here, Franco."

"Thanks, Liz. I have to go make nice with Four. He's been throwing shit around his cave since he found out he's going to be working with Paul and Jonesy. He's been breaking stuff and doing that weird yelling thing he does when he's mad."

"Tell that little shit stain to use his words like a big boy," Liz said.

Matt shook his head. "Good luck, bro. Let me know how it goes."

"Jeez, how are we supposed to handle that guy? I know he's tiny but is he going to go after us? Do we have permission to defend ourselves?" Paul asked.

Matt and Liz looked at each other before Liz answered, "That's a good question. I didn't think he'd go off quite this bad.

I'll have Franco post a guy from M&M with you in his cave until Four gets his shit straight. How does that sound?"

Paul nodded in agreement. "I like that idea. That would be a little much for us to take on."

"Let me show you to your new rooms. Matt, don't go anywhere, I need to finish this conversation," Liz said, hopping off the dresser.

Matt had little free time, but when he did, like most guys his age, he wanted to check out and hop on one of his online games. He was tuned into his game when Liz returned a few minutes later and shut the door behind her. This need for privacy took him by surprise. "Did you get them all situated? What's with the closed door?"

"Does Paul know they are being stashed in a room with the guy who's responsible for him getting shot and for the total destruction of his business?" Liz asked.

Matt sighed. "I haven't mentioned that to him yet. I told him there was a longer story about Four, and that I would get around to sharing it with him. I would feel like a shit dropping that on him now. He's so excited. We really need him. Besides, he has been having a shit time trying to work back at The Basement. I guess he has some PTSD from it. He will be better off away from those distractions."

Liz raised her eyebrows, and said, "I would suggest dropping it on him sooner than later. I would say maybe even grab him before they head out. Once they're gone, then it's going to be really tough to explain your omission."

Matt ran his fingers through his hair. This was exactly what he was trying to avoid. He was already feeling guilty since he *knew* telling them was the right thing to do. "Fuck. Yeah, I guess you're right. I'll go to Table One and talk to both of them."

"I know you haven't heard this in a while, but don't fuck

this up. We'd all hate if Four spilled the beans about the connection they have before you had a chance to explain," Liz said.

"Thanks for the vote of confidence, I'll keep you posted," Matt said. "Let's get out of here. I have some business to take care of."

CHAPTER 24
SPILLING THE BEANS

Matt immediately sent Paul a text asking him and Jonesy to meet him at the table closest to the door in the kitchen. Table One was the only table that could be reserved, and it was used for times just like this, when there needed to be a conversation in a public place, most of the time for safety reasons. Matt hoped that after the Henchmen took Jimmie's Meditation-Mindfulness class at the HTA, it would be used more since the theory was there would be more conversations to have since their first thoughts wouldn't be to threaten and then punch each other.

"Dude, this place is amazing. I feel like I need a map to find my way around. We have to share a room for now, but I'm cool with that. It's fucking huge. The food is so good here too. Wow, all this time we thought you were bullshitting us. It all sounded too good to be true. I really can't imagine you killing people and, well, getting kidnapped. But I have to say, I can't believe you've had such a sweet deal," Paul said.

Matt sat back in his chair and shook his head in agreement. "Yeah, this place is cool. It was a little rough for me when I first got here. That's sort of what I wanted to talk to you about. There is some important information I feel like we owe you before you really take the leap. Some of it has to do with you, and the night at The Basement. I really want to be transparent with some of the stuff that went on here."

"You look so serious, dude. Whatever you have to say would have to be pretty fucking shitty for me to walk now," Paul said.

"It would be hard for me to leave now at this point too," Jonesy said.

Matt could feel the familiar bounce of his legs start under the table. He hoped they didn't notice it. "I don't want you to leave. It's great having you here. So, let me start with the night at The Basement. That shit went down because of Four. At the time, no one knew who he was. He was called the OT, Outside Threat, back then. He was plotting to get a spot on the DMF CM Team, just like you are on now," Matt said.

Paul and Jonesy looked at each other in disbelief. "That little shit? I never saw him there. Are you saying he shot me?" Paul asked, standing from his seat.

Jonesy stood, gently guiding Paul back to the table. "Come on, Matt, you need to be straight with us. That was some traumatic shit that went down that night."

"No, man, I don't want to sit down. I'm pissed right now. How do you think it's ok for us to work next to this guy? How? Please explain," Paul said, pacing the perimeter of the table.

"I'm getting there, guys, hold on. Four didn't shoot you, but the Suits that were there that night were working for him. The salt and pepper guy, that was Fowler, the guy you just met. That night, Fowler was supposed to meet the OT face to face, only he didn't show and sent his Henchmen instead. That's where things got messy, as you saw. We, the DMF Team, spent almost a year tracking him down," Matt said.

"Holy shit. That little jerk caused so much damage! I want to beat his ass now!" Paul said.

Jonesy smirked for a second and said, "Dude, you've never hit anyone in your life. But if you ever were to, he would be the one to hit first." He turned to Matt and said, "Why the hell didn't you tell us this sooner? This is heavy shit, dude. You lured us in with all this money and the house and didn't think we needed to know this first? Nice," Jonesy said, pushing his chair back.

Matt rubbed his hands together. "I know, I know. I made a huge mistake. So much time had passed since that night, I think I just blocked it out. It's no excuse. I'm deeply sorry. I hope you know I wouldn't have asked you if I didn't think you would be safe here," Matt said.

"That Four guy doesn't have a gun or anything, does he? It seems like he's just got a big mouth," Jonesy said.

"Oh shit, no, he doesn't have any weapons other than his mouth," Matt said.

"I suppose we can just put our headsets on and we won't have to listen to him. Does he know who we are, like that we came from The Basement?" Paul asked.

"I'm sure he does by now. I doubt he will bring it up, especially with a Henchman in the room with you. Those guys scare the shit out of him," Matt said.

The three sat in silence, with only glances at each other. As old friends do, the looks given were translated into words, not spoken.

"That's what I thought. Wait here, I'll text Liz and let her know that you are up to speed, and you still want to be here. One last thing, you guys have seen all those cars out back, right?" Matt said.

"Yeah, it's like a luxury car lot. These guys must spend most of their paychecks on cars," Jonesy said.

"Hold on, follow me," Matt said.

He walked them down the hall to the rack of keys that hung

near the back door. The rows of nearly a dozen keys sparkled in the afternoon sun.

"These, my friends, are not owned by the Henchmen. These are cars for us. When we run errands, we use these. What do you think about that?" Matt said.

"Holy shit. I will whip the shit out of that Four dude if he tries to mess with us," Paul said.

"Let's go for a ride, your choice of cars. This is going to be fucking cool to have you both here," Matt said.

CHAPTER 25
BACK TO BASICS

Turns out Matt wasn't as free to cruise the streets with Paul and Jonesy as he thought he was. He wasn't on as strict a lockdown as he was in the past, but since global Rossi sightings were multiplying by the day, Liz went with the 'better safe than sorry' rule and made it mandatory for him to not travel anywhere alone.

The CM Team had a world map hanging in the main room with thumbtacks on each city Rossi was allegedly seen. They used the map to plot his and his decoys' movements to see if there were some patterns to the sightings. The reports of the sightings seemed random, which was what everyone expected. This entire game was random.

OHP was still in full operation mode and pivoted to now work in partnership with Pinky and Amber's European connections. The thought was there had to be a weak link in the Rossi chain someplace, and they zeroed in on finding that link. They guessed it had to be someone with a covert agenda who wanted to see Rossi go down hard. It had to be someone inside the organization. Talk about loyalty, what a joke. A trip to Italy and a couple of other hotspots was on the horizon for the women. The group agreed that using their feminine charms, being Honeypots, in person was way more effective than texting and an occasional phone call. To get the information they were looking for, going there and being the stereotypical sexy, clueless chicks who needed some help was the only way to go. The manipulation game was the one to play. Matt hated to see them go, but knew without a doubt that if anyone could figure this out, it would be the four of them.

Matt had gotten used to his daily routine of a quick morning lift, classes at the HTA, then working the front desk at Pinky's the rest of the day. And now that Paul and Jonesy were working with Four, he made sure to take a trip to the CM room a couple times a day. But with the OHP Team leaving, he was going to have to change it up some and go back to being looked after by David H. He and Matt got along well enough, but it just wouldn't be the same as hanging with the girls.

"Dude, it's not that hard, are you following me? They literally check themselves in, just like you have done a million times," Matt laughed as he tried to train David H. on the front desk duties.

"Fuck off. I get that part! I'm not clear on how to enter the information for a new member or renewal or something. There are a lot of clicks to make for those," David H. said.

Without saying a word, Matt shuffled through the binders on the desk and pulled out the blue binder that was labeled, New Members and Renewals, and laid it in front of David H.

As David H. gave him the DMF death stare, Amber emerged from Pinky's office and said, "You're going to be so bored without us here, aren't you?"

"I'm not sure about being bored, but I will miss seeing you all. I know it's dumb to say I'll worry because I know you ladies can handle anything, but I probably still will worry a little until you're back here," Matt said.

David H. snorted. "Oh, listen to little College Boy being

sentimental. They're doing their jobs, just like all of us. How come you don't worry when I'm out on a job?"

"It's because you aren't as cute as we are!" shouted Liz, who, along with Vanessa and Pinky, had just followed Amber over to the desk.

"I see how it is," David H. said, laughing. "You get to go play around in Europe, while I stay here and go back to being a babysitter to a grown ass man."

"Ouch, be nice! We'll be back before you know it," Vanessa said.

"Are you girls ready to head out? We have to get packing. We leave in the morning. Bring your best gear, ladies! The show's about to begin," Pinky said.

Liz came over to Pinky and put her arm around her, giving her a tight squeeze. "I'm so glad you changed your mind to come with us."

"I know. The more I thought about it, the more I just couldn't let an opportunity like this slip by. I know my gym will be fine in these gentlemen's hands while we are gone."

"This is one for the record books. An all-chicks global errand? This is a pretty big deal for everyone to see. You know the word's going to get out where you all came from once this thing is over, right?" David H. said.

"I wouldn't have it any other way. I'm hoping we can use this to recruit more women to the HTA and we can start to really build that up," Liz said.

"The boys here would love that!" David H. said.

Liz rolled her eyes with her hands on her hips. "I'm sure they would. That's a long way off. For now, we're going to go back to the basics. In a way, I'm glad us girls have the chance to work together and work a plan from beginning to end. That isn't something we get to do very often," Liz said.

"What are you planning to do with Rossi once you get him? Are you going to bring him back here, or what?" Matt asked.

"We have planned for a couple different scenarios, and that's about all the information I'm going to give you. It's going to be a surprise," Liz said.

"There he goes again asking questions to help relieve his anxiety," Vanessa said.

Facing Matt and giving him a lingering, affectionate hug Amber said, "That's not it at all. Matt just likes to know what the next steps are, isn't that right?"

Matt tensed at her hug, feeling awkward, but noticing how nice it felt to be out in the open about the new relationship.

"Oh my fucking God. I'm not sure if I want to see any more of that. And listen, you can defend your boy toy all you want. The way he came here, with all the fuck-ups he made, it's better he asks questions than trying to do shit on his own," David H. said.

"Whatever you say. I think it's time we get out of here. You boys hold things together while we're gone," Vanessa said.

The group waved their goodbyes, and Liz ran back to Matt and gave him a hug, never looking him in the eyes. Amber, however, made eye contact. While Matt had Liz in his arms, Amber stopped before she walked out of Pinky's and locked eyes with Matt. It was a deep soulful gaze that he felt all the way down to his toes.

CHAPTER 26
WHERE DID THEY GO?

THE COMMUNICATION with the OHP Team had been non-existent since they'd left the DMF House. They insisted they needed to go off the grid for a few days. They weren't sure if Rossi could somehow track them, so they thought radio silence was the way to go. If they had a couple of days head start before Rossi knew they were in Italy, it would be to their benefit. They didn't even let Matt know they arrived, which left him unsettled. Deciding it would be best to keep himself busy, he focused on working, homework, and spending time with Paul and Jones to help the days pass quickly. It didn't take long for him to remember how alone he felt when he first arrived, and he wanted to be there as support for them, especially now that they were working in the same room as Four. If it hadn't been for Liz, he probably would have left the House or jumped out a window.

Four was being kept in check with the Henchman being posted in the cave, which was just what Paul and Jonesy needed to get up to speed with what was expected of them in their roles with DMF.

Matt was feeling a little lost and mopey. The OHP Team left for their mission, and he already was feeling pangs of heartache.

He waltzed into the kitchen and saw Franco and David H. They were the few early risers in the House and met regularly for coffee in the kitchen. He was grateful for the few minutes of quiet time without all the grumpy hungry Henchmen who filled the kitchen mid-morning. After coffee most days they would all go over to Pinky's together, especially since Matt wasn't allowed to go alone.

"Are you ready to go? I see you don't have your gear," Franco said, looking at David H.

"I'm ready. I don't feel a hundred percent, so I'll skip the workout today. I'll just work the front desk if that's ok," David H. said.

"Yeah, sorry dude. Too much sushi last night?" Matt asked.

"Something like that, yeah. I've dealt with worse," David H. said.

Paul and Jonesy arrived in the kitchen in the middle of a heated discussion. Their disagreement caught Matt's attention. "Hey guys, you may want to keep it down. Do you not realize that there were other people listening to the content of your conversation?"

Jonesy stopped with a startled look on his face and turned to Paul. "Dude, that's something you need to tell them about. You know it is. I don't know why you're hesitating; they won't think you're overreacting. That Liz girl said it's always better to be safe than sorry."

"It wasn't that big of a deal. It just caught my attention, that's all. You're the one making a big fucking deal about it, just stop," Paul said.

Matt became even more interested when they dropped Liz's name. He knew these two well enough that there wasn't a whole lot that would rile them up like this. They looked flustered and very unsure about the rules of the House.

"Fellas, why don't we take this conversation into another

room? Sounds like it may be something, or it may be nothing. Fill your mugs, and let's meet in the conference room," Franco said.

"Now look at what you did. I'm going to look like an asshole. Thanks a lot," Paul muttered to Jonesy.

David H. laughed. "No one's getting in trouble, relax newbies."

Franco waited at the door of the conference room until they arrived with full mugs of coffee. He shut it slowly after they sat in the oversized office chairs.

Paul looked like he needed some sleep. His hair was messy and his eyes puffy. Jonesy didn't hide the fact that he was nervous and worried they were in trouble so soon after they began work.

"Like David H. said, you aren't in trouble, but let's just talk about what got your attention," Franco said.

The two sleep deprived guys looked at Matt as if asking his approval to answer the question. "Fellas, just go ahead and answer," Matt said.

With some hesitation, Paul took a deep breath, and told them what he was tracking. "I've been noticing the same random words across the message boards that made me think they weren't random, you know?"

"We've been seeing the same word over and over, and it just doesn't seem like a coincidence," Jonesy said.

"Like what? What words did you hear?" Matt said.

"You know Rossi has a code word, right? Only his inner circle of Henchmen, or those working with him, are supposedly privy to it. When someone drops the code word, you know it's safe to talk. It's such a stupid word too. It makes no sense, it's not a word you can just use," Jonesy said.

"I didn't know about a code word. I think that's new information. Good work on figuring that out. But what's the word?" Franco said.

"Like I said, the only reason I picked up on it was because I kept reading it," Paul said.

"Tell them the word!" Jonesy said.

"Skittles. The word is Skittles, like the candy we all love. Totally fucking stupid. They keep having to squeeze it into conversations, and how do you do that? They say stupid shit like, 'I heard they have a special new flavor of Skittles coming out next month,' or 'I found some Skittles in the park by my house today.' It's all so obvious if anyone really paid attention," Paul said.

"So, you figured out the code word, but what got you so curious today?" Matt asked.

"They started saying things about having friends here, in our town, that are enjoying the new flavor of Skittles, and this is the fucked-up part," Paul said, leaning forward. "Their friends who were sharing Skittles in Italy left to come here because the Skittles there were too sweet, like they had been dipped into a honeypot."

"Fuck, they know the girls are in Italy. We need to let them know! Are they in danger? Were you able to determine if they found them?" Matt asked.

"They talked about them, it was no secret they showed up. They were almost expecting them. But I didn't hear anything dangerous, it was more like, 'the stupid girls came, what a joke.' They were very disrespectful and oblivious of the job they could do. But what bothered me more was the fact that I really believe he's here. I think Rossi is here, the real Rossi. What are we going to do about that?" Jonesy asked.

"Wait, well hold on, why do you think he's here? What did you uncover?" Matt said.

"Well, because they basically said so. They aren't too smart, as we all know. The OHP Team is turning the place upside down. They are throwing parties and dangling themselves around the Henchmen. The message that we read said, 'These girls are turning our men into boys. We need our leader here to set things straight and to remind them to act like men.'"

Matt's stomach turned and hoped that alcohol and flirting were all that was going on there. Franco was already on the phone, presumably with Jimmie. He was nodding and responding with a lot of *Okays*. Matt saw the stress on Paul and Jonesy's faces. In a sense, it was heartwarming to see, since it made Matt feel like the decision to have them come to work there was on point. They had integrity and wanted to be productive members of the Team. Franco got off the phone and sat back down at the large conference table. To know that Rossi was close by made his stomach turn almost as much as thinking about the OHP Team flirting and drinking with the Italians. But the stomach turn he felt about Rossi being here was more rage filled. *Now that's a guy I wouldn't mind seeing get hurt*, he thought.

"What did he say, dude?" asked David H.

"You know him, he's putting together a plan. He originally wanted to let someone else grab the dumb asshole, but now, he's over it and wants it done right," Franco said.

"What about the girls? Are they coming home then?" Matt said.

"Dude, they're going to be fine. Relax. Did you forget who they are? They're badass chicks who can take care of themselves. Rossi is a dumbshit, they will be fine," David H. said.

"Fucking Skittles," Paul said.

CHAPTER 27
CODE WORDS

MATT WANTED this crap to stop. He also wanted the OHP crew to be home and to get back to normal, with everyone just running errands like the good old days. Problem was, no one could make contact with them, any of them. Everyone knew there must be a good reason for their silence, but Matt was the only one to openly worry about it. He spent time in the cave with Four, more than he wanted to, to be the first one to hear that they had made contact with the outside world.

While in the room, he saw Paul and Jonesy, who were monitoring the chatter on the dark web, jump up out of their chairs, pulling their headsets down around their necks.

"Why do they keep talking about the training videos? Did you see that? It came up more than once. What training videos?" Paul said.

"Who ever heard of there being training videos for Henchmen? That's fucking nuts," Jonesy said.

"Wait! Hold on a sec. Who's talking about that?" Matt asked.

"There is a newer thread talking about the Flying Monkeys in the Wizard of Oz, and other weird shit about Henchmen that you never realized were Henchmen," Paul said.

Matt smiled. "That was them, I know it. When I first got here, Liz gave me over thirty movies to watch that all had Henchmen in them. It was my job to watch all of them and see how *real Henchmen* worked. That has been one of *our* code words, since I liked the Flying Monkeys the best," Matt said. He was relieved and knew that only reason for the girls to mention the Flying Monkeys was to let him know they were just fine. Only Liz and Amber knew that reference.

"Ok, well, that's unusual, but at least it makes sense now. They didn't really give any other information, so it seems like that was how they are letting you know they are safe," Paul said.

"Yup, I agree. Say something back like those monkeys don't fuck up like the rest of them. They know the rules," Matt said.

"How does that help? More code that we don't know about?" Jonesy asked.

"Right, it is. I used to be known as the king of fuck ups, and that I didn't follow the Five Rules of being a Henchman. I don't think anyone else outside of DMF knows about those rules, or about me being a total fuck up when I arrived," Matt said.

"Oh, that's news to me that you were a fuckup," Paul said.

"I can vouch for that. One of his ultimate fuck ups landed me with a bullet hole in my shoulder," Franco said.

"Whoa dude, are you serious? And you're still here? Franco, you're like the boss here, aren't you?" Paul said.

Franco smiled. "Well, now I am, sort of, but back then I was just a number one, and we were on an errand that went bad. You aren't going to believe this, but Four is actually the one who shot me. He had never fired a gun before. It knocked him on his ass."

Both Paul and Jonesy stood in shock with their mouths agape and eyes wide. David H. shook his head.

"The bullet was meant for me, but he was just a really bad aim," Matt said.

"I guess you *forgot* to tell us that part too. Wow, dude, what kind of mess did you bring us into?" Paul asked.

"He wasn't working for us when that happened. He's still a shit stain that poses no threat to any of us. He's so fucking weird. All he *ever* wanted was to work with us cool kids here at DMF. Believe it or not, he's mellowed out since we brought him back here," David H. said.

"Even so, I think we would like to have a Henchman posted with us a little while longer, just in case he goes off the deep end again," Jonesy said.

"That can definitely be arranged. Things are slow now, and we have the resources to give you," Franco said.

"I think we need to get over to the HTA and have a sit down with Jimmie about all this. Garrett should be there too," Franco said.

"Isn't Jimmie there now with his friend who's teaching a yoga class?" Matt said.

"Oh shit, yeah, he is, but let's go there now anyway so we can grab him before he leaves. Can you call Garrett and get his looney ass there too?" Franco said.

"Teaching yoga. Let's fucking go right now. I've got to see these big goofy ass men being Zen, unreal," David H. said.

"That's not something I would ever think of as a combo, Henchmen and yoga. Never a dull moment here," Paul said.

CHAPTER 28
PUTTING THE PLAN INTO ACTION

THEY FOUND Jimmie in classroom B, where Gabe taught his combative classes. This classroom had no desks in it, only mats on the floor and walls. The only windows, which faced Pinky's gym, were eye level range for the Henchmen six-foot-four and above and about twelve inches wide, small enough so no one could be accidentally thrown through one while learning hand-to-hand combat. The door was left open, and Matt watched from the hallway and could see the yoga teacher, prepping the classroom for the first class of its kind at the HTA.

"Dude, did Jimmie tell you about this chick? She's hot," David H. said to Matt.

"Yeah, she is. I think Jimmie said her name is Crystal. He's vetted her for the job," Matt said.

"Christ, you two. Matt, you have enough to deal with now. Don't go messing with it, and David, you have a baby, keep your hands off," Franco said.

The three lingered outside the classroom just a little longer than they should have. Franco put a hand on each of their shoulders and said, "Let's go, fellas. Let her get to work."

Matt saw the Henchman assigned to Crystal's class were wearing their new official HTA sweats and T-shirts, waiting in the hall until Crystal was ready for them to enter the transformed combatives classroom. Crystal looked like she could be a yoga-wear model. Her tall, tan, tone body fit the expensive, dark gray leggings and black midriff top she wore. She stood at the door with Jimmie and waved the Henchmen over, pulling her light brown hair into a loose bun, with a fresh daisy pinned behind her left ear.

She was busy setting several battery-operated candles throughout the room, filling a decanter with essential oils out, and of course getting the ever-present floating music to set just the right tone.

There had been plenty of harsh jokes made about the addition of yoga into the HTA. None of the Henchmen wanted to openly admit they were curious about taking yoga, so instead they made fun and decided they would not be going *full-on hippy* after completing the class. Jimmie made the class mandatory. Not completing it would mean withholding their certificate of completion. For Jimmie, this was the first step in creating a holistic section of the HTA. He was also planning on teaching meditation, but only after the prerequisite of yoga was complete. He hired Crystal as a consultant for both the yoga and meditation class. Crystal was the perfect fit to bring in. She was the free-spirited sister of Benji, one of the Henchmen who had been with DMF for a few years. She knew enough about DMF and the HTA that there was nothing to explain to her, except that they were introducing yoga as a required course. She had been teaching both disciplines, yoga and meditation, for many years and Jimmie knew she could handle any heckling she may get from the Henchman in her class. When he saw her, Matt's thoughts drifted off to his sisters. They were yoga nuts and were big advocates of doing yoga several times a week. It reminded him that he hadn't touched base with them for a while.

"Welcome to my class, it's wonderful to meet all of you. Please leave your shoes in the hall. We never wear shoes in the studio. Thank you kindly."

The slightly-irritated group grunted to pull their shoes off and made their way into the classroom. "Shit, what's that smell? I kinda like it," Tyler said. "The room looks so different with no lights on."

Standing in the doorway, Matt turned to Franco and said, "We have seriously got to watch this class. Is it being streamed on the CCTV?"

"Yes, it is, but she's also recording on the iPad there so we have a catalog of all the classes. We are hoping the guys really like it and want to take the class over again. But you can go in Pinky's office and watch live if you want," Jimmie said with a wink.

"Good plan, let's go watch this. I think it will be entertaining," Matt said. "Besides coming over here to watch this class, we have some information from OHP."

Jimmie held onto his mala beads thoughtfully and asked what they had to share. Matt could see concern in his body language. He noticed Jimmie held onto those beads when they were speaking of tense situations or discussing what next steps in a project would be.

"What is the news? It's unsettling you needed to deliver the news in person."

Matt shook his head. "No, it's nothing bad. We were coming over here and figured we would just let you know the OHP Team contacted Paul and Jonesy. Everything is good. It was the code word they used that we thought was funny, sort of."

Jimmie took two steps closer to Matt, getting in his personal space. "Oh, I get it, this was a just for fun visit then?"

"I guess you could say that. I'm sorry, I guess it wasn't

funny to drop this on you. But the code word they used was Flying Monkeys, that's funny right?" Matt asked.

Jimmie took steps back to a normal distance from Matt's face, and said, "Ok, since you delivered the message to me, you have nothing else to do then. I'm going to strongly suggest that you join the others for Crystal's class."

Matt knew it wasn't worth arguing, and that Jimmie didn't suggest that as a joke. Franco and David H. were laughing and gave each other a fist bump.

"Have a great class bro," David H. teased.

"Better hurry in. You don't want to be late. There are some extra mats in the back of the room. Let me know what your experience is," Jimmie said, walking away.

"You got burned, dude. You thirsty? We can go grab a nice latte and then come back and watch the class," Franco said.

Matt shrugged his shoulders, turning to enter the class-room. Of all the things they had asked him to do, this wasn't the worst he could think of. It was something more he could share with his sisters the next time they spoke. *They always encouraged him to take a yoga class*, he thought.

The six Henchman, and Matt, stood around looking very awkward, not sure where to go or whether to sit, or stand, or lay. The Henchmen noticed Matt taking his shoes off, preparing for class, only giving him slight nods as acknowledgement.

Crystal gently shut the door to begin class. "Oh, my. I'm so sorry I didn't give you better instructions about how the class will begin. You may all choose a mat to sit on. Please have a seat."

"Aren't you Benji's sister? I think I've seen you before?" asked Mario.

"I am his sister, but for now, let's just begin to let go of what is outside the door. Have any of you ever taken a yoga class?"

None of the Henchmen raised their hands or spoke. "Well,

ok then. Seems like we need to lighten up the energy here. Let's start by saying hello to your neighbors. Usually in my studio, we give hugs, so let's try that too then," Crystal said with a kind smile. When no one moved, she laughed and lightly placed her hand on one guy' shoulders. "Oh, go on now. Give your neighbor a hug."

"How about we just shake hands? We aren't really the hugging type, ma'am," Mario said.

"I see that. Handshakes then. I want you all to know that I will guide you through this gentle practice. We will do a Yin yoga practice that is all about relaxation and is a more meditative practice than what you probably have in mind. I want you all to pay attention to your bodies. If anything feels uncomfortable, or if you experience any sharp pain, please let me know. Some discomfort is ok, but if it gets more than that, I can give you some alternative poses. It is important to me that you all feel comfortable and know that you are in a safe space with me for the next forty-five minutes," Crystal said.

Tyler scoffed loudly. "Forty-five minutes? How hard can that be?"

"I'm sure you will all do wonderfully. Let's start in child's pose. I will demonstrate for you."

Matt was glad she was going to show the poses. If he'd never heard of them, he was sure none of the others had either. The dark chill vibe of the room was slowly helping with his anxiety of not knowing what the hell was going on. As class went on, the grumblings lessened, and the mood shifted to deep rhythmic breathing and stress releasing sighs. It had been rare for him to feel relaxed and calm since being at DMF. But this class really helped him and the other Henchmen to downshift to a gear they'd not reached before while on shift.

As the class finished and the Henchmen were slowly coming out of the final pose, savasana or corpse pose, Crystal thanked the Henchmen for allowing her to guide their practice. "It has been my honor to guide you through your very first yoga practice. Please take some time today to drink some water, more than you usually do. If you are interested, I have some yogi tea prepared and waiting for you at the front desk."

"That was amazing, dude. I don't think I've ever been this relaxed in my entire fucking life. How does it only take forty-five minutes to help me unwind like that?" Mario said to Matt. "I don't think I could drive home even if I wanted to. I'm still not sure of this HTA thing, but this was very cool."

Crystal smiled and bowed her head with her hands in a prayer position. "I'm so glad you liked it. Just remember that yoga is for everyone. We all need yoga in our lives. I look forward to seeing you all next time."

Matt aimlessly wandered out of the classroom, walking up to Franco, who was standing at the front desk with David H., who said, "I think that was one of the funniest fucking things I have ever seen. Those bodies in there are not suited to bend and fold into some of those poses. We watched the whole class from Pinky's office. You guys really zoned out."

"After seeing that, I am not really looking forward to taking that class. I have it on my schedule for the next session. I feel like I should start stretching now. I don't think my knees could take that first pose they did. You get to take a nap after class? That doesn't sound too bad," David H. said.

Crystal was sipping her tea after the class watching the Henchmen come out of the class. "We do savasana after every class. It is a way to complete your practice, it seals in all the relaxation you created while in class," Crystal explained. "Too bad you guys didn't join too."

Garrett walked up to the group, holding his phone up. "I watched it on my phone. It doesn't look so hard to me," Garrett said.

Garrett's loud frat boy voice startled Matt who was just beginning to tune into the world again.

"You made it, I didn't see you come in, glad you are here," Franco said.

"Of course, I want to hear the latest garbage as much as anyone. Before we start, I need a coffee. I'm headed to the Bean, do you guys want anything?" Garrett asked, walking toward the front door.

"We're good, we just were there. We will be in Pinky's office when you get back. Crystal, we'll see you next time. Thank you for being part of this," Jimmie said.

"It was my honor, until next time," Crystal said, turning to leave.

Speaking to Garrett, Jimmie said, "You showing up here must mean that something significant has come up, let's head to Pinky's office so we can talk." Matt and Franco debriefed Jimmie on the code words seen on the dark web, and the possible in-town visit from the real Rossi.

"Seems like it's time to make our move. I'm don't think we need to focus on the whereabouts of the OHP Team now. Their chatter on the dark web doesn't indicate they need any assistance. But if the asshole is here, then we need to grab him. I want to do it so that no one, and I mean no one, can trace it to DMF. I don't want anyone thinking we took this guy seriously. Just get him off the streets," Jimmie said.

"We'll let the CM Team know. Four actually loves to hear shit like that. When he thinks he is the only one to know something, it feeds his ego, and he works even harder. Takes a minute to figure him out, but once you do, he's easy to read," Franco said.

"Have him bait Rossi with false information and get Rossi to believe we think he's back in Italy, and the OHP Team are hot on his tails," Jimmie instructed.

"That shouldn't be too hard to do. From what Paul and Jonesy said, they aren't too strategic or bright," Matt said.

"Perfect, and in the meantime, we can put together a plan here. This is what I want to be kept code red, only the Team assigned knows what's going on. Franco, you select the Henchmen you trust. We can go from there. Matt, you and David H. maintain a routine that won't cause any distraction or attention," Jimmie said.

"Simple but effective, I like it," David H. said.

"Hopefully by the next round of classes at HTA, we won't have this ridiculousness in our lives," Jimmie said, then he looked down at his watch. "What happened to Garrett? He missed the whole meeting."

CHAPTER 29
SURPRISE!

Per usual, Garrett was late to the start of almost any meeting, especially the morning check in which is scheduled for eight. "You are going to want to see what I just saw. Come over here and watch this shit on the monitors."

Matt, along with Franco and David H. followed Garrett to the monitors in Pinky's office.

Garrett stared intently at the security video monitors holding the remote in his hands, arms crossed over his chest. He rewound footage of the front parking lot of Pinky's, eyes narrowed. Garrett paused it and slammed a hand on the table. "That was him. God damn it, I was right."

"What are you yelling about, dude?" David H. asked.

"He was out front again. I was walking to the Bean, and I got a weird feeling about this piece of shit car. Usually, I wouldn't look twice at a 1990s Toyota Camry, but the guy driving, alone, may I add, watched me a little too closely, you know?" Garrett said.

"You're sure it was him?" Jimmie asked.

"I took out my phone and walked toward him so I could take some pictures of him. As I got up to the car, he fucking tipped his hat, flipped me off, Italian style, and drove off," Garrett said.

"He's so fucking strange, but that sure sounds like him," Matt said. "Well, that makes our job a little easier. He's begging us to nab him. But why us? What's his deal with DMF?"

"Duh. Right now, who's his biggest competitor? He probably only brought us in on the NFT project to get more information on us. He's probably laughing that we have you and guys like Four working for us, no offense. But his snooty ass probably thinks we are getting sloppy and not as refined as him," Franco said.

"He wants to throw us off our game. He's mistakenly lumped us with the rest of the ordinary, uninformed Henchmen. Surprise!" David H. said.

"This could be interesting to see how this all plays out. I'm going to go share the news with Fowler, and then I will get moving with my part," Franco said.

"I can't wait to see what we do with him once he's ours!" David H. shouted.

Matt spent the next few days bouncing between the cave collecting intel on Rossi's whereabouts and strategy meetings on how to nab him. As much as Rossi's inept Cyber Team tried to convince the world that he was globetrotting, only stopping briefly here and there, the guys in the cave, Four, Paul, and Jonesy, knew better. The Skittles talk had stopped. It seems like whoever was the author of the chats had either gotten bored with it or it had become too difficult to try to weave into chatter. Matt was fascinated with the strategy meetings; the details were so precise. This mission needed to be coordinated for specific times and places, just so many details that Matt had never thought of. He had to remind himself that this wasn't an ordinary errand like he used to run in the good old days. That shit was simple, most of the time. Stopping by some startup and acting like an asshole was about all it was. There were occasional snags where there needed to be surveillance, but those were rare.

The finishing touches were coming together and the plan, or plans if needed, were ready to run. Matt had received a lengthy text from an "unknown" number. He smiled when he saw it was from Liz, he guessed, catching him up on the latest movements. He read the OHP Team was working, however, they were also using the time to connect with old friends. Liz was the only one who didn't have connections in Europe, but Pinky was boss lady over there. She spent most of her life living all over Europe when she was traveling with the circus, eventually creating her own Team of Henchmen. She actually had teams spread out throughout the continent, and that was how Vanessa got the gig at the Rossi villa. And Amber, she had no home. The world was her home, which led her to have many old friends to visit with. It wasn't exactly a girl's trip or vacation, but once they determined Rossi was not on the same continent, why not have a little fun reconnecting?

Through these unknown numbers, they kept Matt in the loop. He could picture them sitting around laughing about how worried he must be if they didn't keep proper communication with him. He learned that since things had calmed some, the OHP Team purchased a couple burner phones instead of relying on the message boards of the dark web. Being able to communicate easier made Matt happy, and it relieved some of his anxiety about their safety. They still had to speak in DMF code, and the texts became more and more creative as the days and weeks went by. He was glad for the list of training videos, as they became names they used, situations, and outcomes they referenced to keep things personal. It wasn't hard to decipher who was texting through their different tones and personalities. Liz handed out more practical and useful information, while Amber's messages were a bit more personal and fluffier. Vanessa's were most infrequent, and usually only if Liz was working and couldn't send the updates. Liz's texts included things like 'Yes, the sun is still shining,' or 'We're getting bored with the same meals every day.' Amber's texts would include 'Sitting alone again at dinner tonight,' or 'I've been so bored. I'm missing my kitty, Mr. Big.'

"OMG, are you still texting random dumb shit to the girls? That must get old. You need to get a life, dude," David H. said.

Matt laughed. "You caught me at a bad time, it's not what it looks like."

"Sure, whatever you say. Grab your phone and come with me. We need to run downtown to pick up a couple of things from the DMV. *Someone* didn't get the tags on one of the vehicles renewed in time. In our line of work, you never want to be pulled over for something random like that. Let's go," David H. said.

CHAPTER 30
PLEASE PICK A NUMBER

"I don't understand why they have the fucking DMV on the tenth floor," David H. spat.

A woman who was sharing the elevator with them shot David H. an enraged look. "Excuse me, but would you please watch your language? My kid doesn't need to hear that."

"Oh shit, my bad," David H. muttered.

"That's a bad word too, mister," said the little boy.

The woman clapped her hands over the boy's ears, her mouth in a tight, unhappy line.

"Sorry," Matt said to the woman. "He just forgets where he is sometimes, you know?"

The woman ignored them, trying to shield the boy from them with her body.

Matt was relieved when the doors opened. With quick nods to the mother and her son, they walked to the DMV kiosk to get their number and wait to be called.

"The lines are not as long as usual," Matt commented hopefully as they took their seats.

"Yeah, only a few hours to go," David H. said with a long sigh.

"Jesus, what did we all do before we had phones to occupy

our time?" Matt asked, pulling his phone out of his jacket pocket.

"Fuck if I know. Wake me up if something other than *this* happens," David H. said with a yawn.

Matt was on his phone when he noticed two men come in who looked out of place. For one thing, they were Henchmen size, and two, they had suits on. He quickly noticed that they didn't have a little paper number in hand, possibly indicating that they were only there to look for someone. By this time, David H. was in deep slumber, and Matt didn't want to disturb him if it was a false alarm. But he just couldn't shake the feeling that something was about to happen that would wake him up anyway. After a few jabs to David H.'s arm, he woke.

"There better be a good reason for you waking my sleeping ass up," David H. said with his eyes still closed.

"Dude, I think some shit's about to go down. When you open your eyes, look at nine o'clock," Matt said.

David H. shifted in his seat, putting his head between his knees before raising his arms over his head to take a good morning yawn and stretch. His expertly trained glance knew exactly who Matt was referring to.

"We aren't doing anything. You hear me? Let them make the first move, if they do. But good call to wake me up," David H. said, patting his side, indicating he was armed and ready to rumble if needed.

"How many more numbers do we have until we are called?" Matt asked too loud, and too obvious.

"*What are you doing?* Oh my God. Do you know what playing it cool even means? Act fucking normal," David H. said through tight lips.

Matt put his head down to show he understood, and that he was embarrassed for looking like a total rookie, again.

Matt and David H. played on their phones with slight

glances at the pair of Henchmen for the next twenty minutes until there was some commotion at the front kiosk and reception desk.

"Fucking kids, make too much noise," David H. growled.

The blond Henchmen in the navy suit stood and walked to the front of the room. Matt and David H. sat up straighter, but this time didn't try to be nonchalant. They watched him until he left the room, his bald Henchman partner sat in silence, giving Matt the death stare.

"God, I hate that. I wish he would stop," Matt nervously said to David H.

"Something isn't right. Stay here. I want to go check this out," David H. said.

"Wait, what should I do? Shit, I'll just wait for you to come back," Matt said to deaf ears.

Matt awkwardly pulled out his phone and pretended to be occupied by his screen. He felt the eyes of the bald Henchmen bore into his own private space. *God, how do they do that?* The Henchman was all the way across the room, yet Matt could feel his stare.

CHAPTER 31
I SURRENDER

Everyone in DMV simultaneously looked up from their phones when the faint sound of what Matt knew to be gunshots echoed through the nearby hall. There were questioning looks, like, *Is this really happening?* since mass shootings were an unfortunate common occurrence. He quickly glanced to the bald Henchman, who didn't seem to have heard the shots and seemed more into listening to his podcast than working. Matt questioned whether he had heard gunshots, since he seemed to be the only one to not be concerned. A few of the waiting people shuffled in their seats, whispering to each other about what was most likely the same thing as Matt was trying to decipher.

A concerned look on the face of the women sitting across from him spurred Matt to console her. He quietly said to her, "I don't think we have anything to worry about." He smiled to her, and her face relaxed again.

Matt heard David H. before he saw him. David H. was talking very loudly so the whole room could hear him. Matt shook his head in disbelief at what he saw. The whole room gasped and the people waiting for their turn looked to be in shock. There stood David H. with his hands in the air in an *I surrender* position. Next to him was Rossi, with a perplexed look on his face, his hands also in the air. The blond Henchman had his gun pointed at them both. Matt could feel his body tense when he saw Rossi. His first instinct was to run to him and punch him in the throat. He quickly read the room and knew he needed to see how this played out. *No need to be reactive, that's what we are learning not to do* he thought through a clench jaw.

"Look who's so fucking smart now! You DMF guys think you are so fucking cool? Well, who's getting the money now? We are!" shouted the blond Henchman, letting out a deep laugh. "You didn't even notice that the old Italian man followed you here. What idiots you are! Did you see how easy I grabbed them, Vincent?"

Matt noticed the bald Henchman, Vincent, hadn't moved and was just watching the whole scene play out. It was as if they hadn't planned this far in advance, so he wasn't sure how to contribute to the in-plain-sight kidnapping attempt. Matt stood to get a better view of the shouting Henchman and to see if he could read David H.'s face for any type of clue as to how this was going to play out. All he could decipher was that David H. showed no signs of stress or panic. He looked as calm as he did when he left the room in the first place.

"Hey asshole, you can take the crazy old bastard. We don't want him. Just let all of us go. Take him, who gives a fuck?" David H. shouted without turning to look at the blond.

"Oh no! Please, do not give me to him. I do not want that to happen. This wasn't the way it was intended to happen!" screamed Rossi.

"Tell him to shut his fucking mouth, Tommy!" yelled Vincent.

Matt noticed that many of the people in the waiting room were on their phones, presumably calling 911 or at least the building security. Vincent finally stood up and shouted to the crowd, "Put your fucking phones down, now!" He turned toward Tommy. "Lock the door!"

"You lock the door! Can't you see I'm busy?" Tommy shouted across the room, waving his gun in the air.

Vincent stood for a moment before he walked to the front doors to shut and probably try to lock them if he could figure it out. The thought of trying to tackle him and restrain him crossed Matt's mind, but a quick glance to David H. confirmed he should let things play out and not try to be the hero.

Rossi looked like he was going to drop, his eyes looked crazed and confused. His breaths were short and rapid which, as Matt had learned, was the absolute worst thing to do in a stressful situation.

Vincent rubbed his hands together in front of the door. "Dude, where is the little security guard we saw earlier?"

"Your tough guy here knocked him out in the hallway. Can you just let these people leave? They don't need to be here. Take the old man and go," David H. said.

"Shut up!" Tommy shouted to David H., knocking David H. in the side of his head with the butt of his gun. The crowd of people let out an audible gasp, but David. H didn't waver as blood dripped down the side of his head. Tommy turned to his partner. "Hurry and lock the doors, man! We need to get this under control!"

Vincent was still struggling to get the door to stay closed, much less locked. Under less stressful situations, one could figure out that the pin needed to be removed from the top hinge mechanism. Vincent kept trying to pull it shut without putting it all together. Looking frustrated, he went to the where the fire extinguisher hung on the wall and violently pulled it from its mounted wall bracket. Matt wasn't sure what Vincent would do next. Was he going to use it as a weapon? Instead, he began to bash and smash the fire extinguisher against the door handle and the hinges, disabling it from being able to open or close.

"Hey asshole, why are you trapping all these people? At least let the women and children go! Come on, man, it doesn't have to be like this," David H. said.

"For the last time, shut up! I know what I'm doing. With all these people here, I bet I can get over five million! Isn't that right, old man? You will pay me more if I keep all these hostages!" Tommy snarled.

Rossi just nodded. "Whatever you want, I will pay you if you let me go!"

"Everyone, get out from behind your desks and come sit in the middle of the room and sit with everyone else! Now!" yelled the bald Henchman.

The DMV workers stood and made their way to the empty seats left in the middle of the room, and the people who were already seated made room for the staff to sit. The energy in the room read fear and confusion, mixed with a sprinkle of panic. Matt desperately wanted to do something that would be helpful, but David H.'s cool, calm responses had set the tone.

Matt heard sirens coming closer. The Henchmen paced with their guns drawn.

Vincent laughed. "Good! The stupid cops are showing up. That's what we want. The more attention we get, the more money our Italian will pay."

Matt couldn't take being a silent hostage any longer. "Hey numbnuts, this isn't funny. You guys getting out of here isn't going to happen. You fucked up, and you had your chance, but you shouldn't have been so greedy. The cops are going to blow your fucking brains out," Matt said.

Tommy squinted at Matt. "Aren't you the one they call College Boy? I recognize you from the meme on the dark web as somebody you don't want to be, it was pretty funny. You don't know how this works. Vincent and I have a plan. You two fools are going to blamed for this! We're going to look like the heroes, not you two."

"Oh, ok. Like that's going to work. But sure, I bet all the people in here will get us confused and blame us," Matt said.

"God, you're so stupid! Why do you think we are getting more money from the old man? So we can pay everyone in here to tell the cops it was you two! It's a perfect plan that will make everyone happy," Tommy said.

"Jesus, what a fucking stupid idea," David H. snorted. His face came to life with anger. "I'm going to ask you one last time to let the people go, otherwise shit's about to get real, my friend. I don't want people to be more traumatized than they need to be. But, I *am* going to fuck you both up."

With a slight turn of his head in Matt's direction, Matt knew he would go to Tommy first, then Vincent. Matt was ready for whatever happened next, hoping that it would be quick with minimal bloodshed.

CHAPTER 32
DEAD ON ARRIVAL

MATT WAS WATCHING this all play out, not making any moves. No one expected, least of all Matt, that Rossi would make the first move. Matt figured Tommy had patted Rossi and David H. down when they first entered the DMW waiting room. Tommy had confiscated their holstered weapons, but he clearly had not taken the time to pat down their legs. If he would have, he would have discovered that David H. never left the house with one weapon. Matt let out a sigh of relief when he realized that David H. was still armed. He knew David H. could handle his business.

Rossi looked as though he was going to faint. *I wouldn't be surprised if he did,* Matt thought. *I've seen him carried into his house for Christ's sake.* The room watched as Rossi bent at his waist, making it look like he was attempting to catch his breath but instead reached for his weapon in a loaded ankle holster. He fired, immediately striking Tommy in the side of his head. Tommy dropped to the floor, dead before his body smacked the ground. David H. already had his weapon in hand, and Matt's legendary Henchman instincts kicked in. *This asshole's going down.* While Vincent stood dazed and confused looking at the body of his dead friend, Matt already was in his defensive tackle mindset, sprinting to blast the unaware Vincent. Matt hit him so hard it knocked them both off their feet. Matt landed on top, trying to keep the advantage by putting Vincent in an armbar hold.

The room turned into pure chaos—crying, yelling, screaming people trying to figure out what do next. Having to step over Tommy's dead body made the panic heighten. The frantic people rushed to the door. The first person to the door tried pushed it open, not realizing that it has been disabled earlier. The door remained jammed into a closed and locked position.

Matt had the upper hand in the fight of his life. With the chaos in the room, he continued to wrestle Vincent. He was only focused on keeping control of the brawl, but unfortunately for him, Vincent was an expert in hand-to-hand combat, and just stronger and more agile enough to make this an unevenly matched fight, not in Matt's favor. It was more of a heavyweight wrestling match than the two going blow for blow.

Matt and Vincent were both grunting with sweat pouring out of just about every crevasse of their bodies. In a gutsy move, Matt released his grip and spun himself around to the backside of Vincent, gaining control in the match. Matt held Vincent firm in his favorite grip, a tight headlock. Matt squeezed as hard as he could to keep Vincent from slipping out and reversing the hold. Vincent was twisting and turning, trying to get out of Matt's powerful grip, almost foaming at the mouth. Matt knew it would only last for so long. Either Vincent would pass out, or he would run out of adrenaline. Matt was facing David H., who was searching for Rossi in the panic filled room. When David H. saw Matt and Vincent clashing, he turned to run full speed into the unprotected belly of Vincent. The force with which he hit sent both Vincent and Matt up against a wall. Matt's head slammed into the wall, and for a split second all he saw were stars. The vicious blow David H. delivered left Vincent without the capacity to take in a breath. He could only make it to his knees, trying to crawl away. This was his fatal mistake. David H. lifted a folding chair and swung it with incredible force before the ailing Henchmen knew what hit him.

"I'm not going to shoot your sorry ass in front of all these people! They don't need to see that shit. You can go sit in jail!" David H. shouted.

Matt was still slumped against the wall. David H. and rushed over to him. "Sorry dude, you'll be fine, I need to find that fucking old man right now," David H. said then, looking like a rabid dog acting only off instincts, asked Matt, "Did you see where the fucker went?" Matt could only shake his head back and forth.

With much of the chaos contained, the crowd huddled against the door, desperately wanting to get out, which made it easier to find Rossi. David H. turned to the crowd and said, "Look, I'm really sorry about this shit. If you can get out, go! But I'm going to stay here and get the old man. What he did was wrong! You hear that, old man? I'm coming to find you! This game of yours is over now!"

Matt was startled by a sudden movement to his left.

"Hey mister, I know where he is, I saw him go hide," the little boy from the elevator said.

Matt quickly smiled at the small child. "Can you tell me where? Just whisper it in my ear."

The boy crawled closer to whisper that Rossi was hiding under the desk in the far-left corner where there was a row of windows.

"You're the man! Thanks kid, I owe you one," Matt said with a wink. He scrambled to his feet, reaching David H. He stumbled into him, losing his balance after his first couple of steps. Before he could speak, David H. had his gun pressed against his forehead.

Matt didn't say a word, he just looked into David H's eyes, until he could see David recognized him. He'd never seen David so hyped up.

David drew his gun shaking his head, rubbing his hand over his mouth. "Dude that was fucking stupid. I was going to fucking kill you. Don't fucking sneak up on *anyone* like that."

"I know better. My balance is all fucked. But I know where Rossi is," Matt said, tipping his head toward the desk in the far-left corner.

David nodded and patted Matt on the arm, taking off to grab the old man hiding under a desk. "Real fucking manly," David H. muttered.

David H. moved closer to the far edge of the room, gun drawn.

"Watch out, David! He's armed, he's not being taken prisoner!" Matt shouted.

"That's right, I am armed," came Rossi's thick Italian accent. Matt turned to see Rossi standing with his gun pointed at the crowd. "I do not want more bloodshed today, but I will not become anyone's prisoner."

"Then put your gun down, old man. You're scaring the shit out of the kids in here. Fucking put it down! You started this game. This is on you," David H. growled, taking a slow step toward Rossi.

Rossi pulled the safety off the gun. Matt heard people in the crowd weep.

"Listen," David H. roared. "It's me taking your ass down, or you get to go hang out with some nice American criminals in our prison system. Those are your two choices here."

"I don't like either of those options," Rossi said as he spun around, aimed, and fired at the row of windows, shattering three of the panels.

The glass rained down in millions of pieces, landing on filing cabinets, bookshelves, and a couple of desks. Rossi ran and jumped up on one of the desks before promptly climbing out the window onto the narrow ledge ten stories above the ground.

"Jesus, what the fuck is he doing?" David H. shouted, running to the open windows. "Don't fucking shoot me, old man. I'm coming out on the ledge too."

"David, wait! Don't go out there, he's not worth it. Let him jump!" Matt said.

Matt's pleas went unacknowledged. David H. kicked away some of the broken glass, grabbed the window frame, and hoisted himself up to the ledge ten stories up. As woozy as Matt's legs were, he got up and staggered over to the windows. What he saw came straight from a movie, but this time the Henchman was a hero. This Henchman was in charge and was incredibly brave and methodical, not reactive.

Rossi stood with his back against the building, a terrified look in his eyes, more like a wild animal that was trapped against his will. David H. stood with one hand holding the window frame, not willing to get any closer.

"Drop the gun, Rossi, it's over. Just fucking stop this. How do you see this thing ending?" David H. asked.

"I wish I could jump. I don't have the courage to do that. Can you get me out of here? I have a lot of money. I can pay you, just get me out of here," Rossi said.

"I don't give a fuck about the money, you hear me? Now toss the gun. I'm not asking you again. I will come out there and toss your ass," David H. said.

"Ok, ok, I will drop the gun, I want to come inside now," Rossi said. He was holding the gun with his thumb and pointer finger, like it was a rotten piece of flesh, and he tossed it to the ground.

"About time, old man. Matt, get those people out of here. I called the CUC when I first left to check out what was going on in the hall. I figured better safe than sorry, I could smell some shit brewing, they can help me get him out of here," David H. said.

"But the police are here too, they want to get in here first. What are we going to do about that?" Matt asked.

"We have to time this perfectly. The CUC, I'm sure, will come up the back set of stairs. If you look, I bet they are already there. We need to slip out as the police walk in. With all the people at the door, it may help us out as a distraction," David H said.

Matt wasn't sure if it was aftereffects of his head being smashed or not, but he stood with his hands in the air. "What back set of stairs?" He spun around to look again, only confirming that he had another concussion, almost falling mid spin. "Shit, this not going to feel so good, pretty quick."

David H. did a quick chin nod to the far back corner of the DMV. "Dude, come on, always know where your out is!"

"Christ, yeah, I know. I'll go check the emergency exit stairway and see if they are there. Hold on," Matt said, racing to the emergency exit stairway. The emergency exit, which hadn't been utilized by the frantic crowd, most likely due to it being off to the corner in an inconspicuous similar shade of off white as the rest of the walls, was now their only way out. Poorly planned escape route for the general population, it seemed more of an afterthought than a useful escape.

Matt opened the door slowly to peek his head into the dark stairway when he was grabbed and thrown into the patented Henchman hold, face smashed against the wall, one arm twisted behind his back, and his attacker's arm pushing against the back of his neck. He sure as shit hoped these were the guys from the CUC.

"Fellas, look, I'm here with David H. He sent me to escort you in, he's on the window ledge with Rossi. I work at DMF, you've actually cleaned up a couple of my messes."

"Let him go, Sam, let him go. I know who this is," the CUC Henchman said.

"Thank you. Christ, let's get this going. The police are outside the DMV office doors, there are about twenty people near the door, Rossi and David are on the ledge," Matt said.

"Fine, get out of our way. Let us do the work," the CUC Henchman said.

Matt noticed that the four CUC Henchmen were dressed in casual, non-descript clothes so they would blend in with the rest of the people trapped in the DMV office. They were not oversized humans like traditional Henchmen either, and they carried backpacks like many other *normal* people. But Matt knew that their backpacks weren't filled with what normal people would bring on a trip to the DMV. The desk phones had been ringing the entire time, and the first thing the CUC Team did was answer each phone until they got to the one with the police hostage negotiator. The CUC Henchman answered the phone in a feigned panic.

"Hello? Oh, I'm so glad to finally speak to you! We couldn't get to any of the phones until now! We are all ok, except one of the assholes in here."

One of the CUCs went to the crowd to calm them and assure them that everything was going to be ok, and that it was almost over. The remaining two went to the window to help coach Rossi off the ledge. Matt heard David H. urging Rossi to come in, but Rossi wasn't having any of it. He was terrified of every option available to him now, stuck in freeze mode. He kept screaming this wasn't how it was supposed to happen.

"Well, old man, this is how it happened. Now let's go in or I'm afraid I'll have to leave you out here all alone. The police will be in this room soon, and I'm not sticking around for them," David H. said.

"I don't know what to do! I'm frozen with fear, I don't think my legs will carry me back in. We are so high up," Rossi cried.

The CUC Henchman was losing patience. "We don't have time. The door is going to be opened really fucking quick here, and we all have to be gone before that happens. It's now or never. I'm counting to five, and we are out."

David H. gently held out his hand for Rossi to grab. "You got this. Just look at me, don't look down. Take small steps, and go slow, keep looking at me."

Rossi was sniveling with tears rolling down his face, but he summoned the courage and took David H's hand. He clung to David H.'s hand and slowly shuffled his feet across the ledge until he was close enough that the CUC Henchmen both grabbed him, throwing him to the ground. The crowd cheered as Rossi was pulled in off the ledge. The police had moved in from their tactical positions in the main hall after the phone call and were busy unscrewing the door hinges from their angle.

"Move away from the door! Once we take this last screw out, it's going to fall, move away!" shouted the police.

The CUC Henchmen, David H., Matt, and Rossi knew they had to escape the room as quickly as possible. As soon as the door hit the ground, they all rushed out of the emergency exit. Matt assumed they would run down the stairs to safety, but instead, the CUC Henchmen ran up the stairs. Matt wanted to ask why but followed without explanation. David H. threw Rossi over his back and ran up the flights, with him bouncing up and down. It was an impressive feat of strength that David H. was able to keep the fast pace of the others with a man pinned across his back. The group ran up five flights of stairs and only stopped to open the door marked *Roof*.

They kicked the door to the roof open, and to Matt's surprise, there was a helicopter waiting. Seconds after the group entered the helicopter, it took off again, gliding across the cityscape to an unknown destination.

CHAPTER 33
IN THE AIR

MATT LOOKED out the window of the sleek black helicopter and felt instant relief. The stress had subsided, but his head hadn't stopped hurting, and he felt a wave of nausea set in. His neck stiffened, which were side effects he was familiar with. The newest concussion he received during his fight with Vincent was turning into a whopper of a migraine. He knew when those hit, he needed to be in a dark quiet place, not in a noisy, bright helicopter. Although he was glad to be in it and not having to explain what happened to the police, he just needed to close his eyes until they landed, wherever that was going to be. Rossi appeared to be agitated and was fidgeting in his seat. The CUC Team looked bored, with blank, emotionless expressions. David H. looked as though he were reflecting on the last ninety minutes of his life.

The CUC Team had handcuffed Rossi. They didn't want Rossi's irrational behavior to continue while in the air. They had also used duct tape to keep him in his seat. Apparently, they had several rolls of the duct tape in their backpacks, and as soon as they took flight, three of the CUC Henchmen swiftly taped Rossi to his seat. One took his feet and ankles, one took his upper chest and arms, and the third his mouth. There was no confusion about who would tape which part of Rossi's body, it was routine. *Such precision*, Matt thought.

"What's next with him?" Matt asked as the helicopter began its descent to the ground below.

None of the CUC Team acknowledged his question. David H. waited to speak over the roar of the chopper.

"The CUC Team is going to take him to have a little chat. After that, who knows?" David H. said.

"Just a chat? I wasn't sure what his future would be after the shit he pulled. I wonder if his Henchmen will come looking for him," Matt wondered.

"You always ask this many questions? Why don't you just leave it alone? This doesn't concern you," The CUC Henchman said.

"Matt likes to be in the know. I guess I'm used to him by now. He's just a little anxious little guy," David H. laughed.

"Whatever. We got him from here. You don't need to know anything else about it," The CUC Henchman said.

"You guys are acting too much like the fucking CIA," Matt said. When the four CUC Henchmen turned to look at him with daggers, Matt held his hands up. "That's not a bad thing. We need guys like you on our team. Thanks guys, it was cool to see you at work. I've only ever just heard about you. What you do is really impressive. Maybe one of you can come talk to a class at the HTA. They could learn a lot from the way you handle yourselves on the job."

"Look, bro, the *only* reason you even saw us today is because of the nature of the situation. We only show our faces when the general public is in danger. We won't be coming to any HTA classes," the CUC Henchman said.

David H. gave Matt a look that translated to *don't open your mouth again*, which Matt obliged. The helicopter landed gently, and the blades slowed to a complete stop. Without pause, the CUC Henchmen cut the tape off where Rossi was taped to the seat, leaving the handcuffs on. Matt was glad that Rossi's mouth had been taped shut. He wasn't in the mood to hear his winey bullshit. Rossi was quickly escorted off the helicopter and ushered into a waiting windowless van. Rossi did not go willingly, and he tried to run away, slipping and falling after only a few steps. The CUC boys didn't skip a beat, as if this was to be expected. They each grabbed a specific part of Rossi, and out came the duct tape rolls. With efficiency Matt never seen, they hogtied Rossi with duct tape. He squirmed and rolled to no avail, as the CUC Henchmen each grabbed an arm and lifted him not too gently into the van. Matt wondered when he would, or if he would see him ever again.

Skippy was driving the Suburban that brought Matt and David H. back to the DMF house. Franco was riding shotgun. "Well, that was some fucked up shit," Franco said.

"David was awesome. He managed the whole situation really well, like a trained professional," Matt said.

"Thanks dude, you handled your business too. How's your head feeling?" David H. asked.

"I think it's a bad one," Matt said.

"What the fuck? You knocked him out? I need to hear this," Franco said.

"You want to know the whole story? You can watch the video; it's blowing up online. It's gone viral," Skippy said.

"What does that mean, gone viral mean exactly? I've heard the term, but never wanted to ask what it meant in case I sounded like an idiot. It sounds like I have a disease," David H. said.

Skippy reached for his phone and removed it from its charging stand. He had one eye on the road, and another on his phone, scrolling through until he found the video. "This is crazy. I can't believe the entire thing is online. Those two Henchmen were really fucking dumb," Skippy said.

"Hold on, let me see that," David H. said.

Skippy handed Matt his phone with the video still playing. Matt quickly turned up the sound so they all could hear, and Franco spun around in his seat to watch the scene play out.

"What does going viral really mean? I don't pay attention to that shit," Franco asked.

"It means a fuck ton of people have seen this, like close to a million," Matt said.

"Shut the fuck up, a million people watched that?" David H. asked.

"Nearly, yes, they have. This may not be such a good thing. When this shit happens, it draws attention to whoever is on the video. We may want to put a plan together for how to deal with this," Matt said.

Skippy was back on his phone looking at the latest notification that popped up from a local news station. "So guess what? The freaking news got the video. You are on the news, man. Oh wow, this is *not* good. They have pictures of you with the caption, *DMV Hero*."

"No, they don't! That's just stupid," David H. said.

"Oh, this is not good," Franco said.

"No, it's not good," Skippy said.

As the Suburban turned onto Oakwood Drive, the street where the DMF house was located, the usually quiet low-traffic street now was lined with cars and local news station vehicles. There were so many cars, and people milling about that Skippy thought better than trying to get up the DMF driveway. There were several reporters standing at the iron gates trying to get a glimpse of anyone on the property.

Matt's phone buzzed in his pocket. It was a text from a random overseas number, but he knew it was from Liz. The text read, *What the absolute fuck is going on there? It's all over social media.*

Matt said, "We better find another place to stay tonight. Liz even has it in Europe."

Franco was already on the phone with Jimmie to figure out how to contain the video and maintain some sense of their much valued and tended to privacy.

CHAPTER 34
UNWELCOME MEDIA BLITZ

The Suburban drove by the DMF House and headed to Pinky's. Skippy figured that was the safest place to go. If there were reporters there, at least they could park behind the gym and use the HTA entrance. Since the video hadn't been viral for too long, they thought maybe not enough time had passed for anyone to uncover anything about the HTA. Matt and David H. were watching the clips on several different streams when they arrived at the HTA parking lot, presumably undetected.

The Henchman filling in at the front desk seemed oblivious to what was happening on social media and beyond. The gym was empty except for three Henchmen who were just finishing up their workout.

"Close this shit down now!" shouted Franco.

The Henchman in the gym swiftly moved without asking why and turned the lights off, locked the doors, and took an inventory of what cars were in the lot. Two stood on either side of the entrance while Franco and Matt fired up a couple of the laptops from the HTA. David H. and Skippy stood beside and watched as they scrolled through the various social media applications and the local news stations to see David H.'s face as the number one story of the day. Besides seeing David H. in action, there were interviews with some hostages from the DMV playing too. The news reporter asked a twenty-something woman in a light blue Nike sweatshirt, "Karen, what can you tell us about what happened behind those locked doors? Do you know what happened to the man who was seen out on the ledge?"

"I don't know where he went. As soon as the doors came down, we all got out of there as quickly as possible. That old man shot someone dead. It was cold-blooded. We were all in shock when he did that. The guy who got him off the ledge was a hero to all of us. He kept his wits about him and really made getting all of us out safely his priority. I would really like to thank him," the interviewee said.

"So, you're saying that he laid his life on the line so that you could all get out safely?" the reporter asked.

"Yes, he did. As crazy as this was, it could have been so much worse if he hadn't kept it under control. And he saved the old man from jumping to his death," the interviewee said, smiling.

"Do you know who this hero is? Did you happen to catch his name?"

"Uhm, yeah. The guy he was there with called him David, at least, I think that's what he said."

"David, we would sure like to find you to thank you properly. Thank you for sharing your story with us, Karen. I hope that one day, you will be able to give thanks to the hero that saved so many lives. This is Susanne Blake, reporting back to you in the studio," the reporter said.

"What the fuck are we going to do about this shit? I don't want my name out there or anyone to know my business. Can you take it down, delete it, or something?" David H. asked.

"It's out there for everyone to see, forever. It's only a matter of time before they find out everything. We need to get a plan together on how to spin this. How can David be interviewed, but in a way that gives as little information about DMF and the HTA as possible?" Matt said.

"Hell no. I'm not going to be interviewed. The CUC will take care of that," David H. said.

"The CUC will take care of you not having any police interviews, but the news stations are going to be searching for you," Franco said.

"Excuse me, fellas, but a news van just pulled up out front. Do you want me to take care of it, or should we just leave it alone?" Sal, the Henchman guarding the front door, asked.

Matt, Skippy, Franco, and David H. all looked at each other for the right answer. No one wanted to make the call about what to do next. The van pulled into a spot out front. Skippy interrupted the silence.

"Maybe they won't get out. Maybe they will just wait out front," Skippy said.

"Sal, let's just leave it. I'm calling the CUC right now. They need to get over here, or at least give us some cover. This could be a long fucking night," Franco said, walking away with his phone to his ear.

"I'm going to try to call Liz too. They need to be back here for this. I don't know how to handle this shit. Whatever we do, we need to all be on the same page," Matt said.

"Did someone order a pizza?" Sal asked.

"Dude, seriously? Why do you ask that?" David H. asked.

"Well, because there is a guy coming to the door with a couple of pizzas. He must be a fake," Sal said.

"I am hungry, but yeah, he's a fake. No one ordered any food. Can we at least open the door and grab the food? I'm up for that," David H. said.

"Listen, we may be here a while. See if he actually has food. If he does, throw him some cash and grab the boxes. Let us get out of sight first, but then go ahead. I'm sure he's a reporter or something," Matt said.

"You got it. But I don't have any cash," Sal said.

David H. offered Sal forty bucks to toss at the fake pizza guy, then took cover behind a large potted plant. Sal opened the door, intending to grab and toss. With the door only open a crack, the delivery guy dropped the pizzas and gave a vicious two-handed shove to the door, catching Sal off guard.

The pizza guy was inside before anyone saw it coming, and right behind him were two more Henchmen, weapons in hand. It happened so fast that the two DMF Henchmen stationed at the door could barely draw their weapons. The fake delivery men were screaming in Italian, with some *fuck yous* scattered into their ranting.

"*Dov'è lui? Dov'è lui?* We have come for *Signore*," shouted the Henchman.

"These are Rossi's Henchmen! Guys, you need to calm down. Rossi isn't here," Matt said.

The Italian Henchmen were outnumbered but had the element of surprise on the Henchmen posted at the front door. Franco was crouched hiding behind Pinky's desk. Matt wasn't going to be called out on this as not being prepared or having a plan in place, like he should have at the DMV. He would plan his own surprise if needed. Quickly, he made mental note of where people were standing, how he could include them in his plan, either as human shields if needed, or to help him take cover. He knew his advantage over the Italian Henchmen was knowing the floor plan of Pinky's and the HTA. He heard Franco had already been on the phone with the CUC, and knew they were already on their way. Franco texted to update them on the arrival of Rossi's three Henchmen.

"Hey dumbshits, Rossi isn't here. You should have done a better job protecting him. He made a real asshole out of himself today. Why do you play his games and keep his secrets?" David H. asked.

"We need him to bring him back home to our Italia. He is needed there. You must give him back to us. We cannot return without him," the Italian Henchman said.

"That's not going to happen. Not today, not anytime soon. Put your fucking guns away, and let's try to sort all this out," Matt said.

There was a loud knock on the front door, which startled everyone. Sal rushed to the door to see it was the reporter from the news van. The small blonde woman dressed in a pale business suit and small notebook in hand looked too perky for the situation. She had no clue what she was walking into. Matt recognized her as Susanne Blake from the news clip they watched earlier. As Sal opened the door, Susanne edged closer to try to either get inside or to at least see what was going on inside.

"Hello, my name is Susanne, from channel twelve, KTVW. I'd like to come in and have a word with David," she said, looking down at her notepad to make sure she had the first name correct.

"He's not available to speak to anyone at the moment. I'll tell him you were here. If there is nothing else," Sal said, attempting to shut the door.

Matt didn't need to try to be the hero today. The CUC timed it perfectly. Susanne at the door distracted the Italian Henchmen. The stealth CUC Team didn't let that opportunity go by. Coming in the back door undetected, syringes in hand, one steady plunge of the needle into their necks, and the Italians dropped like flies. Matt learned that their drug of choice was etorphine, which was a sedative and worked almost instantly, rendering the person immobile and unconscious within seconds. At any given moment, the CUC Team could restructure a crime scene within seconds.

"Wait! What happened to your pizza? Why was it thrown to the groundout here in the parking lot? Is everything ok in there?" Susanne shouted.

"Lady, everything is fine. Why don't you find someone else to bother? I'm sure you can find something more important to report on," Sal said, fully shutting the door and locking it.

By the time Sal turned around, the Italian Henchmen were gone, and Matt and Franco were back on their laptops, watching more videos of the scene from the DMV.

"Where did they go? asked Sal.

"The CUC is quick, dude. They scooped them up and took them away. Probably will take them to where they are holding Rossi. It'll be a little family reunion for them all," David H. said.

When the CUC Team moves in, Matt learned it was best to just step aside and let them go to work. They were so precise. Each time he'd seen them in action, they never flinched once, asked a question, or made a false move. One of the most impressive things was that they never spoke to one another. The seemed to work purely off of instinct and intuition.

Susanne stood by the door for a few more minutes before giving up and sliding back into the passenger seat of the van. The news van pulled away, only to turn around once more when a black Suburban pulled up out front.

"Jesus, now who's here? Another vehicle out front. I'll just go fuck them up if you want?" Sal said.

The Suburban sat idle for a moment. With the windows tinted, in the evening light, it was hard to determine who was driving the vehicle. There was tension building in the gym, with the Henchmen ready to pounce on the passengers. The Suburban's four doors opened simultaneously. The identity of the drivers and the rest of the passengers was quickly revealed. Liz, Amber, Pinky, and Vanessa exited the vehicle, heads on swivels, ready to engage.

CHAPTER 35
DMF FAMILY REUNION

"OPEN THE FUCKING DOOR, YOU FREAKS!" shouted Liz.

Matt was the first to the door, fumbling with the lock, then he gave Liz a warm embrace.

"Get out of the way, we all need to get inside, but it's nice to see you too, Sport," Liz said.

"Did you bring us any food?" David H. asked.

"You haven't changed despite you being famous now! How does it feel to be a hero?" Amber gushed.

"David! You were amazing there today! All of your course work has paid off! You handled yourself with such poise," Pinky said, giving David H. a big hug.

"Thanks, Pinky. But things are getting out of control here. I'm glad to see all of you. We need to get your expertise on how to handle all the attention," David H. said.

"It was perfect timing. We were headed back anyway, and Vanessa was the first to pull up the video while we were riding in from the airport. What do Fowler and Jimmie know? Do we need to get them in here too?" Liz asked.

Franco looked up from his laptop. "I have been keeping them informed. If you had seen the insanity out in front of the House, you would know why we ended up here."

"We figured it would be a shitshow over there. I see one rando is here. She seems pretty relentless. Maybe she is someone we can use to our advantage," Vanessa said.

As if on cue, Susanne was back knocking on the front door, asking for an interview.

"I'll handle this. Watch and learn, boys, watch and learn," Amber said, skipping off toward the front door.

The group watched as Amber opened the door with confidence and greeted Susanne with a cheery hello. With skill and intention, Amber stood in the doorway in a way that blocked most of Susanne's view into Pinky's, but also showed enough for her to see there was nothing unusual going on. The group maintained their *discussion*, giving no hint that they were paying the uninvited guest at the door any attention. They instructed David H. to move out of Susanne's view, not wanting to dangle too much candy in front of her. Amber's tone never wavered when pelted with questions from Susanne, leaving her with a knotted brow, signaling confusion. Nothing seemed to rattle Amber, even with the mention of David H. being a hero in the eyes of the community and beyond.

Susanne, edging closer to Amber, asked, "Can you tell me more about how Pinky's Gym has anything to do with David's career? People want to know how he was able to keep such a cool demeanor when there was every reason to panic. From what I could tell, it seems like he had been in this sort of situation before." Standing on her tiptoes, stretching to get a glimpse of David, Susanne continued, "Does the gym offer some kind of class on terrorist negotiations? Is that what this place is?"

Matt and Franco exchanged looks, eyebrows raised, at Susanne's last question.

"We are in deep shit if she is going to report that kind of bullshit," Franco mumbled under his breath.

Amber gave a slight turn of her head towards the group

before she answered. "Oh, goodness! My dear, that is a huge assumption to make! Terrorists? That sounds so scary and intense. Doesn't our government take care of those types of situations? Pinky's is just a little local gym. The classrooms that you see have been recently added. We offer different types of, let's say, yoga and workout classes. Nothing as unusual as how to negotiate with a terrorist for heaven's sake."

"Yoga? I will have to hear more about that sometime. I can't imagine men this size enjoying a nice yoga class. For now, I would really like to speak with David. Is he around, please?" Susanne asked, this time inching even closer to the door.

Amber did not budge, she simply closed the door behind her so that both women were now standing outside of the gym.

"Oh shit, should I go out there? I can't hear what's going on," Matt said.

"Sport, did she look like she needed *your* help? I think she's got it covered," Liz said.

Sal was still standing at his post near the door, behind the tall plant. His eyes were trained on the two women still speaking to each other. "Shit, she's good. She has her arm around the reporter and is walking her to her the van. What the fuck? She hugged her goodbye."

"I rest my case, Sport," Liz said.

Sal opened the door for Amber to return inside Pinky's. She strode in as if nothing had happened. "How was that? I think we're BFFs now."

"We need to get a handle on how to deal with the unwanted attention. She will be just the first of many that want access to our world," Franco said.

"You got that right. Do we even have a social media expert in the CM Team? I don't think we do," Liz said.

"That is a good place to start. I will get a hold of Jackson and ask him. I don't remember anyone talking about this shit, though," Franco said.

Franco left to go to Pinky's office to make the call to Jackson. In a weird way, for just a couple of minutes, Matt was enjoying watching the rest of the Team struggle and not know what to do, feeling lost. He was way too familiar with being confused and frustrated, not knowing which direction to go. He also knew the Team well enough to realize this was a temporary moment of anxiety and they would put together a kick ass plan. The rest of the group was silent with looks of distress on their faces. Even Pinky was at a loss for words. It was anyone's guess about how this would eventually play out. The concept of sharing their very private world was not something they'd spoken about. Just having Matt show up at their doorstep at the DMF House had been a shock to their system. His arrival had thrown off the homeostasis, and it took weeks to get it back on track.

Pinky shut her laptop a little too violently. "Well kids, let's get something planned, at least tentatively. We can't sit here like this forever!"

"What do you have in mind? I think it's going to be up to us, and we need to incorporate the entire Team for it to work, whatever we decide," Matt said.

Franco came out of Pinky's office shaking his head. "Well, that wasn't good news. Turns out there really isn't much to do, except to insulate David as much as possible and to coach him through interviews. It's not a matter of if it's going to happen, but when. Jackson said that what we need more than a social media expert is a PR type. This is definitely a public relations nightmare."

"We've never worked with a PR person before. How are we going to find someone we can trust who understands our business?" Liz said.

Pinky walked to the middle of her gym and loudly cleared throat. "Listen. I know just the right person for the job. Do you all trust me on this? I'm sure I can get him here ASAP. I've worked with him in the past, and he is just what we need. He knows enough about our world, but isn't curious about it either, if you know what I mean. He doesn't ask a lot of questions. The man does his job."

"Are you talking about Jace? Wow, I hadn't thought about him in years. He would be perfect," Vanessa said.

Liz walked over to give Pinky an unexpected hug. "I knew you could sort this out. Thank you."

"Wait until you see him. Believe me when I say no one will confuse him with being a Henchman," Vanessa said with a laugh. "He is, how should I say it, flamboyant. Last time we worked with him, he was into wearing feather boas with every outfit."

"What the fuck is a feather boa?" David H. asked.

"It's not something you would ever wear, guaranteed. Think drag queen. It's like a scarf but made of feathers, right?" Matt said.

"Ok, got it. I don't give a shit about what the dude wears as long as he can get me out of this craziness," David H. said.

CHAPTER 36
FEATHER BOAS TO HIGH HEELS

THE GROUP SPENT the night at Pinky's. Matt woke up stiff and sore from sleeping on the floor of Classroom C, the combatives/yoga room with matts on the floor and walls. It was reminiscent of a middle school sleepover, minus the midnight pranks. The group was exhausted from either a long overseas flight, or the events of the day at the DMV.

Skippy, Pinky, and David H. left early to scoop Jace from the airport. Matt was grateful for the downtime while they waited for them to bring Jace to the group.

Vanessa, the most anonymous of the group, was nominated make the coffee run. No one was more grateful than Matt that DMF had kept the Vanilla Bean Coffee shop, aka the Bean, on the payroll after the HTA rollout and purchase of the retail strip mall.

Matt was getting impatient to hear what the OHP Team had pieced together while in the villa. Part of him wasn't sure he wanted to know. His imagination ran wild, telling him stories of how far the flirting actually went. *Maybe I'll try some flirting of my own.* He was watching Amber while she gave Vanessa her coffee order. There was no doubt about it, he felt something for her. With a tilt of his head and a slight smile he walked over to Amber. She was scrolling on her phone when she noticed him. He reached for her hand and gently guided her down the empty, dark HTA hallway. If it was possible for someone else to hear your heart beating, this would be that moment. This was real. What he felt was not just a schoolboy crush. He leaned her against the wall, keeping his eyes locked on hers, placed his oversized hands on the sided of her face and moved closer to her. The kiss was a kiss that neither one would ever forget.

Matt stepped away, breathless. "Holy shit. That, was fucking amazing." Crossing his arms across his chest, feeling awkward about what was to happen next.

Amber shook her head, pulling her shirt back down into the correct place. "Well, amazing yes. I literally had an out-of-body experience, I felt like I was transported to another galaxy. Intense."

"I'm not sure I ever want to stop, or that I know how to stop."

"Are you two done playing kissy face? I thought you wanted me to tell you about our trip. Now I'm not sure you even care," Liz said from the entrance of the hallway.

"Crap, now she's pissed. I better go have a talk with her," Matt offered. "We can figure out what's next another time?"

Amber gracefully walked to Matt, and laid another long, sweet kiss on his lips. "Absolutely we will."

Liz was sitting at the front desk, trying not to notice when Matt walked up and gave her a brotherly hug. The hug almost knocked her off the stool she was sitting on. She slapped his arms away, and said, "You are a goner, dude. Head over heels. No time for me now, I guess."

"Hardly the case. You are my best friend, Liz. You aren't going to be pushed aside. I promised you that once before, and I meant it."

Liz crawled into his arms, for one of the shortest hugs he'd ever given, but it was Liz after all. "I'm really happy for you, for the both of you."

In an instant, Liz packed her emotions and had her game face back on, like it never left.

"So, what do you want to know?" she said, getting back to business and emotional unavailability. Matt's hands were in his pockets, and he swore he wiped the little grin off his face, switching gears to match Liz's haughty tone, but he was having trouble focusing.

Liz rolled her eyes, and said, "Do you want to talk about *it* first?"

His mouth said it all, his wide smile and nod. "It was mind blowing."

"Ok, now we have that out of the way. Good for you. Can I tell you about my adventure now?"

Matt sighed and jumped up and down a few times. "Yup, I'm good, all ears."

Her story was pretty much what he had imagined. It was hard to listen to how stupid and gullible men were around beautiful women. She explained that there wasn't one Henchman that they hadn't been able to crack. Vanessa introduced her and Amber as flight attendant friends who liked to have a good time. The Henchmen ended up all vying for their attention. Their Italian machismo was off the charts, according to Liz. The OHP Team fed them with their smiles and ouhs and ahhhs, fumbling over their physical prowess. She shared stories of how they would have push up contests to show off for them, and other 'manly' tests of strength.

"It was pretty gross most of the time, especially for me," Liz laughed. "But you would have been proud. I played the dumb, clueless flight attendant from Iowa."

Matt looked down at his shoes, his knees began the familiar

bounce, and he asked, "Just flirting, or was there more? You know what? Never mind, I don't want to know."

"Sport, we didn't *need* to do anything else than flirt. We got all we needed. Which was information about Rossi and his ridiculous scheme. Turns out the best intel we got was that there is a guy named Leo who is supposedly the brains of the operation. He used to be Rossi's right-hand man. But it seems now he has manipulated Rossi into playing along with this shit they are pulling now."

Matt studied her face to see if there was any sign that she may be holding something back. She wasn't letting on that he had anything to be worried about.

"That doesn't sound too complicated then, right? I know you weren't there as long as you thought, but you did get some good information. I think I met that Leo. He sat in one of the evening chats Rossi and I had. He seemed pretty slimy to me."

"Oh, you got that right. He was a totally slime ball, right Liz?" Amber said, joining them and rubbing Matt's arm while she spoke.

Matt and Amber smiled at each other as if they had a secret no one else knew about. Liz greeted Amber with a colder glare than Matt had seen in a while. It was the same death stare that he'd seen before, when Amber first arrived at the DMF House. Liz took a deep breath before she responded, "Yeah, I guess you're right. He actually gave me the creeps. I think we all agreed that he is someone we need to keep tabs on."

Matt was relieved when he noticed he noticed Liz's glare become less intense.

Sal quickly grabbed the door for Vanessa, whose hands were balancing a tray each of four coffees.

"I never imagined my time as a flight attendant serving drinks would come in this handy, bloody hell. Thanks for getting the door and not making me kick it open."

The group swarmed her, grabbing at the drink trays as if they were the last drops of coffee on the planet.

"I fully admit my caffeine addiction. Thank God for coffee," Matt said, almost spitting out his first swallow at the sight from the parking lot. He wasn't sure what or who he saw walking into Pinky's. David H. was walking shaking his head fumbling with his phone, Pinky was arm in arm with whom Matt assumed to be Jace. Jace was also wearing a suit; however, it was not a traditional Henchman suit. This was a hot pink, double-breasted suit. Jace was a tall slim build, his long legs made longer by the four-inch sparkling pumps he was wearing. The large white flowered brooch nearly reached his chin. His bleached blond hair was short and very tidy, like he got a trim every few days. At first glance, Matt could have sworn he had pink nail polish on. Jace laughed with Pinky as he entered the gym.

"Jace has arrived my friends! Pinky, you never told me what an adorable place you have here. Oh my, and who are these lovely souls? Let me guess, you must be Liz, love the hair by the way! And no doubt this is Matt. I see what you mean, Pinky," Jace said, winking at her. "Amber. What can I say? You are amazing. Love the outfit, Prada? And last but not least, Franco. My, my, you are a big boy, aren't you?"

Matt stood speechless, as did the rest of the room, until Vanessa broke the silence.

"Come here and give me some love, mate!" shouted Vanessa.

Strutting to give her a hug, Jace squealed, "My sweet little Nessie, I didn't see you there."

"It's great to see you. It's been a while. Way to make an unforgettable entrance. I know the pink suit and nails weren't a coincidence," Vanessa said, smiling.

"You know me! Never want to look out of place or underdressed. Oh my, who is that hiding behind the plant? I'm sorry I didn't see you there. Don't want you to feel left out. You must be Sal," Jace said.

Sal's reply was a simple nod and then back to eyeballing the parking lot. No other suspicious vehicles had made an appearance since Susanne the other day. Matt joked that knowing her, she had given her rival news stations false information about David H.'s whereabouts to throw them off her scent. "She's probably fed them a load of shit about her 'leads' on where you are hiding out, David. She's helping us out without even knowing it."

"It gives us time to get Davey all prepped and ready to go. I was briefed on the way here, and I am so impressed with Davey's demeanor. I'm sure this will all end up being beneficial to DMF in the long run," Jace said.

"Do you need to have some privacy? How can we help?" Liz asked.

"Beautiful girl, thank you, but no. I want everyone here to see how I work, what I expect, and to answer questions for me. Typically, I would usually never let anyone see me without my heels, but my feet seem to have got puffier than a blow fish during the flight. Does anyone mind it I take them off?" Jace asked.

"You do you, man. I don't think anyone cares if you take your fucking shoes off," David H. said.

"Davey, that's not the thoughtful responses we are looking for. What happened to that charm I saw on the ride here?" Jace said with a wink, gently removing his left silver, glittery pump.

The group made their way to Classroom A, which was set up like a traditional classroom with rows of chairs and a whiteboard in the front of the room. Jace strutted to the front as if he still had his heels on. The rest of the group followed with David the only one sitting in the front row. Sal remained at the front door, protecting his Team from unwanted guests. There were still a few local customers that arrived to use the gym, only to see the shades pulled and a sign on the door that read, "Closed until further notice."

Jace wrote out his strategies on the whiteboard. His handwriting was filled with large loops and looked like calligraphy.

"That is the best cursive I've ever seen. It's like art!" Amber said.

"Why, thank you. Let's discuss when everyone's done reading," Jace said.

The list was titled: `Interview Principles 101`

1. Answer only the question asked. Don't give any more information than they ask for. The goal is to answer with a yes or no if at all possible.
2. When possible, end your response with a question back to them, or a personal complement.
3. Smile a lot. Look at them like you could be their best friend.
4. Always look them in the eye. Make them look away first.
5. If a question comes up you aren't comfortable answering, respond with, "Please follow up with my agent," and then smile.
6. There is to be no cussing.

"I don't have a natural smile. That is going to be the most difficult part. Not going to lie," David H. said.

The room filled with laughter.

"Oh David, I think that is something I can help with. I wasn't the most smiley little girl either," Amber said.

"I have to learn how to smile? Great."

"You can look awfully scary. I saw that face when we were at the airport. I mean, if looks could kill," Jace said.

"See! It's not just me. That death stare gets me every time! I refer to it as the patented DMF death stare," Matt said.

David H. turned to give Matt one last look which sent chills down his spine. "Stop dude, that fucks with me big time, it's like PTSD."

"She's baaacckkk!" Sal shouted from his lookout station.

The group left the classroom without hesitation. Susanne had her nose pushed up against the window with her hands cupped around her eyes when she shouted, "There he is! I see him! David, David, can I speak to you now?"

CHAPTER 37
OH NO SHE DIDN'T

"WHAT THE FUCK? Shit, it was just instinct that I came out too. God damn it. Now what should I fucking do? Jace, buddy, better get out here and put your heels back on. We have a situation," David H. said.

Jace came running out, slipping his heels back on. "What is it? What happened? Oh, I see. Ok, not to worry here, Davey. She won't be granted an interview. It's just plain old rude to show up unannounced, and I will tell her so myself. She can come back when we say so. I got this, hun."

Jace motioned for Sal to unlock the door. Jace tossed his short blond locks to the side, took a deep breath, and marched out the door. He turned to Sal and said, "Keep it locked until I say so."

From what it looked like to Matt, Jace was scolding Susanne. He had one hand on his hip and the other hand was shaking his pointer finger at her as if to say, *back it up, sister.* Susanne's body language went from perky and curious to shameful, with her head down, looking only at Jace's magnificent heels. After the tongue lashing was done, Jace turned and spun on one foot and walked with what Matt could only describe as fierceness. No super model could have done better. He pointed to the door and threw his arm back over his head like he had just finished a ballad.

"We are all set. She won't be back until her scheduled interview for this coming Thursday at noon," Jace said.

All the group knew what to do was clap. Jace, on cue, bowed and curtsied.

"We won't be having any more drama from Little Miss Cheap Pantsuit any longer. We have some time to work with David. I took her down in seconds. She will be easy to work with, Davey. She's not a dumb one, though. Don't let her fake blonde hair fool you," Jace said.

"Back to the classroom, you heard him," Liz said.

The group settled in for what was going to be nonstop coaching and roleplaying. Matt's and David's noses went up in the air like hungry animals when the smell of food entered the space in the HTA.

Vanessa said, "I hope you don't mind. I took the liberty of ordering eight large pizzas. I know how predictable guys' stomachs could be. This time a proper delivery, not from an imposter, eat up boys!"

Matt was practically drooling. None of the guys were facing the front of the classroom anymore, noses following the scent.

Liz rolled her eyes. "It seems like we need to take a break for the feeding frenzy to be over."

Jace shouted to the group, "Be back in twenty minutes! And did someone remember to order me a vegan meal?"

Hours later, after dinner, Jace called it a night.

"Thank God. I'm so over this," David H. moaned.

With his hands on his hips, Jace said, "What was that? Look, I know this is a lot, but you are doing so well. This first time can be intimidating, but it is so important to get this right. This will set the tone for everything else in the future. Going from Henchman to hero can't be easy."

"That's what they're saying. I guess it isn't. I think I got it, but I'm ready for everything to go back to the way it was before," David H. said.

The group looked around at each other. Matt wondered who would be the first to tell him that it would never go back to the way it was.

Franco was the first to speak. "Dude, it won't. We all just landed on a new planet. This is big, and not going away. I never thought it would be like this, with you being the spokesman for DMF and the HTA. It's unfortunate, but this is the way it is. We had a good run. This is our new world. Maybe we should have seen something like this coming, but we didn't. You got this, bro, and we are all here to support you."

"I need to go out back and have a smoke. Is that still allowed?" David H. asked.

"Hold up, I'll go out with you. I know what it feels like to never be alone," Matt said.

Franco motioned to Sal, for him to follow as well.

"Are you kidding me? You still don't trust me?" Matt complained as he pushed the back door open.

"I'll be standing right here. You guys do your thing. I'm not going anywhere," Sal said.

David H. started pacing and taking long drags off his cigarette. Matt stood by the door silently. He wanted to say something thoughtful to David, something that would let him know everything would be ok, but without it sounding like fluff or that it was just bullshit. The only sounds were from David H.'s footsteps as the whir of a helicopter sounded overhead. Sal instinctively ran to grab David H. and bring him back inside.

Shots rang out as the helicopter dove lower in the sky, getting closer to the tree line. The three men scattered to different places around the parking lot to take cover. The door had closed behind Sal and was now locked. Someone had to push the code for it to open. The door was being peppered with bullets, which made it off limits for the three to get back in.

CHAPTER 38
ARE YOU KIDDING ME?

Matt ran to take cover behind the large blue dumpster that was pushed near a wide branched tree. This vantage point gave him a clear view of the helicopter and both David H. and Sal, who were not as fortunate. They had run toward the parked cars and were darting in between them taking cover under the larger Suburbans, the only ones they could squeeze under. Since it was dusk, the helicopter didn't have the line of fire they were perhaps looking for. The cars were being riddled with bullets, and Matt was wondering how long it would take until one or all of them exploded. Was even possible, or did that just happen in the movies?

Suddenly, the back door was kicked open. Matt instinctively motioned to run inside, but what he saw stopped him from making a fool of himself. Franco, Liz, and Amber, all heavily armed, began to fire in rapid succession into and at the helicopter. What had been a free for all for the sleek back helicopter turned into an all-out battle for it to stay in the air. It didn't take long for the helicopter to make its way off into the dark skies, leaving an eerie silence behind.

"Is everyone ok?" shouted Franco.

Liz saw Matt was ok and raced to help Sal and David H.

out from underneath the damaged vehicles. Amber made a beeline to Matt, grabbing his arm and pulling him into a warm embrace. "I'm so glad you weren't hurt."

Matt immediately felt comfort in the embrace. It wasn't awkward or unnatural like it may have been before the kiss. In the world of cold-hearted, emotionless Henchmen, he was grateful for the human connection he felt when he was anywhere near Amber.

Franco was on the phone, anger filling his voice. "What in the actual fuck was that? Who were those assholes? You guys need to get on that ASAP! It was a fucking ambush!"

"Come quick! Sal's been hit!" Liz yelled from behind the parked cars.

Franco shouted again, "Find out who did this, and how they fucking knew they would be outside! Yes, I know that they must be listening! Now go do your job and find them!"

Matt ran to where Liz had yelled. Liz had Sal's head in her lap. He was still conscious with labored breathing. They had shot him in the right thigh. David H. had taken his shirt off and was holding it on the wound.

"Those Italian fuckers," wheezed Sal.

"It had to be them, right? I mean, who else would pull that shit?" David H. said.

Matt looked around for what he could do to help. They needed to get Sal back to the medical suite at the House. "Are all the vehicles damaged? I can run to the front. What should I do?" Matt asked, looking at Franco and Liz.

With a quick nod, Liz motioned to the front. "Hurry. Franco, did you call ahead?"

Matt didn't listen to the response and ran to look for an undamaged Suburban. Sprinting to the front desk and double checking he grabbed the correct set of keys, he jumped into the driver's side and drove it around back to load the injured Sal into the back. As Matt was opening the door for them to put Sal in, everyone's phones buzzed at the same time.

Franco was the first to react to what he read. "Are you kidding me? They tried to shoot up the DMF house? What fucking idiots. There are still some TV news crews there! It would all be filmed. Why would they do that? Jesus Christ."

"They must have only flown by to cause our security system to be alerted. They want us to know they have the place wired and can swoop in and fuck with us whenever they want to," Liz said.

"Let's get Sal to the medical suite. We can figure the rest of this shit out. I've seen some bold stunts, but this is just stupid," Amber said, helping lift Sal, laying him gently into the back of the Suburban,

Matt wasn't sure who should stay and who should go with Sal.

Franco looked around before making the call to organize the next steps. "Matt and Amber, you stay here with Pinky, Jace, and Vanessa. Liz, David, and I can handle getting Sal back to the house."

"Got it. You guys were amazing. I think you must have hit the shooter too, did you see him let go of his grip on the mount?" Matt said.

"I think you're right. We blasted those pricks. Let's go, Sal needs to see the doctor," Liz said.

———

Back inside, Pinky was on her phone speaking what sounded like Russian. Her voice was calm but stern, her hand waving in the air as she spoke. She was even-tempered until she ended the call and then stood, shaking with fury. "Those nasty little fuckers. They play so many goddamn games. They just can't be straight with me. It was Rossi's idiot Henchmen, I could confirm that. But this could be a bad thing, no one seems to know who's in charge now. From what I could gather, it's chaos in the Rossi organization."

Vanessa was in Pinky's office, also on her phone. She sat in Pinky's desk chair with her feet up on the desk, looking way too relaxed for the situation. Several times, Matt saw her throwing her head back and giggling like she had just heard a good joke. It was disturbing for Matt to see her not taking this whole thing seriously. Didn't she know Sal was injured?

Matt continued to watch her, and as she ended the call, the smile disappeared. As she left Pinky's office, Vanessa's face showed concern.

"Hey mates, we need to talk. I just got off the phone with some friends from my stay in the Rossi villa. You won't believe what I have to tell you. That old man is a bloody monster."

CHAPTER 39
THE JIG IS UP

"More of a monster than we already knew Rossi to be? How so, what did you hear?" Pinky asked.

"It's brilliant, if you are twisted in that sort of way. Matt, I'm sure you will appreciate what I am going to tell you."

"Christ, I can hardly wait. I know he is a crazy old man who holds grudges for fun," Matt said.

"Let's have it, spill the beans," Amber said.

"Ok, so we all know that his Henchmen are not the most talkative guys. Well, I thought they were just trained to be that way, but I found it odd that they never broke character so to speak. They didn't show emotions, at all, in any situation. Amber, I'm sure you know what I mean," Vanessa said.

"Oh, I sure do. I've got to say, I don't miss that part."

"I can only imagine, but I did think it was odd. They had a zombie quality about them," Matt said.

"Let me ask you a question, Matt. How much wine did they try to shove down your throat? I guess what I'm saying is, wasn't there a lot of it? Even for being in Italy?" Vanessa asked.

"It was everywhere, with every meal, and lots of it. They always brought me a bottle or two and they were opened. I figured they just wanted me to get drunk and pass out," Matt said.

Vanessa hopped up on the front desk. "Oh, they wanted you to be drunk, and also to drug you."

"He didn't! I can't believe he pulled that shit! I'm the one who gave him the idea. I never thought he'd pull that on his own men!" Pinky said.

"I've heard about that. That's just dirty to do that to your team," Amber said.

"Do fucking what? What are you talking about? And they drugged me? I know I slept a lot, but drugged?" Matt said. "I thought it was jet lag or something. I remember it getting harder and hard to concentrate and to focus. Even when I was just chilling watching something on Netflix, it was like time went by and I got lost in the plot of the show or movie I was watching, I was getting super confused at the littlest things."

"Rossi's vineyard is his pride and joy. He loves it and is so proud of it. I was there when he designed the label for his new red blend. Along with the wine, he was including a mild tranquilizer into each bottle. The bottles would have a hypnotic drug like Klonopin, which puts you in a zombie-like state. So, he trained them, gave them free wine, and encouraged them to drink lots of it. After a few weeks of that drug being in their system, he made it mandatory they all see a 'special doctor' to have their chips implanted. They were told the same thing you were, that the chips just helped you get around the house without getting zapped, which they did. But they also kept them loyal to him. They were basically programmed to always follow him and never divulge his whereabouts. That's why no one could find him for so long."

"I knew it! Those chips were more than what he said they were. Those poor dumb bastards," Matt said. "It all makes sense now, why Rossi was so fucking obsessed with the loyalty part of the HTA. All he kept saying was how important that was, and that it couldn't be taught. Well, no shit it can't be taught, but you can zap guys' brains to make them loyal."

"I feel like there is something else you aren't telling us," Pinky said to Vanessa.

"Oh, there is. The reason for the chaos in the house now isn't just because Rossi is gone. Turns out, one of the Henchmen claimed he was allergic to wine and never drank it, and somehow avoided being chipped. We were right to believe it was Leo. Well, seems Leo's no dummy and saw what was happening. Instead of being the zombie Henchman like the rest, he took matters into his own hands. Leo played along into Rossi's immature ego and even encouraged Rossi to follow through with his idiotic plan. This guy was the mastermind behind the whole thing. He brainwashed Rossi!"

"Holy shit. What a mess," Amber said.

"Let me guess, this Leo dude didn't figure out how to deactivate the chips, and the team sees him being in charge as straight up anarchy, not loyalty," Matt said.

The group nodded with thoughtful looks on their faces, still trying to piece this all together.

"Pinky, you know all about a *coup d'état*, am I right?" Vanessa asked with a smirk.

"Stop it," Pinky said, laughing, "I could write a book on the subject."

"What is this guy's end game? It sounds like he absolutely knew someone would eventually catch Rossi. He's not planning on coming to get him, is he? He's going to take over the organization," Amber said.

"He knew the Henchmen he sent here on the *rescue mission* would remain loyal to Rossi. But he also knew they had no clue how to set up a rescue operation, no clue how to navigate around the United States. None of the Henchmen who volunteered to come here even spoke English. It played right into his hand," Vanessa said.

"It was a setup. This guy's not stupid, that's for sure. So what do we do? How do we respond? Do we just mind our own business?" Matt said.

Vanessa hopped off the desk and walked to Matt, looking up at him. "Do you really think your Team is going to let one of theirs get hurt without some type of retribution? I can't see that happening, and frankly nor should it."

"I would think the CUC has already located the helicopter. They will have their hands full with Rossi and his 'loyal' Henchmen all locked up with no place to go," Amber said.

"What happens to them? Or do I even want to know?" Matt asked.

"Yeah, you probably don't want to know. It's not pretty. Let's just say that if they do walk out, they don't look the same, or walk the same. Most times, they get the shit kicked out of them, and left for dead," Pinky said.

Matt's phone buzzed in his pocket. "Hold on, let me grab this, it's Liz."

Liz relayed that Sal was in surgery and they weren't sure how severe the damage to his leg would be for some time. Matt filled Liz in on the chaos at the Rossi villa and the new villain, Leo, putting her on speaker.

"Are you shitting me? What the hell? We won't sit this one out. I'm going to have to tell Jimmie and my dad about this. I have a feeling they may want to go to war. Rossi's assets may be worth it. This is an opportunity to expand DMF to Europe. This could be huge for us. I think Leo and what's left of his shit show of a Team may be headed right for that iceberg."

CHAPTER 40
INTERVIEW DAY

"On top of everything else, I have to deal with a nosey ass reporter today. That is the last fucking thing I feel like doing," David H. said as he opened the now repaired back door of the HTA.

Matt and David H. had just returned from picking up Jace from his hotel. He absolutely refused to sleep in the combatives room with everyone else, or even at the HTA. No one thought it such a horrible idea that he skipped being at the DMF House since he wouldn't have anyone there to show him around, and he most certainly wouldn't fit in on his own. After five long days, the reporters' presence near the DMF House was dying down, however, with Susanne's upcoming interview with David H., they knew the heat would be back on as soon as it was released.

"You are going to be fine. You have done amazing in our roleplays. In fact, I have to say I have never seen anyone pick it up as quickly as you," Jace said to David H., skipping along into the HTA.

"He's not bullshitting you. I mean it. I think you got this. I know it's a pain in the ass, but it's also kind of cool that we get to share our *product* with the world," Matt said.

"If it's so cool, then why don't you take my place? You were there too, maybe she wouldn't care who she spoke to, just that it will be loads of airtime for her," David H. said.

Matt rolled his eyes, then batted his eyelashes and said, "But Davey, you are so much more photogenic than I am."

"Fuck you, College Boy. And don't ever call me that shit, it's bad enough coming from Jace," David H. said, reaching for his coffee from the Bean.

Pinky rushed up to David, grabbing his arm. "Now boys, you be nice. We just need to support each other through this today. David, sweetheart, you follow me. Amber is going to pretty you up even more."

David H., looking defeated, obediently followed Pinky into her office where Amber was waiting with a blow dryer and brushes.

"Poor guy. The way he walked looked like he was walking to have his last meal on death row," Liz said.

"He's just saving all his good energy for when he's on camera, that's all. I have created more than one masterpiece in my time. Davey is a diamond in the rough, my specialty. Please have faith," Jace said.

"We do have faith, just seeing him so uncomfortable is hard," Liz said.

———

At noon on the dot, there was a knock at the door. Benji, who had replaced Sal at the front door, waited until they gave him the thumbs up to open the door for Susanne and her crew. She entered Pinky's with much more respect than the first time she appeared at the door. "May we come in? We can wait outside if you aren't ready for us."

The DMF group looked at each other with eyebrows raised at the different approach she used this time.

Since the kiss in the hallway, Amber and Matt were physically unable to *not* stand next to each other. Oftentimes, she would grab his hand and pull him closer, which he couldn't get enough of. Matt whispered in her ear, "I would give anything to know what the hell Jace said to her. It's actually pretty impressive. She's like a different person."

Jace took over from there and invited her in. With quick introductions of the DMF group, he took the KTVW crew into Classroom A, where had they decided the interview would take place.

"Jace, what do you think about moving the interview into the front of the gym? So much better light," Susanne asked.

Jace walked with Susanne with their elbows interlocked, and said, "I see your strong and capable men have portable lights, I think those will be more than sufficient, don't you?"

As the KTVW crew completed their set up and audio and video tests, Jace motioned to have David H. brought in. Amber walked with him into the mock TV studio with her hand gently resting on his shoulder. David H.'s face looked relaxed and almost unrecognizable. His usually tightly knit eyebrows were slightly raised, and he had a slight smile on his face, instead of the almost constant DMF death stare everyone was used to seeing. He turned one last time to look at his crew for a look of moral support. All eyes were on him as he gracefully walked to meet Susanne. Since she was a petite woman, David H. was more than a foot taller than her, even with her heels on.

"I'm so glad you could make it today. It's wonderful to finally meet you," David H. said.

Matt and Liz tried not to laugh, giving each other small pokes to each other's sides. Vanessa stood in the corner whispering to Amber as David prepared to do battle with Susanne in the most gentlemanly way.

The interview began with Susanne giving a brief but detailed overview of the *Terror on the Tenth Floor*. David H. sat patiently, waiting for the first question to be asked, keeping the slight smile highlighted.

"Here we go," Jace said, tossing his head back and lifting his chin in the air with a sense of pride.

"David, after seeing that video, what do you have to say about it? Walk us through what you were thinking when you saw this horrific situation taking place," Susanne said, leaning forward.

"Susanne, before I answer that question, I would highly encourage and recommend you provide a warning for parents to not let their young children see that video. It was unfortunately violent, and it could have lasting effects on children if they saw that. That is something I feel very strongly about," David H. said, not budging an inch in his seat, which made Susanne wiggle back to her original position in her chair.

"Oh, of course we can do that. Our youth is so important to our community," Susanne said.

"I would really like to use this platform to bring awareness to violence in our community. What happened on the tenth floor was unnecessary and an absolute tragedy for the young people who had to see that. It upsets me greatly to know that those children saw what they did. It was my priority to keep the violence to a minimum, particularly for their benefit," David H. said in a voice and tone that none of the DMF group had ever heard from him before.

This tactic threw Susanne off her script of wanting to report on a story filled with drama and gory details. Her training as a reporter clicked on, not missing a beat. She tried to hide her confusion by feigning a slight cough, clearing her throat. "Well David, how admirable of you to put the mental health of the children first. I would love to hear how, and perhaps where, you learned to be so cool in a deadly situation. Because of your actions, no one else was hurt or injured. How did you learn your first-class crisis management skills?" Susanne asked.

"I'm glad you asked that. I have been working in the *security* field for a few years now. It was *not* something that I learned to do while on the job. You see, I didn't have any training. Because of my physical size, I was chosen for the job. It was dangerous for myself and my team since we had no prior training on how to solve problems without using violence. Traditionally, that was what was expected. We were reactive, and no one seemed to care. There was such a significant amount of collateral damage. But I was recently trained on how to be a better communicator, be less reactive, and use violence as a last resort."

Jace was almost mouthing the words as David H. spoke. He was nodding his head up and down as if to say, *Yes, you are still on the script.* It was becoming evident that Jace's masterpiece was to shape David H.'s interview into an infomercial for the HTA. He had coached David H. into shifting the interview away from drama and celebrating violence to talking about how others in his profession of *security* could come here and learn to become an expert in their field.

"So you're telling me that the Henchman Training Academy, the HTA, is an actual place? That people in the *security* field can come here and be trained to learn how to be more collaborative when tense situations arise while on the job?" Susanne asked.

"That's it, yes. And to be transparent, my team handles the security of my company, but we are in all actuality real life

Henchmen. Similar to the ones you see in the movies and perhaps associate with comic book characters," David H. said.

Matt wasn't aware that David was going to drop the H word, Henchmen. Did he miss something, or did no one else know either? It was obvious Susanne didn't know either. She was lost. *I really feel like this is something we should have talked about as a group. This could go poorly in either direction,* Matt thought.

It took Susanne a moment to calculate how to follow up with what David H. just laid on her. "Well, David, that is just about one of the most unique businesses I have ever heard of. Tell us, how does one, say apply to join your, uhm, Academy?"

Looking like he'd done this hundreds of times, he responded causally, "At the moment, there is a waiting list, as you can imagine. Once we open the list back up, the people who need to know how to find us will be able to."

"So mysterious. I think this about wraps things up here. Live from the HTA, a new training facility housed in a scrump-tious little gym called Pinky's, this has been Susanne Blake with KTVW, closing for now with a true Henchman to hero."

CHAPTER 41
THE AFTERMATH

"Did you know about this?" Matt asked Liz in a loud whisper.

Liz was chewing her gum with a serious look on her face, her arms crossed. "I knew, Sport. I just didn't think I would have the time to explain to you. We knew this day would come, right?"

Matt felt like he was gut punched. How could she keep something like that from him? "I thought we were a team. I trust you to give me the low down, I need that from you, Liz."

She kept from making eye contact with Matt, which only agitated him more. *If she was keeping this from me, were there more secrets?*

"Well, do you have time now to explain? I'd sure appreciate it."

Liz finally turned to look at Matt. He could read some indecision on her face. He asked, "What are you thinking about? I can tell you want to say something."

Liz walked over to the trash can and spit out her gum. "So here is the deal, Sport. Jace got the green light from Fowler and Jimmie to go ahead and blast the existence of the HTA for the world to see. They told me their thoughts and discussed it with me. They determined with the help of both Max and Jackson, there really was no way to contain this story, so why try to hide it? Jimmie was all for the altruistic aspect of the HTA and saw this as a perfect opportunity to give back to the communities organizations like DMF worked in."

Before Matt had a chance to respond, he heard the producer say, "That's a wrap, folks."

"I need a smoke," was all David H. said after they stowed the camera. He didn't say goodbye to Susanne, and his familiar scowl was back.

Jace took Susanne to the door and escorted her to the news van, waving his final goodbye.

"What, no applause this time? What did you think? Wasn't he just marvelous?"

"He was indeed. I am never surprised by the quality of work you turn out," Pinky said, giving Jace a kiss on his cheek.

"He was almost too good. This place is going to turn into a shitshow. We need to start preparing for the onslaught of curious onlookers. I wish someone would have given us a heads up," Matt said, looking at Jace. "We have some work to do for sure. We need to set up a more secure system to handle the people that are going to show up. Are we thinking we should let them join the gym?"

Franco stepped forward. "I'll tell you what we are going to do. Right now, we are getting the fuck out of here. I'm seriously not sleeping on the floor one more night. No offense, Pinky. But the news idiots will zero in on this place now, and I am not going to get trapped here. Now that David's face is out, we can go back to the House."

The back door slammed shut, and everyone spun around to see David H. "Fuck yes. I'm all for that, let's get out of here and head back home."

It was a welcome relief for everyone to get outside again.

They quickly and efficiently grabbed their personal effects and headed out. Benji was going to stay, with two additional Henchmen arriving, for door duty. Pinky's sign on the door indicating that they were not open would be left up for an indefinite amount of time. Before heading out, Amber and Vanessa checked the security cameras to ensure they were working properly, since they could be valuable to see who was sticking their noses up against the windows of the gym.

With David giving Susanne an exclusive interview, there were only a sprinkling of media people near the gates as they drove back to the DMF House. Most of the local media hadn't taken in the fact that this was a real place. They were a little slow to wrap their heads around the fact that there are real Henchmen in the world, not just in comic books, and movies.

"Those assholes must be hard up and desperate to keep their jobs if they are still here," David H. spat. As the group walked back into the familiar kitchen at the DMF House, no words were spoken, and everyone went their separate ways to their rooms.

Matt, sighing, fell into his bed only to get a text from Jimmie asking him to meet in ten. "Christ, I just wanted to sit and chill and play some games."

Standing in the doorway with a couple of Blue Moons, Liz said, "I see you got the text too. I know it's tempting to want to check out for a bit, but you have to admit we have a lot to plan. Not only with the arrival of randoms at HTA, but with the crazy fucker, Leo."

"I know, you're right. Let's at least enjoy these," Matt said, reaching his bottle to tap the neck of Liz's. "Sometimes this shit tastes so good. Let's see who can down these quickest on the way to the office. Warm beer is a big turnoff, and I don't want to leave them sitting while we talk for God knows how long."

"You're on, Sport." Liz didn't get halfway through her Blue Moon before she coughed and spit out the mouthful she had left. "You win. It went up my fucking nose."

"No burps? Is there something wrong?" Garrett asked on the way to Fowler's office.

"Garrett! Great to see you man! Are you headed to the meeting as well?" Matt asked.

"Dude, why wouldn't the in-house counsel be at a meeting like this one? Of course," Garrett said.

"That was a pretty stupid question, Sport," Liz said.

Franco, David H., Amber, and Vanessa were already huddled in Fowler's office, with chairs wheeled in from the adjacent conference-meeting room. Fowler sat behind his desk and said, "Before we get started, we ordered some food for you all. I'm sure whatever you were eating at Pinky's wasn't enough or very good."

"Thanks, Dad, what we ate wasn't too healthy," Liz said.

Jimmie slid in behind Fowler's desk, standing in his typical Jimmie-stance with his arms crossed over his chest, and said, "Congratulations to all of you. I feel like a proud papa. This is a momentous occasion for us here. You handled yourselves with grace and dignity."

"Yeah, sorry. I should have started with that. You guys were fucking awesome. That Jace is quite a character, am I right? David, your transformation was incredible," Fowler said.

"Thanks, I guess. I'll never admit it outside of this room, but it was sort of entertaining to be someone else for a moment," David H. said.

"I know that's right," Amber mumbled under her breath.

The kitchen staff arrived with trays of sandwiches, chips, and fruit. They also dropped off a case of Blue Moons, Matt was especially happy to see that. The crew went for the sand-wiches immediately, not even sitting to eat.

"I guess you were hungry! Holy shit," Garrett said, laughing.

"Let's get started while you guys inhale the sandwiches. Jim, do you want to share what you came up with?" Fowler asked.

Jimmie moved out from behind Fowler's desk, stood oppo-site the table of food, and said, "We have been given a gift. We all should be grateful for this, but I want to add that in case you weren't aware, things will change here. The good old days are long gone. Change is inevitable and sometimes gets a bad repu-tation, but in this case, it was years in the making. I hope you can see from the perspective I have that we are going to change the world."

The group stopped chewing simultaneously and looked at each other. With a mouth still full of food, Matt said, "You're serious about this then? That wasn't an act you fed to Jace? We are really going global and offering this up to all Henchmen?"

"You bet your boots we are! The rest of my businesses are global, why not this one too?" Fowler said, taking a swig from his Blue Moon.

"I think the next steps would be to put together criteria for admittance and how we are going to support the HTA staff with the new interest popping up," Jimmie said.

"I know we have only been thinking so far ahead as how we can get Henchmen to enroll, but I was also thinking, how will we know they have learned everything they need to in order to become a modern-day Henchman? They should have an assignment or task. When I was in college, we had to take a final exam, write a paper, or give a presentation to show what we learned at the end of each class. What is the Henchman version of a final?"

Garrett was the first to speak. "I actually had been thinking along the same lines, but from a legal standpoint. How are we going to show that they benefited from their time here? I don't want their organizations to say anything like their Henchmen are no different from when they left and now they're out fifteen thousand dollars."

There were quizzical looks from the group. Fowler asked, "I assume you have something in mind Garrett? Have you thought this through?"

Garrett jumped up and down with excitement. "Yes, yes, I do! I have been thinking of this really rad idea. I think it's perfect, but of course I want everyone here to be onboard. I thought about the golden ticket concept. You know what I mean?"

None of the group seemed to know what he was getting at, exactly, but Vanessa asked, "You mean like the golden ticket in the Willy Wonka movie?"

"Yes! That's it exactly. We would make it a scavenger hunt of sorts. Instead of golden tickets, it would be HTA graduation certificate tickets. I think it would be cool to make them purple tickets, you know instead of gold, to make them stand out. I feel like putting them out around the globe and making it a little game would produce excitement about hopefully the recent grads finding one of the tickets, or graduation certificates. And, most importantly, it would sift out the lazy Henchmen. Only the ones who want it badly enough will work hard enough to find the hidden tickets," Garrett said.

"That's bloody brilliant!" Vanessa said.

"Jim, do you agree? I think it kicks ass," Fowler said.

Jimmie was holding his jade mala beads, smiling. "It's a yes from me."

"Glad you all like it! It's going to be a blast finding the places to hide the purple graduation tickets!" Garrett shouted.

"We can also use Paul and Jonesy to announce the clues as to where they are. I'll have to set something up with them so we can get this rolling," Matt said.

Liz leaned up against the wall and slid down to a seat, taking a deep breath, then letting it out. "So whoever finds the ticket, they what, just bring it back to the HTA to have it verified or whatever? And that is a way to verify their passing grade?"

The room was filled with lively discussions about how to print tickets that have some invisible watermark or something on them to signify it being an authentic purple HTA graduation ticket, when Fowler said, "Listen, I know I'm not even sure what a fucking NFT is, but could we use that on the tickets so that they couldn't be forged?"

"Pops, they won't be forged. The guys who bring them in will have to have been enrolled in the HTA, so I don't think we need to worry about that happening. This will only be for the Henchmen who have completed the whole curriculum. But making an NFT for the graduation certificate sounds like a cool idea," Liz said.

"Well, let's get on this then. Garrett, thanks for the suggestion. Back to what we were discussing, how to get Henchmen here," Fowler said.

After some discussion, they agreed that since Paul and Jonesy had been spending their days on the dark web, they would be best suited to take on the job of 'advertising' the HTA to the Henchman-for-hire message boards. They were posting on them regularly and had a better sense of what was going on, and maybe how it would be received by the rest of the world. When the time was right, they would begin a thread on the Henchmen-for-hire boards and give them links to how to receive an invitation to apply.

"Are the new recruits going to have to be affiliated or unaf-

filiated? I thought we decided we only wanted to take unaffiliated Henchmen to avoid issues between opposing Henchmen
organization," Liz said.

"That's a great question. Yes, we are going to take affiliated
Henchmen from reputable organizations. We didn't want to
turn candidates away that weren't connected, so we are going to
open it up to unaffiliated Henchmen," Jimmie said.

"Are you sure about that? I've worked with unaffiliated
Henchmen, and they are the worst! They're terrible. How's
that supposed to work? There is usually a reason an organization has not picked them up. I may sound like a snob, since I
technically was an unaffiliated Henchman, but that was my
choice, not because I was a fucking idiot like most of them are."
Amber said.

"The more idiots the better I say. Less dangerous untrained
Henchmen running around causing undue pain and suffering.
That is after all the premise behind the HTA," Fowler said,
reaching for another Blue Moon.

Garrett thoughtfully reached across the desk with the
bottle opener in hand to pop the top on Fowler's beer, "I
thought this through, from the legal aspect. I don't think it will
be more paperwork for me. And my higher-ups agreed that we
go big, or not at all."

"In that case, who's paying for this?" Liz asked. "The affili-
ate's organizations, or the unaffiliated will have to pay out of
pocket?"

Garrett took a swallow from his beer, and said, "the affiliated will pay the tuition for the Henchmen they send. I
thought about how the unaffiliated will pay, and I came up with
a plan."

"Well let's hear it then. I don't want to be stiffed for these
guys," Fowler said.

"I have created a data base. These guys and all their information will be collected. When someone wants to hire them full time, then they will be required to pay an sort of finders fee. You won't necessarily make back the money right away, but as they keep getting hired out, they will end up being able to repay the tuition fee. Once we cap out at the fifteen grand, then they will not be considered to be in our debt."

"What you are saying is that we will eat for the first few years on these guys, but we will be paid up front with the affiliated. I guess I'm good with that structure, for now." Fowler said.

Matt thought about giving his two cents worth about his experience as a newbie Henchmen but chose to keep his thoughts about how irresponsible it was of DMF to have zero training to offer the new guys. "At least these guys coming in will already have experience on the job, and this will just be more refining of their skills. You know what I mean, they won't be like me, is what I'm trying to say."

The room was silent. The looks they had on their faces were as if they were remembering back to when Matt first arrived at the DMF House. Amber came to stand next to Matt, she gently put her arm around him, and looked at the rest of the people, "Oh, come on, was he really that, uhm, confused when he got here? I can't imagine it was all that unpredictable."

Jimmie shook his head with a half grin on his face. "Do you want to tell her the time you decided to go for a ride on your own, without permission, or should I?"

Matt laughed. "I didn't really get too far though did I Jimmie? You made sure of that."

Liz punched Matt in the arm. "The walk of shame through the kitchen, well that was memorable."

"Or how about the time I had to throw his ass up against the wall in the atrium, when he flat disrespected Franco?" David H. added.

"Ok, we could go on with more examples, but there were some good things too, right?" Amber asked the room.

Fowler walked over to Matt, looking him square in the eye. "If it wasn't for him, I would be dead, so yeah, there was some good stuff too."

"Here, here, a toast to Matt, Sport, Kid, College Boy, whatever name he goes by, he's tried his best to understand our world. Cheers to the not-so-new Henchman, Matt," Franco said.

Matt was humbled by the toast, putting his head down, to not show his emotions like a true Henchman. He felt part of the DMF family, as unique and non-traditional as it was, he was part of something. He knew that they would have his back, no matter what. In fact, they gave a new meaning to having your back. It was a deep-seated loyalty that trumped even sports teams' level of devotion toward one another.

"Thanks, guys. Who needs to be chipped to feel family and loyalty? Let's get the Henchmen signed up and get this party started."

"Unaffiliated, and affiliated, let's get them to be friends. Well, maybe not friends, but at least sit in the same classroom together. You kids all look wiped out. Let's call it a night." Fowler said.

Liz ran up and kissed her father on the cheek. "Thank you, from all of us. I'm so proud of us."

CHAPTER 42
SLEEP OVERS

THE ROOM FILLED with a collective sigh. Matt could tell everyone was tired and wanted to go to their own beds and sleep. Liz, Amber, and Vanessa hadn't been in their own beds for much longer than Matt and were still on European time.

The room was silent before Fowler spoke. "Listen, I know you kids are tired. How about you get me up to speed on what that Leonardo is hoping to accomplish by leaving Rossi locked up with us here?"

Liz took the lead in getting Fowler and Jimmie caught up on the intel they have been able to get. The big question for the two leaders of DMF was should they intervene with the debacle? If so, then would DMF just completely take over, or would DMF just let Rossi go on his merry way like nothing ever happened?

"Forget the coffee, Vanessa," Jimmie said, opening the door for them to leave.

No one argued with being dismissed and sent to their rooms. Matt immediately collapsed on his bed. He was absolutely done talking for the day. Video games didn't interest him either. Putting his phone on silent mode was a no-no, but he thought about it anyway. Henchmen had to be on call twenty-four-seven. After changing into his sleep clothes and brushing his teeth, his phone buzzed.

"You have got to be kidding me. Who is texting me at this time of night?" Taking a quick glance at his phone, he saw it was from Amber. His heart began to race, and he had to sit down from the rush of adrenaline that hit after seeing her name pop up on his screen. The text was simple, but effective, it read, *I just want you to know that I'm thinking about you.*

Matt flopped down on his back and let out a long sigh. He wasn't sure how to respond to her. Was it meant to be flirty, like 'come to my room,' or what? After the kiss, they hadn't found time to do much more of that, not that he didn't want to. The House was not the place to have such encounters. Since it was late, he figured a quick text back would be the best move. His response was, *Thanks for letting me know, I was thinking about you too. Have a good night.*

If Amber was to text back, it would have to wait until the morning. Matt could hardly keep his eyes open. He turned his back to his phone, but when it buzzed again, he quickly rolled over. Amber had responded with the blowing a kiss emoji, *What a great way to start the day. But hang on, screw the emoji. I want a real kiss.*

Matt threw some clothes on and set off to Amber's room. He was hoping he didn't run into anyone else this early in the morning. He knew he would feel obligated to explain where he was going. When he was in the girls' hallway, only steps from Amber's door, he could feel his confidence growing, replaying what he would do when she opened the door. He was just going to grab her and kiss her like he had nothing else in the world to do, focus only on her. He was so lost in thought, he walked smack into the back of Garrett, who was trying to be stealth leaving Vanessa's room. Garrett spun around to see who collided with him. Neither of the men expected to see the other at that time of night in that hallway. With an awkward nod, Matt said, "Sorry dude, didn't see you there."

Garrett finished buttoning his shirt and ran his fingers through his hair. "No worries, bro. I was just, you know, on my way back to my room."

Amber and Vanessa opened their doors at the same time. "Gar, you forgot your jacket . . . Matt?"

Amber turned to look at Vanessa, then at Garrett. "Garrett? That's your blast from the past who you've been spending all this time with?"

All four sets of eyes darted back and forth, met with confusion and laughter.

"See, I told you it would be awkward getting caught. Should have just told them in the first place," Garrett said.

"How long does this story go back? I want to hear all about it," Amber said.

Garrett and Vanessa looked at each other, and did a quick two out of three rock, paper, scissors, to see who told the story. "Garrett, mate, you're up," Vanessa said.

He ran his long fingers through his messy bed head hair before he spoke, "I don't know how far I'll go back on this, except to say that Pinky thought we would hit it off some years ago. I was in Italy for work when she played matchmaker. That was at least what, five, six years ago now, right Ness?"

Vanessa put her arms around Garrett's waist and hugged him tightly, "But this is the first time we've ever really stayed in the same place. We are making up for lost time."

"We understand that, don't we Matt?" as Amber pulled Matt into her room, but it didn't go as Matt had planned. She made the first move this time. She was still in her pajamas, looking like the commotion had awakened her in the hall. Matt had never seen her in anything but relaxed clothes, and not make-up. She looked more beautiful to him than he could remember. He was about to speak when she held her finger to her mouth to quiet him. Their eyes locked. She got closer, and he felt his knees go weak, and his stomach did the familiar flip-flop. But this time, it was an actual flip flop onto the bed.

Amber expertly had him in a hold and flipped him onto her bed, where she graciously followed him, and whispered, "I've been waiting for you."

They set the follow up meeting for after lunch, which was perfect for Matt and Amber. Getting alone time was not always an option, but they took full advantage of being lost in her room the rest of the night and morning, shutting out the rest of the world.

A knock on the door snapped them back into reality. They both giggled before Amber went to answer. It was Liz, and to Matt's good fortune, she stood in the doorway with a smile on her face. "It's about fucking time. I'll have to check and see who won the bet."

Matt got up and put his shirt back on over his messy bed head. "What bet?"

"Honey don't you know? The Team had bets when you would get up the courage to come knock on my door."

"Oh shit. Well, this was a foregone conclusion then? I hope I made someone some extra cash then."

Liz plopped on the bed like it was her own. "Yes, you did, but I don't think anyone had bets that Garrett and Vanessa would connect as quickly as they did, and before you two. I think that's a good match."

Amber came out of the bathroom dressed and ready for the day. "I do too. They are so cute together. Matt actually bumped into him leaving her room this morning. And just so you know, this isn't as new as you think. Pinky set them up years ago."

"Oh, now that makes sense. Love it," Liz said.

"I feel like a dumbshit. I had no idea about those two," Matt said.

The two women laughed. "No comment from me," Liz said.

"Nice. Well, I'll leave you two to gossip some more. I'm going to head down to grab coffee and some breakfast. You guys want anything?"

Amber and Liz both shook their heads. "We're good, honey, thank you," Amber said. Matt's cheeks flushed when she referred to him as Honey. *I liked the way that sounded*, he thought. After a quick trip to the kitchen to grab a coffee and bagel, he went straight to his room and logged onto his computer. Playing games gave him a sense of normal and helped to relax him, something he hadn't been able to do in quite some time. After the way his day started, he needed to not think about anything else. Paul and Jonesy were also online. It felt like old times, Matt was finally in his element, until his door burst open. Matt sighed, removing his headset and standing up from his desk. It was David H.

"David, what's up? You ever heard of knocking, bro?"

"I knocked for fucking ever. You probably couldn't hear me with that nerdy ass headset on," David H. grunted.

Matt scratched his head sheepishly. His headset was sound blocking, so he probably hadn't heard. "Is everything ok? I don't think you've ever been in my room before."

"Dude, no, I haven't been in here, at least not to see you. Only time I've been in here was when this was Franco's old room. He was in here when he first arrived," David H. said.

"Now there's some DMF House history. Did you want to sit down?" Matt asked.

Matt still wasn't sure what David H. wanted, but he knew it was something that was difficult for him to talk about. Matt took a seat back in his gaming chair. David H. sat on the edge of the bed looking uncomfortable, not like the version of David H. who was a smooth talker while being interviewed by Susanne. He looked more like an oversized child sitting on his parents' bed, needing to have an awkward conversation about life. He was not making eye contact and was picking at imaginary specs of lint on the bedspread. This was not the same foul-mouthed Henchman Matt had come to know.

"Dude, you are freaking me out here. What the fuck's going on? Are you dying or something?" Matt asked.

"No, I'm not dying, I'm already dead."

Matt spun in his gaming chair to close the door and said, "That's rather cryptic. Maybe you can clarify?"

"It's like I disappeared. I don't know where I went. I used to wake up and know what my day was going to be like. I knew how to do this job, I knew how to handle life, my life. I knew myself. Now, it's all fucked up. It's confusing me. I don't like waking up now, man. The Team is looking at me funny, no one is just shooting the shit with me like they used to. They are fucking with me and asking for my autograph. I feel like I'm a fucking outsider. It hit me, this is exactly how you must feel, or must have felt when you first got here."

Matt sat back in his chair and crossed his arms. He was hesitant to say too much and thought maybe just listening was the best response for the situation. He had never heard David H. show any introspection and wanted to make sure that he had the space to continue if he wanted to.

"Well, College Boy? I'm asking you, what should I do? How do I make things go back to the way they used to be, to a world that I knew all the rules for? I don't know how I fit in here anymore. I know how to be really good number two, I got that. But now, I need a fucking PR person to help run my life? And me, me being the spokesman for the HTA? I didn't get a choice in that. The shit with the DMV, I keep going over it in my mind. I should have had someone else get the plates renewed, I should have done a lot of things differently. If I would have, then I wouldn't be where I am now," he said, falling onto his back on Matt's bed.

"Jesus. I hear you, man. I didn't think about it like that, but yeah, when your life gets ripped out from under you, it fucking sucks. It's a lot to take. I feel you," Matt said.

"Really? It sucks? That's your advice?" David H. asked.

"Well, it does. But it also gets better. You have support and friends here. If I have learned anything while being here, it's that going with the flow is best. It is what it is, everything happens for a reason kind of thing. Yes, it's new and not what you were used to. But that can be ok. Life is all about learning things. And it sucks that it seems you don't have a choice in the new version of you. But I have to say, you were *really* good with Susanne. You're a natural, and if this had never happened, how would you have known that you had the skills to be on live television, and never show any signs of being intimidated? Look, what I am saying is that it just takes time. Don't fight it, because the balls are already rolling," Matt said.

"Ok, *Jimmie*. What the fuck was that bullshit?" David H. sighed. "But yeah. I get it, sort of. I'll keep at it, and if you tell anyone I was here, I will break your fucking nose, you got me?"

Matt laughed and clapped David H. on the shoulder. "There's the David H. I know! See, he's still in there."

CHAPTER 43
SHOULD WE STAY OR SHOULD WE GO?

THE MEETING about the Italy mess was moved to the conference room. They resumed where they left off the night before. Jimmie started off by saying that he had received an update from the CUC on the status of the Rossi clan still in their custody. "There are no changes to report. There have been no attempts to reclaim the Rossi clan. It's been radio silence. Rossi is still babbling about his mistakes and wanting to go back home. Since we discovered the intel about the use of the chips, we had them removed from the Italian Henchmen we captured from their failed rescue mission. Apparently, he is so completely annoying that they needed to be separated from him. The CUC have arranged to isolate Rossi for his own safety."

"Why am I not surprised? He was acting like an entitled child when the whole DMV thing went down," David H. said. "It's no wonder he had to drug and chip people to be loyal to him, or even care if he lives or dies."

"It amazes me he's gotten as far as he has with his business holdings. He must have a hell of a structure in place to keep things moving," Fowler said.

"So now what? Do we leave them and see if anyone ever

claims him? It doesn't seem like anyone gives a shit about him. Why would Leo bring him back at this point? Loyalty is in the toilet now," Liz said.

"I think we can all agree Rossi really has no allies. But we need to weigh out our options. What will benefit us in the long run? Do we let him go back to business as usual, knowing that it will eventually collapse with the Henchman all de-chipped, or do we keep Rossi and do our due diligence with Leo and remove him from his inherited seat at the top of the organization?" Jimmie asked.

Franco stood to pace the room, and said, "So, you propose that we possibly remove Leo, and what, have DMF swallow up Rossi's assets? Honestly, we have a lot on our plates with the HTA opening up to the world. Do we really have the manpower to set up shop in Italy? To even plan that sort of thing seems like a huge undertaking."

"Honestly, I want to take him all the way down. I don't want to watch it happen. I want to make it happen and take it all. Fuck old man Rossi. He's out of control, and that is exactly what we don't want. I say we take it all," Fowler said. "I have faith that the Team you put together will put this whole thing together. It's apparent that there is no urgency on Leo's end."

Jimmie was pacing the room with his head down. The pacing usually indicated that he was processing next moves. Matt was curious to see what Jimmie's thoughts would be on what angle to take.

Jimmie spun and turned with what looked like an aha moment. "Let me be sure I have this correct. Leo has only been able to keep some of his Henchmen onboard, right? His Team is not working at full strength. But he also doesn't seem to think this is a problem? I say he's ripe for the picking."

"Let's let him hang himself. The fucker doesn't know what

he's got. He's going to think we are letting this go. The word 'ambush' comes to mind," Liz said.

"I like the sound of that. The more we watch the more we can observe what his next moves are. That is just more information for us to find his weaknesses and see where we can most effectively infiltrate," Jimmie said.

"If you need me to go back, I would be willing to do that," Vanessa said. "I know people there. I even met Leo a few times. I could slide right in where I left off. It will take a minute for me to convince everyone why I came back and left DMF, but I know I could do it. This is kind of my thing; I love to be the fly on the wall as you say. I am brilliant at being there, but not, if you know what I mean."

"That could be a little tricky. Are you sure? Maybe we could have some of Pinky's European connections come to the villa so you would have some support. I've had to go back to places I left, and it can take some time for them to accept you back in," Amber said.

"See, this is why I have faith in you guys. We just worked out some significant shit here in a matter of minutes. Vanessa, you have our full support with whatever you need. I haven't paid Pinky a visit in some time. I will take care of asking her about lending us some of her Team," Fowler said.

"Pinky will love a visit from you, Pops," Liz said, with the others laughing.

Fowler actually blushed and got up to leave the meeting. "Good work today. Thank you, and I am glad you young ones with all this creative energy are on my Team, and not against me. That asshole Leo won't know what hit him."

CHAPTER 44
NFTS

Matt put an inquiry to the CM Team to see who, if anyone, could create the purple graduation ticket NFT that would be used as a certificate of completion of the HTA. Apparently, it's easier to create one than it is to understand what they really are. The first response Matt received was from Paul and Jonesy. They both had already made a couple NFTs that they sold successfully for a ridiculous amount of money. They were flattered to be part of this new global sensation and were excited to get started on the project. Things with Four had calmed down now since the whole Rossi thing had blown over. The small Team of three had been moved to learning more about social media since the DMV incident. This extra free time gave Four some of his freedom back, which in turn helped his usually sour mood. Even so, he still found things to whine and complain about.

Matt was pouring his second mug of coffee when David H. slapped his arm around him, causing him to spill part of his perfectly concocted mix of coffee and creamer. "Dude, watch out. I had the perfect mix going on there."

David H. gave him a *I really don't give a fuck* look and said, "You are pulling me into the same room as that asshole Four this early in the morning. You kind of deserve to spill a little. You're lucky I don't dump it on your head. That guy still bugs the shit out of me."

"Can't argue there. It will be quick, and we are there to talk to Jonesy and Paul."

David H. threw open the door to the workroom, which startled Four, Jonesy, and Paul. The three spun around in their chairs. "Good morning, people. Four, before you start your shit, we aren't here to talk to you. We are here to talk to the other two."

"Why do these guys get to work on the purple ticket? You know I could produce one of those in my sleep. I don't get it, oh wait, I remember now. I'm trapped in a place that finds no value in my intellect! The disrespect continues!" shouted Four across the workroom.

"Did you bother to read the email that asked for people's help? I suppose if you would have, you may have been picked," Jonesy said with a cool tone.

Four sniveled and wiped his nose with the back of his hand. "Whatever. It's probably because you're friends with the Precious Prince. That's all. Anyway, it doesn't matter. I can still out-code any of you, with my eyes closed!"

"You don't need to be pissed off at them, Four. Get off their asses," Matt said, walking closer to Four than made either one of them comfortable.

Four tried to take a step back, but Matt followed. "Ok, I'll say it again. Back off, man! You're crowding me, and I don't like it. Take your little friends and go make your stupid NFTs."

"Fuck off you little freak," David H. spat. "God, it feels so good to swear and intimidate. I've missed it."

Four straightened, trying as best as he could to puff out his chest. All one hundred and fifteen pounds of him didn't look very intimidating, but he was trying to match the same

Henchman stance that men over two or three times his size took when they wanted to look like a badass. He drew his right arm back, as if it were on a spring ready to punch, with his head turned slightly to the left. "You can't talk to me like that! I demand to have some respect here!"

David H. and Matt looked at each other and laughed, a deep belly laugh, the kind where you have to hold yourself to keep it under control. David H. was the first to speak. "Respect. Yeah, ok. And if I refuse that, what are you going to do?"

"No, he'll probably hire some Henchmen to do it for him. Oh wait, he can't do that anymore!" Matt snorted.

Four stood down, crossing his arms, "Very funny. I really do hate you all. I'm going to tell Jimmie how you are treating me. This isn't what you learn in your stupid classes with him I bet."

Matt grabbed Jonesy and Paul's shoulders and directed them to the doorway. "Feeling's mutual Four."

Matt and David H. brought Paul and Jonesy to the kitchen to give and to get details on what they wanted, and how long it may take to get the NFT created.

"It really doesn't take long, but we should be able to get it to you in a week or so. And you said you want them on a USB stick, right? I've read that it is the safest place for anyone to store them," Paul said.

"Yeah, that's what we were thinking since we have to hide them in just a couple places. Some will be located in a DMF European holding, and some here in the US," Matt said.

"Creating a QR code won't take long either. Wherever you place them, here or in Europe, it can really just be a piece of paper, you know, printed out. It sounds like you will need them to be encrypted as well. We can do that. Whoever finds the specific DMF location, they will scan the QR code, which will open a link to the purple NFT, or as we call the HTA graduation certificate ticket. That way, if for some reason it falls into the wrong hands, we will have a way to track them." Paul said.

"You guys have thought of everything, that's really helpful," David H. said. "So, did you make any mockups of what you think it will look like? I'm just curious."

Paul and Jonesy smiled at each other and pulled out their phones. They scrolled through their apps until they both giggled, and Paul said, "You go first, you show them yours first."

"Ok, if you're sure! Here you go, what do you think?" Jonesy said.

David H. took the phone from him and leaned back, sharing the screen with Matt. The purple ticket was a motion design. There were several little purple men running around the edges of the rectangular certificate. They each had a miniature purple ticket in their hands, waving them as they ran. The middle had a golden star that flashed when it opened, with the text, *Congratulations from the HTA.*

"What the fuck, that's awesome! It's like three dimensional, I think this is perfect. But did you say you have another one too?" Matt asked.

Paul and Jonesy giggled again before Paul pulled up his version and handed his phone to David H. for review. This NFT was more like what a traditional certificate would look like, however, the lettering caught Matt's eye, literally. It was as if the digital art knew what you were looking at, and as you read the words, each letter would rise above, giving you the impression it was floating, along with fireworks as your eyes moved to the words, *Congratulations from the HTA.*

"Can we choose more than one? These are both fucking impressive," David H. said, handing the phone back to Paul.

"We had fun making them. Thank you for the compliments. I can send the files to you, and you can show them to the

Team and let them decide. Either one you pick will make us happy," Jonesy said.

"I don't think we need to change much on either of them. Such a strange thing to put value in, but I guess if people have the money, they will spend it," Matt said.

"Now we just have to figure out where we are going to scatter across the globe, and where, for that matter," David H. said.

"Are we going to be the ones monitoring the message boards and communicating with the Henchmen searching? I think we are pretty fluent in the way everyone speaks and don't mind shifting our time to that project. Since we will be the ones who embed the code and will have to set up steps to verify the stick as authentic," Paul said.

"That is a perfect fit for you. I will pass the information along to Fowler and Jimmie for the final decision. These are great, I'll keep you in the loop as to the timeline we need these," Matt said.

"I don't think I've ever heard of a scavenger hunt across the globe to find the QR code that leads them to the NFT. I think this will be the first of its kind. Fits with the theme of the HTA being the first of its kind," Jonesy said.

Matt and David H. got up to leave and saw Four coming into the kitchen, trying to be incognito. It was obvious he was trying to eavesdrop on their conversation.

"What the fuck are you doing? You weird little shit," David H. said across the kitchen.

Four just ignored the comment, looking frustrated that they saw him, and grabbed some snack bars and a coffee.

"He didn't say anything? That's out of character for him. Wonder what that's all about," Matt said.

"Who cares? No one does. He's an awful human being.

Let's go pick some sweet places to hide these bad boys. Four isn't a threat to us anymore, thank Christ," David H. said.

Matt wondered if that really was the case. Was Four innocently grabbing snacks while they were meeting about a very important DMF initiative? Maybe they need a decoy. Matt had a strange sensation at the same time. He couldn't believe it, but he thought for a moment that he felt a pang of compassion for him. *Shit, where did that come from? I mean, it must suck to be him. Maybe he's got some personality disorder that he can't control.*

CHAPTER 45
HIDE AND SEEK

During the Wednesday planning committee meeting, it was agreed upon that the HTA would initially open up to eighteen affiliated Henchmen and to twelve unaffiliated. The planning team changed from the original idea of having more unaffiliated for the first class. The change in plan came after Fowler voiced concern over costs. By offering it up to affiliated Henchmen, who had to pay their tuition first, they would be able to be profitable. The unaffiliated would have their fees and tuition paid for after they graduated. This way, they would get a huge payout at the beginning. Garrett was working on the legal forms needed as well as the application. Once those were in place, they would be available to forward to reputable, well-vetted organizations that wanted to have their Henchmen Team trained to be effective in the twenty-first century Henchman etiquette. A select DMF Team that comprised the Top Five, Liz, Jimmie, and Garrett would review applications. All the applicants could follow threads on the Henchmen for Hire messages boards to get clues as to how to apply to be an HTA applicant.

For the graduation certificates, the majority of the QR codes would not be randomly placed under a rock in a park in some obscure country. They were going to be given to very trustworthy people from DMF business holdings. The first rough draft of the plan was deemed too confusing. The original plan would have included current Henchmen from Pinky's European Team, or retired DMF Henchmen, across twelve cities picked for the distribution were mostly in Europe and the United States.

Jimmie finished reading the now pared down, less complicated plan. "I like this better. This will be less to keep track of. Two places for them to go, not twelve. Much improved."

Fowler, staring at Liz with a look of concern, said, "This sounds so easy, but this is going to take a fuck-ton of planning. How in the hell are we going to keep track of sending out clues and all that shit?"

"That's my thing, Pops. You know I like to be organized. You know, consider me an Excel expert. It's been amazing. I'm going to make a spreadsheet for each city and clues needed for them to get to the ultimate end point," Liz said.

"Amber, Pinky and Franco will work on getting the list together of possible middlemen, the guys holding the NFTs. I can't imagine anyone not wanting to do this. If I could, I would be one of them. It's got just enough intrigue that I think I would find it rather invigorating," Jimmie said.

Fowler laughed. "You want back in the action? I love hearing that, old man."

"Hey now, watch who you are calling an old man. We did go to school together, in the same grade," Jimmie shot back.

"We could use you in this project if you want to know the truth. How about you head up the European hunt? You don't have to sit and be the middleman, but you could be there to monitor and make sure things run smoothly," Matt said.

"Let me think about that and get back to you. It keeps

sounding more and more like something I would like to be part of," Jimmie said.

———

Matt and David H. were selected to be Jace's personal chauffeurs. Moving forward, each morning they would roll out of bed to go pick him up and bring him back to the DMF House. Jace was an early riser and liked to get his day started almost as soon as he got out of bed. It was such an early wake up, Matt and David H. didn't even grab a coffee before heading out. Neither of them were morning people, which worked well since neither felt the need for smalltalk on the drive to the hotel. Without fail, Jace was standing at the pickup point waving like a madman despite no one else being up at that ungodly hour.

"Jesus, look at him. How could we miss him? There is no one else out here," David H. groaned. "He's a nice guy, but the spunky energy this early almost hurts."

Matt got out to open the door for Jace, who was wearing an exceptionally bright lime green well-tailored suit. Not a suit like Matt and the Henchmen wore. This one was all about style rather than comfort. There would be no way a Henchman could work in a suit like that. Matt wondered how he could even bend his knees with as fitted as the trousers were. Plus, the fact that Jace always had high heels that went with each outfit. Matt didn't even know they made four-inch, or even six-inch pumps in men's sizes. Today, Jace had a more muted shade of ivory to go with the lime suit.

Jace stopped waving to bend and pick up his black patent leather briefcase. "Good morning boys! How are we this bright and beautiful day!"

David H. didn't answer. His hair was still messy from last night's slumber, and Matt gave a short grunt in return.

"Oh, come on boys, why the sour faces? Do you love my new suit? Is it too much? The boa was dyed to match the suit, a couple shades lighter. I am so in love with the whole look! You boys wear such dark suits, hazard of the job I imagine."

Matt turned to look at Jace in the backseat and sighed. "Jace, dude, can you tone it down just a bit? We haven't had any coffee yet."

Jace put a pout on his face. "Of course I can, but I probably won't." He laughed. "Don't hate me for it. I find that being authentic suits me best. When I used to try to conform and be and look like everyone else, I was filled with anxiety. It wasn't a good look for me. Now that I am my true authentic self and literally don't give a fuck, excuse my language, about what anyone thinks, I feel so free."

"You be you, bro, just respect us being us," David H. said.

"Point taken. What's on the agenda for today?"

Matt and David H. glanced at each other to see who would answer. They did a quick two out of three rock, paper, scissors to see who it would be. Matt ended up losing the first two games, David H. tipping his head towards the backseat.

"We're meeting with Paul and Jonesy to decide which design of the new NFT ticket we are going to use."

"Did you say design? May I attend the meeting too? That seems right up my alley," Jace said, smiling with his hands framing his face.

"That would be fine. Once we get back to the House, meet us in the conference room next to Fowler's office," Matt said.

Only a few sets of eyebrows were raised when Jace waltzed into the conference room.

Amber was sitting next to Matt when she whispered to him, "Well, that was generous of you to invite him."

Matt wasn't sure if he ever should have told her that he liked when she whispered softly into his ear. It helped remind him they were a team all of their own. It also made him want to grab her and take her into another room, shut the door, and let whatever happened happen.

Amber gently placed her hand of Matt's shoulder. "Jace, what a lovely surprise to see you here. I have to say, the suit, wow. Amazing."

The look on his face said it all. He was beaming. "Why, thank you. You know the color would be fabulous for your skin tone."

During the meeting, it was decided that they would use both the NFT designs they came up with, which was the politically correct thing to do. Paul and Jonesy were delighted both of their designs were met with approval from the executive committee. The next task at hand was for them to work on the clues to be divvied out as the hunt began. It was determined that this part of the project was going to take longer to pull together than creating the NFTs. Research on the various cities with well-qualified DMF employees and how to write clues up that would be informative, but not in a totally obvious way. Once everything was lined up, they would send a couple of the DMF Team to do a dry run to each city. They would use these dry runs to figure out any errors or gaps that may turn up. This was not anything that was to be rushed due to the fact that the locals have been clamoring to get more of the Henchman to hero, David H.

"Pinky's has turned into a circus. There's a steady stream of curious onlookers wanting to know more about how David H. had been trained so well in such a dangerous profession," Franco added.

"What are we going to do about that? Keep the extra security in place?" David H. asked.

Franco nodded. "Indefinitely. But we are most likely going to have to create some type of waitlist. We are being pummeled by walk-ins, emails, and phone calls about memberships."

Jace waved his hand in the air, "Can I just give a little update too?" No one protested, so he continued, "Just a little behind the scenes work going on. I'm maneuvering more interviews for David H. I've even been able to get David H. an invite to one of the local high schools to speak to the graduating seniors about choosing Henchman as a possible career path."

Confused looks appeared across the faces of the Team. Franco was the first to speak. "Wait a minute. Are you telling me you are encouraging kids to pick this as a profession? Is that wise?"

"Well of course it is! He's a hero now. Don't we want to encourage the youth that are on sitting on the fridge of society to have productive and fulfilling lives?" Jace answered.

"Who in the actual fuck ever thought we would be saying the word Henchman out loud to the general public? I feel like I landed on another planet. This is way out of my comfort zone. Not too long ago, we almost took Matt's head off the night he showed up at our door. We kept our privacy as number one priority. Now we are blasting our business everywhere. I'm still trying to wrap my head around how this is ok," David H. said.

"This is the only way to go. Once that video went viral, there was nothing to do but show the world what you got! It was going to happen at some point. It's the way the world works now. Being incognito just isn't a thing anymore," Jace said, blowing on his hot tea.

"But talking to a school? I hated school. How do I go in there and not fuck this up? I'm more nervous about this than I was with that reporter chick. It's like I'm having flashbacks to high school, and let me tell you, that's no place I ever want to go back to," David H. said.

"David, if he could whip you into shape with Susanne, you know he will get you prepared for this. They won't be asking so many stupid questions either, which will help," Matt said.

"Fuck. Ok, but is anyone other than Jace coming with me? I could use a friendly face in the crowd," David H. said.

Amber smiled and placed her hand over David H.'s and said, "Matt and I will be there. Isn't that right, Matt?"

He was caught off guard by the invitation but eagerly nodded. "Of course, David, we will be there."

———

Matt often thought about what his life could look like past the DMF House, especially since he and Amber were now officially in a relationship, at least that is what he would call it. Would they be able to last on the outside, in the real world? Have more normal job, a nice little condo to call home. *You don't want to jump too far ahead of yourself, maybe start with asking her out on a date.* The last date didn't go so well—she kidnapped him, for Christ's sake. He wasn't sure if it was even ok for them to go out together in public. Matt knew he needed to ask Liz for some guidance on this one. He really didn't want to wait to set it up, so he picked up his phone and texted Liz; *I want to take Amber out on another date, is that cool?*

Liz's response was a thumbs up emoji, followed by, *We knew you would ask sooner than later, so I already got an answer for you from Jimmie and Fowler.*

Matt smiled before sending back, a smiley face emoji. *Thanks for letting me know earlier!*

With permission officially granted to ask her to dinner, he marched down the long DMF House hallways to reach her room. He was reflecting on the planning and security that took place the last time he tried this with her. *What a fucking relief that's over with*, he thought.

He knocked on her door, and quickly stuck his hands in his pockets, his comfort zone stance.

Amber's hair was messy, hanging loosely around her beautiful round face, her green eyes sparkling the light off the hallway. "Hey, Matt!" She reached up and gave him a kiss on his cheek. "What's up?"

Matt rocked back on forth on his heels, and said, "Hey, yeah, well I was just thinking that since we, are, well, together now, I probably ought to take you on a real date. Would you please have dinner with me sometime next week?"

Her response didn't need words, she planted a long deep kiss on his mouth. The kiss went on for what Matt felt like forever, only to be interrupted by Vanessa, who was walking to her room. "Get a bloody room you two."

CHAPTER 46
STRUCTURED CHAOS

Days after the Susanne and David interview, Pinky had opened the door to her gym once again. They had taken the time to prepare for the increased interest in locals getting a membership. There was such a wide variety of people stopping in that there were at minimum six Henchmen dedicated to being in the gym at all times. Two needed to remain on door duty, two worked the front desk and fielded questions, and two gave tours of the facility, making sure no one headed down the hall to the HTA. The hallway to the HTA was roped off and the lights in the classrooms were usually kept off. Matt wasn't feeling as safe and secure in Pinky's now. It used to be a casual space where he knew most of the people there. It was getting overcrowded, and it just didn't seem like things would be manageable if shit went down. He made a quick note in his phone to bring this up in the next meeting, he simply wrote, *It's too full, cut out membership to outsiders.*

"What the matter, Sport? You look more fidgety than usual," Liz said.

Matt's eyes were scanning the crowd, he was on edge. "This isn't cool. There are too many strangers in here."

Matt and Liz spent most days working out of Pinky's office,

which gave him firsthand experience of who was showing up and asking to be members. "This gym isn't big enough to hold the crowds that are signing up. Do we put a cap on the number of people? Have you seen the line outside to get in? It's being treated like we are some sort of freakshow. I don't like it." Matt said. "It makes me nervous, brings back not so nice memories for me."

"I don't think ninety percent of these people will be here in a month. They are just paying to be nosey. Most of them come and sit in the lounge area, very few actually work out. I've heard them talking about David and wanting to see if there are any other hot Henchmen hanging out," Pinky said.

Matt laughed. "Hot Henchmen? Wow, I'll have to make sure and let David know about that. I won't tell him that until he is done with the school visit later today."

"I haven't seen too many guys signing up, it seems like it's mostly chicks," Liz said. "I wonder if they are interested in seeing the hot Henchmen, or if they are wondering if there is a place for them at the HTA?"

"Let's just get this under control, finish the scavenger hunt. If there are women who are interested, then we can take them. I mean who's to say they can't keep up. I think since we are opening it up to current Henchmen, and some newbies like I was. You know what I mean?" Matt asked.

"I guess so. I think we will have to put together a protocol, so the guys won't mess with the girls. Speaking from experience, that needs to be addressed at the orientation," Liz said. "For now, let's just get the people out of the lounge area. They don't need to be sitting here all day."

"That's a good point Liz. We need to get things off to the right start. You've always done a good job with keeping boundaries with them," Pinky said.

Matt stood and grabbed a set of keys. "It's time to head over to David's school visit. You're coming, right?"

"Duh. I wouldn't miss this for anything. This is going to change everything, and I want to be there to see it."

Benji came into the office looking agitated, sweat was forming on his forehead. "I just wanted to ask, do you guys know these guys?" He pointed at two Henchman size guys working out in the free weights section.

"The dude over there in the black sweats and white shirt and his pal? The big guy?" Liz asked. "No, I haven't seen him here before, why do you ask?"

"I don't know if it's anything to worry about, but I'm pretty sure I heard them speaking Italian. It's probably nothing, but it just gave me a weird feeling, so I thought I better say something. That mindfulness class taught me something," Benji said with a slight smile. "I'm heading back to my post at the plant."

"You definitely did the right thing. That's suspicious to me. Let me go out there and see what I can figure out. Bet they don't know that I speak a little Italian myself," Pinky said.

Matt mustered up the best DMF Death Stare as he could manage, while he stared intently at the Henchmen in question. He was trying to remember if he'd seen them at the villa. He was so bad at facial recognition, it was almost pointless for him to try and place them. *See, this is why I don't want everyone bopping in and out like this, these guys are just the ones I don't want in here.*

"You ok, Sport? You have a look on your face like you need to use the bathroom real bad," Liz said.

Matt didn't answer, he was lost in holding the death stare until Pinky returned from speaking to them.

"It's fine. Pinky's got this. You can relax," Liz said patting him on the back.

Matt looked at her. "Aren't you a little suspicious of them?"

"I've been suspicious of people since I was a kid, so no, not particularly," Liz snorted.

Matt and Liz watched as Pinky nonchalantly walked the floor of her gym. She briefly stopped and talked to some of the new members, smiling and chatting it up with them. They watched as she paused near the free weights, she smiled at the two Italian Henchmen, putting on her best *dumb blonde* routine. Her body language was flirty, lightly touching the Henchmen's arms, covering her mouth when she was laughing, and clearly pretending she didn't speak a word of Italian, as she was using hand motions to point things out. She waved a quick goodbye to them and waltzed over to the treadmills lingering just enough to hear what the parting comments were.

"I love watching her work. She needs to teach something at the HTA. Maybe she and David M. can work together on the bullshitting course. Between the two of them, who knows what they could do to unsuspecting stupid people? They are both skilled Honeypots," Matt said.

Pinky skipped her way back into the office, turning and giving one last wave to the Italians who were watching her every move since her conversation with them. "Well, they are definitely with Rossi. They must have sent in a new crew to try and find him. They must be the few who escaped getting their chips removed. They are still fiercely loyal to him."

"How do you know that? What did they say?" Matt asked.

"When I first walked up, they said, 'That's her, she's the one. She is the one *Signore* told us about. She is the one who can help us find him. She is loyal to *Signore*.'"

"That's fucking creepy. We need to put a watch on you. I don't know that you are safe here, Pinky," Liz said.

"Liz is right. You can't be alone right now," Matt said.

"You two, such sweethearts. I think I will be fine. They aren't the brightest bulbs on the tree if you know what I mean.

When I was walking away, they said basically that I was a dim-witted little woman and that they would have no trouble convincing me to help them. They have no idea what I'm capable of. They thought I was a *scherzo*. That pissed me off," Pinky said.

"*Scherzo*? Pinky, we don't speak Italian, what does that mean?" Matt asked.

"It means they think I'm a joke. If it would make you happy, I will let you watch out for me. But please know that I am not a *scherzo*. I will get rid of them in my own way, after I find out if Leo has anything to do with sending them here," Pinky said.

Matt knew he would never want to fuck with Pinky. He would love to know more about her, the real story about her past. Of all the people he'd met since being with DMF, she was one of the biggest badasses in the whole organization.

CHAPTER 47
CAREER DAY

Jace had picked out a light blue business casual shirt and black slacks for David H. to wear to the visit to the local high school, claiming he wanted *Davey* to present as approachable and not scary. A suit and tie may come off as a little too threatening to a bunch of high school seniors. Jace, staying true to his authentic self, showed up in a gold jumpsuit, gold platform shoes, and a white boa. Matt thought he looked more like an Olympic figure skater than a director of his own PR firm.

Amber was already backstage with David H. and Jace when Matt and Liz arrived. She was wearing a form-fitting sage green dress. It was professional looking, not one she would wear on a date, but Matt couldn't take his eyes off the way it fit all her curves in just the right places.

"You made it! I was beginning to wonder, he is just about to start," Amber said, kissing Matt on the cheek. He still flushed at her touch.

"Sorry, we had some foreign visitors right before we left. Pinky took care of it. You look amazing by the way."

Amber held Matt's hand. "Foreign visitors? Anything I need to be updated on? This is so exciting. I was thinking back to my life a year ago. I would never have imagined being part of something like this, or meeting someone like you."

Matt smiled. "No, we have everything covered concerning them. But I can say the same thing."

As David H. was introduced, Matt reminisced about his start at DMF and entering the career of Henchman. He remembered one of his first pillow talks with Jimmie where they discussed the history of Henchmen after Matt personally did research and wasn't able to find any evidence that anybody wanted to know what a *day in the life* of a true Henchman looked like. That was what motivated Jimmie to create the training video list of thirty movies that reflected a day in the life of a Henchman. Matt knew that times were changing after the fateful day at the DMV. David H. was seen as a hero, not a bad guy. Kids that were "misfits" like the Henchmen needed to know that there were other career paths to take. They didn't have to all turn into degenerates with nothing to work toward. After getting to know this team of Henchmen on a personal level, Matt felt proud to be part of helping the fringe kids have hope that there was a place for them to go in this world of too-perfect people.

This was a perfect career for those outsider kids that didn't include hanging out on the streets or being bouncers at the neighborhood clubs. Until working at DMF, Matt never knew there were not-so-big guys working as a subset of Henchmen. The cyber minds were just as important as the meat and muscle guys. Some of those introverted, computer genius, base-ment-living guys could be considered modern day Henchmen as well. The HTA was making Henchman a reputable profes-sion, something these kids had never heard of.

"Quit fidgeting, Davey. You look amazing, and you did the roleplays perfectly," Jace said, using his lint roller on David's shirt.

David H sighed. "Christ, I can't believe I'm doing this. Can you see my pit stains? I'm sweating like a motherfucker."

Matt grabbed David's shoulders with a hand on each shoulder and said, "David, look at me. Focus and breathe. Long, deep breaths. You got this."

David H. groaned and ran his hand through his styled hair, much to Jace's horror. "I don't know who to look at while I'm talking. It was easier with just stupid Susanne there. One set of eyes. This is ridiculous."

Jace quickly combed David H.'s hair back in place. "We practiced this. Look past everyone, no one will know that you aren't making eye contact with someone. You have us to use too. Look just above their heads and remember to hold onto the podium. That will help keep you present."

The school guidance counselor called David's name, and the pain on his face was almost too much to take. Liz, not known for being a hugger, gave David a warm embrace and sent him on his way. Amber gave squeezed David's arm, and Matt patted him on his shoulder.

As he walked to the stage, the applause ceased, and the auditorium became silent. David H. pulled at his collar as if to loosen it up. As instructed, he held on for dear life to each side of the dark wood podium. Matt could see David take a long breath. After the long breath, his face softened, his eyebrows unknit, and his shoulders dropped at least a couple of inches. His transformation was instant, and with that shift, his voice was soft and confident, just like his interview.

"Thank you to the senior class for the invitation to speak to you today. It is quite an honor that you have afforded me today."

"Afforded? Have you ever heard him use that word?" Matt asked.

"No, but it sounds impressive as fuck," Liz said with a wide smile. "He's already got their attention."

Jace had grabbed Amber's hand with both his palms covering hers. He lifted their hands to his heart and beamed as his student worked the room.

David H. began his speech to the senior class with his own experience in high school, how he was an outcast, and how he felt like he had few options with nowhere to go once he graduated. He shared his personal story of how he found the career of Henchman. For a group of sometimes squirrely teenagers, they remained still and seemed enthralled to hear the trials and tribulations David H. had gone through while navigating life after high school, with no real plans on how to make a living as an adult.

Jace, again, was mouthing the words David H. shared with the class. He watched like a proud parent and silently clapped while David H. fielded questions from the curious students.

"So do you, like, kill people too? Like, isn't that illegal?" asked one of the students.

"Kill people? No, we don't kill people, unless, well, they are trying to kill us. It's done as self-defense, kill-or-be-killed type of situation. You may have seen that in the movies or TV. That is a stereotype that isn't accurate. We provide important people with protection. There are lots of important businesspeople who need our specific kind of protection. I will admit that sometimes it can include being physical with people. Just like what you saw on the video of me during the DMV incident," David H. said.

Another student made their way to the microphone in the aisle, and asked, "If you don't kill people, then why do you carry guns?"

"That is a great question. I'm glad you asked that. We don't all carry guns. You can see that today I don't have a gun," David H. said, putting his hands up.

Liz snorted and nudged Matt. "We know that's not true."

Matt tried to hide his laugh. He knew David H. never left the House unarmed. He had an ankle holster on, which wasn't empty.

David H. continued, "Like I mentioned before, we protect people, and sometimes that requires we have weapons. Just like the CIA or the FBI, we also need to be prepared at all times."

David H.'s eyes darted to Matt and Liz, who were standing in the back of the auditorium. That quick glance meant he had reached his limit. Jace didn't pick up on the glance, so Liz gave him a quick elbow to his side. Jace was snapped out of his proud papa moment and marched down to the front of the stage.

"You know, you kids have been a fantastic audience. We are so grateful for the time you have given us, but it seems that Mr. David needs to tend to other Henchman duties. Will you please excuse us?"

Jace motioned for David H. to leave the stage while the guidance counselor gave an awkward dismissal to the students.

Matt hopped back in the driver's seat of the Suburban while the others settled in.

"I will never, ever, fucking do something like that again," David H. said with a cigarette between his teeth. His hands were shaky as he lit it.

"You kicked ass, David. You did it again," Liz said.

"They were mesmerized by you. I like how you talked about yourself too, that made it relatable," Matt said.

"Shut the fuck up. I mean it, I won't do that again," David H. said, blowing smoke out the cracked window.

Jace looked up from his phone and said, "Are you sure?

Already two more schools are requesting you to be their guest speaker."

"We don't have a choice. This exposure is just what DMF is looking for. I'm sorry you didn't enjoy that, but think about this, it was sixty minutes of your time, not too terrible. And without sounding too much like Jimmie, you probably made an impact on those kids," Liz said.

"How come I'm the only one doing this crap? Why doesn't College Boy ever do shit like this, aren't those his people?" David H. said. "He was there too."

"I was, but perhaps you remember I not the leader you were. Look, you are the face of the HTA now. You may as well get used to it," Matt said.

"Trust me when I say that things will just get easier from now on. The first time is always the hardest. You already know what to say, and the questions will probably be the same sort of thing," Jace said.

David H. leaned his head against the window and sighed softly, looking defeated. "I'm just not used to all the attention."

Matt could tell David was shutting down, overstimulated with all of the social interactions that were so foreign to him.

Matt felt a pang of guilt about putting David H. in the spotlight, since he knew this wasn't really his thing. But damn, he did a great job. Maybe they would be able to find a back- up for him too, just to take some of the pressure off.

"Let's change the subject to something way more fun, but ten times lamer," Liz said.

"Oh, that sounds exciting, what are we talking about?" Jace asked, looking up from his phone screen again.

"Do we have to?" Matt asked. He didn't wait for an answer, he knew he would have to tell everyone that he was approved to go out on an official date with Amber.

"Lover boy here is finally going out with Little Miss

Redhead. We are all hoping that it isn't quite as tragic as the first one," Liz sniggered.

"Do tell, do tell!" Jace said with excitement.

Liz recounted the story of the disastrous first date they had where Matt did not follow the very strict safety plan laid out for him, instead got drunk, and was kidnapped by Amber, who was working for as an unaffiliated Henchman hired by an unknown entity. Matt added that the one good thing about it was that she had been able to work the situation so that he wasn't eventually killed by the sloppy Henchmen she was teamed with. Amber had taken out the Henchmen that had kidnapped Matt and made it possible for DMF to track and capture the notorious OT, aka Four.

Jace had his hand covering his mouth while gripping Matt's arm as Liz spoke. "I can't wait to hear how round two goes! Maybe this time you will end up capturing another villain!"

CHAPTER 48
ROUND TWO

There were instructions for this date like there were with the first one, but it wasn't quite as tightly planned since, from what anyone knew, no one had a bounty on their heads. There were still precautions that they had to follow, and they weren't going to totally be alone, but Matt was going to take whatever was offered to him. The plan was for a simple dinner and drinks, and then head back home to the DMF House. Skippy would drive them and wait in the Suburban for them to leave the restaurant. Gabe and Franco had *volunteered* to be in the restaurant while Matt and Amber had dinner. Since they were brothers, it was a treat for them to be able to touch base on what was happening in their personal lives. Having a nice meal while your job is paying is a perk no one would argue with. Since things had been going smoothly, Rossi was in DMF custody, and no one wanted to take ownership, it was deemed a level two threat, meaning they would be able to enjoy a glass or two of wine with their meal.

Matt was nervous with anticipation since asking her out. He wasn't as nervous as he'd been the first time, he had learned a lot since then, but still nervous in the fact his tummy was flipping with excitement.

Liz came to see Matt as he was getting ready. "Hey, you know Vanessa is leaving for Italy in the next couple of days."

Matt was primping in the mirror. "Yeah, I heard that. How's Garrett feeling about that? Is he going to miss her?"

Liz dropped her chin, with an *of course he is* look. "You know she is helping Amber get ready with the girly stuff I know nothing about."

"What's girly stuff, like picking out clothes and shoes?" Matt asked.

"Yeah, shit like that. You know, moral support, kind of like I'm doing here for you now," Liz said.

"Got it, and thanks by the way. It wouldn't be the same without you here. I was thinking that this time, I won't be alone in sticking to the plan. Amber's well aware of it too. That's better odds than what I worked with the last time," Matt said.

"True, and I guarantee that Gabe and Franco won't let anything slide either. The last time was a once-in-a-lifetime, crazy ass thing to happen. I think she's a decent girl, and I hate to say it, but I hope you have fun. Before you go, like last time, we have to pinky swear that you won't stop being my friend if this thing gets any more hot and heavy."

Matt rolled his eyes and held out his hand so they could pinky swear, and said, "Liz, I promise that you will always be my BFF."

Liz put her head down so as not to show the wide grin on her face and said, "Ok, let's get you downstairs so you don't want to keep her waiting."

He and Liz got to the bottom of the stairs when he saw her. Amber was sitting on the very same couch he sat on the first night here. It was the first time he'd had a panic attack. Liz had been with him then too, helping navigate the attack by instructing him to put his head between his legs and take some deep breaths. He was going to have to take some deep breaths tonight as well after he saw Amber. She was wearing a black strapless dress that showed all her best parts. Her well-toned arms and legs, tanned by her recent runs outdoors, added the sun-kissed affect to the whole look.

Liz waited a moment before she spoke. "Well, if you aren't going to say it, I will. Amber, girl, you look amazing."

Amber smiled, putting her head down shyly.

"Sport, do you have something to say?" Liz asked

Matt shook his head, covering his mouth with his hand. "I do. Liz is right, you look fucking amazing."

Amber walked up to him giving him a short but sweet kiss. "Let's get outta here."

As they walked through the kitchen to the car port, he noticed the Henchmen in the kitchen having a late dinner stop what they were doing, watching them walk by. He felt like he was walking with a real-life movie star. One of the Henchmen shouted, "I have no idea what you got that I don't!"

———

The evening could not have gone better.

After Skippy dropped them off, Matt and Amber sat a few tables away from Franco and Gabe.

Matt was proud of himself for the quick-witted conversation he was able to muster all night. He felt like he could be himself and noticed that he hadn't laughed this much in many years. From what he could tell, Amber was also enjoying the night out. He noticed her looking more relaxed and free to also let her guard down. Most the night they held hands across the table. Matt gently stroked her hand as they shared some jokes about their first date. He had so much more to contribute to the conversation now that he had been on errands. Part of their evening was spent talking about various on-the-job stories. Matt even described the night at The Basement, which led to him being at DMF in the first place.

Amber delicately pushed back a strand of her hair, "You know, I don't think I've ever heard that whole story. You poor baby. Knowing you now the way I do, that must have been such a shock to you. I grew up this way, but to go from your normal life to this overnight, I just can't imagine."

"It was pretty stressful, that's for sure. In a way, it seems like I've always been here. I've learned so much about myself. Like, I never would have imagined that I naturally had the killer instinct. The strangest thing is that I still don't feel any guilt about the lives I took."

Amber smiled. "We have that in common. I haven't ever felt guilty either. I struggled with that, wondering if it made me a bad or evil person. It's so nice to be able to talk to someone else about it. It's been so incredible to find someone like you. Someone I was sure I would never find unless I left the job all together. I never thought I could have such deep feelings for someone and just know they are real. I've never met someone as real and genuine as you."

Matt leaned in to kiss her, savoring her smell and taste. "You are just a smidge different than the last girl I asked out. I wonder what ever happened to Catherine from Tailgaters, she just wasn't you."

Amber pointed to her watch and said, "I'm afraid our time's up. We need to be respectful of the rest of the guys since I want to make sure we can do this sort of thing again. And you'll have to tell me all about this Catherine person sometime."

Matt nodded in agreement and pointed to Franco, who was also pointing to his watch, indicating that it was time to head out.

The four paid their checks and headed out, with Franco

and Gabe exiting first, heads on swivels, mostly out of habit, with Matt and Amber following behind.

"You guys shut the place down, we were the last ones to leave. I'm sure you didn't notice, but the waitstaff was getting irritated with us sitting there," Franco said.

Matt proudly put his arm around his date. "Did you guys have a good dinner? We did, right, Amber?"

Gabe patted his fully belly. "We ate like kings, my man."

Franco stopped and yelled, "Go back inside! Matt, take her and go back inside!"

Before anyone knew what happened, Franco, Gabe, and Amber all had brandished their weapons. Matt, who still wasn't comfortable carrying a weapon on a day-to-day basis, felt naked and vulnerable without one.

"What the fuck is going on?" Matt pleaded. As soon as he asked, he saw what caused everyone to react.

The Suburban sat parked where they'd left it, but the person in the driver's seat was not Skippy.

Amber asked, "Who the hell is that? Is he actually pretending to be Skippy? Like we wouldn't notice?"

A man, wearing a dark hoodie, presumably a Henchman, sat inspecting his nails as if nothing was wrong, almost like no one would notice. The three well-trained Henchmen scanned the parking lot to see what clues were left. They spread out across the parking lot, dashing in between the parked cars to make their way closer to the Suburban with the imposter in the driver's seat.

Matt stood and watched the Team expertly take control of the situation. Franco knew Matt wasn't armed, and gave a quick whistle in Matt's direction, tossing him his weapon from his ankle holster.

He caught it and motioned to Franco that he saw something they didn't.

One of the Italian Henchmen that Pinky had spoken to at the gym was coming up from the opposite side of the restaurant. Matt knew he didn't want to shout at them to watch out, thinking it best to let them get to Skippy as soon as possible. Despite having Franco's gun, he'd rather not use it. His weapon of choice, whenever possible, was his ability to sack the shit out of the any unaware Henchman. Matt switched on his game-day adrenaline and jumped up and down a couple of times, like he used to as he walked up to the defensive line during his games with the university. *I'm going to lay you out,* Matt thought. He jammed Franco's gun into his waist band, picking up his pace, until he hit full speed in the direction of the Henchman, and before the Henchman knew it, Matt had hit him with his full force just like he was an unsuspecting quarterback. The Henchman hit the ground hard, with his gun flying out of his hand across the parking lot. Matt hit him with such force that it knocked the wind out of him, leaving him unable to move. They landed behind the row of parked cars, out of sight from any possible questioning restaurant patrons. Matt quickly jumped on top of him and held his hand over the Henchman's mouth, until he was rendered unconscious. Matt ran to grab the unconscious Henchman's gun and joined the others in their search for Skippy.

There were no traces of a struggle, no blood or broken teeth left on the pavement around the Suburban.

"What the fuck? Where did they take him?" Matt asked.

Without a consensus from the group, Gabe marched over to the Suburban to deal with the idiot sitting in the driver's seat. "Does this asshole really think he's fooled us into thinking he's Skippy?".

The imitation Skippy had his hoodie pulled up over his head and was slouched, mistakenly thinking the DMF Team would just hop in the Suburban and that would be that.

"Gabe, wait. Hold on before you get reactive and walk into their game. These guys are the worst! If Rossi has to drug and brainwash Henchmen, at least he could have gotten men who weren't complete tools," Amber said.

Franco gestured for them all to follow her. They walked a few paces away, and Franco said, "Act natural. Follow my lead."

They walked back toward the Surburban so as not to alarm the driver that they suspected anything unusual.

"Do we just hop in like nothing's wrong?" Matt whispered.

Franco held his finger up to his mouth indicating that no one should be talking just now. "We want to make sure nothing else is going on here. We need to listen to cars coming or more footsteps."

Matt smiled and watched as Amber and Gabe went to one side of the Suburban, and Franco to the other. Matt thought it best to follow him.

The sound of breaking glass caught Matt by surprise. The rear window of the Suburban shattered with thousands of tiny pieces of glass landing on the ground below. At first, he wasn't sure if it had been shot out from outside in the parking lot or from the inside the vehicle. There had been no sign of Skippy or anyone else for that matter. The DMF Team crouched to get their bearings and see what their next move should be, when another shot rang out, this time piercing the rear door panel of the Suburban.

"That's got to be from the inside, it must be Skippy," shouted Gabe. "I'm going in."

Without hesitation, Amber had moved to the driver's side and had her gun drawn and pointed at the driver, who seemed to be fumbling with getting the vehicle started.

"*Lentamente, lentamente*, slowly, slowly come out," Amber instructed him. The door opened, and he slid off the seat and fell to his knees. Amber quickly grabbed his arms and twisted them behind his back, holding them in place with her knee, and pushed the butt of the gun into the back of his head.

Gabe opened the back door with cover from Franco to find Skippy sitting upright with duct tape covering his mouth, wrists, and ankles. The Henchman had confiscated all his weapons but did not think to look in the back cargo area, where the DMF Team always stored extra weapons for situations just like this.

Gabe rushed in and gently removed the duct tape from Skippy's mouth. "Dude, are you ok? What the fuck happened?"

"I'm fine. These fuckers made me spill my dinner. I was hungry, those pricks," Skippy huffed. "I knew right off the bat these guys were stupid shits, so I wasn't really too worried. I knew you would come and take care of business."

Gabe continued to remove the remaining duct tape and helped Skippy out of the Suburban. Skippy walked over to the Henchman Amber had pinned to the ground. He kicked the downed Henchman twice, hitting him in the ribs both times. "Fuck you, asshole. I was enjoying my dinner!"

"What were they trying to accomplish? Did they really think we would fall for the imposter driver and hop right in? Was this supposed to be another fucking kidnapping? I'm about done with that shit," Matt said.

The Henchman Skippy had just attacked rolled over on his back, trying to get much needed oxygen back into his body, and said, "Yes, we take you, we get *Signore* back."

"Wow, that's a great plan. Jerks. I'm calling the CUC now. Go ahead and throw them in the Suburban just to get them out of the line of sight. Use their own duct tape on them. The CUC should be here soon to clean this mess up," Franco said.

After the Henchmen were thrown into the back of the

Suburban, Matt asked the group, "Do you think there are more of these assholes floating around, still being loyal to Rossi? How are we going to find them?"

"Hopefully not like this. This was not how I pictured the evening ending. Is it ok if I go speak to them and see if there is anything I can find out?" Amber asked.

"Go ahead, but the CUC will be here, and usually they don't like people even seeing them, much less talking to the detainees," Franco said.

Matt started to walk across the parking lot to the Italian Henchmen with Amber.

Amber stopped abruptly when she realized Matt was walking with her. "What are you doing? Are you following me? Do you think I can't handle this?"

Matt was surprised by the sharpness of her tone. "No, I'm just going with you, not for any reason, it just seemed like the right thing to do. I mean no offense, Amber."

Her gaze was deep with brows tightly knit, "I just don't want you to see me as weak and incapable now. I'm still a hard-core world-class Henchmen, and don't you fucking forget it. Don't say anything to these assholes, I have it under control, got it?"

Matt threw his hands up in the air, and said, "Be my guest, you run this show."

"Just watch and learn. I'm putting my Honeypot act on for them. I'll get so close they will be able to smell my perfume, you know personally how well that works."

Amber spoke in fluent Italian to the two semi-conscious Henchmen. She left the badass, gun-toting persona behind and was now speaking in a soft tone, smiling at them. Matt watched as she got close enough for them to smell her perfume, which made him uncomfortable. She was his, and watching her be a Honeypot, he realized how much he wanted her for himself.

She slowly and gracefully removed the duct tape from their mouths. Matt assumed she did all this because she could lure them into a false sense of security, hoping they would answer her questions. She even climbed into the back of the vehicle and sat with them, showing she was interested in their well-being.

She nodded and touched their arms, making eye contact with each one as they spoke. Matt had fallen for all this schmoozing in the past, he knew the look all too well. When the CUC pulled up, Amber quickly exited the back, jumping into Matt's arms.

"Go to work boys, I got what I needed," Amber said. "Told you I would! Sorry I snapped at you, I was in the zone, and I just couldn't mix the two worlds right there. I hope you understand."

Matt turned his head and gave her a short but meaningful kiss. "You *are* the best."

———

The CUC took over the situation, cleaning up the would-be abduction by clearing the glass off the ground and determining if anyone was in their parked cars watching the scene take place. One even went inside the restaurant, Matt assumed that was to check and see if anyone in there needed to be reminded of what they actually saw take place.

The CUC lead motioned for Franco to come to him. They spoke briefly, and Franco returned and said, "It's time we get out of here. They are going to transfer them into their van. I feel for them."

"Feel for who, then Henchmen or the CUC?" Amber asked.

"I guess both. I just don't know how you get through life being that stupid," Franco said.

"I'll drive back, Skippy, you've had a night," Gabe said as they helped Skippy into the backseat. He was fine, like he said, but they also gave him a pretty good-sized lump on the back of his head.

"Yeah, I'm good with that. My head's not working too well," Skippy said.

Liz was waiting in the kitchen when they arrived back at the house. Her arms were crossed, and she was tapping her foot. Matt knew what type of mood she was in just by looking at her.

"That is *the* last time you two go out, never happening again. I seriously can't believe the luck you have."

"Oh, it wasn't so bad this time, was it Matt? We worked well as a Team. He's going to walk me up to my room to say good night now, isn't that right?" Amber said.

"I think you both deserve at least that," Liz said, giving Matt a side hug before he left.

Amber took Matt by the hand as they slowly walked to her room. It was a sweet gesture that made him feel awkward, but fantastic all at the same time.

"Here we are. I wanted to properly thank you for dinner tonight. I had a lovely time. I hope we can do it again sometime, minus the kidnapping attempt," Amber said, smiling.

"I had a really nice time too. I wanted . . ." Matt tried to speak but Amber pulled him close and gave him a soft, warm kiss.

"Good night, Matt, have sweet dreams," Amber said.

Matt was only able to respond with a quick, "You too," as Amber shut the door behind her.

What a perfect way to end the night, Matt thought as he floated back to his room.

CHAPTER 49
BACK TO BUSINESS

IN THE WEEKS after wrangling the Italian Henchman in the parking lot, the focus of the planning committee shifted to getting the first round of Henchmen approved to join the HTA. The meetings, which had been held regularly each morning after Pinky's, had taken a backseat to having everyone settle back into their lives at DMF. There had been so much upheaval and unplanned jobs that a unanimous decision was made to take a mini staycation at the DMF House. Not having an agenda for a couple of weeks was just what everyone needed to get their energy and excitement back about getting the HTA off the ground.

The morning of the reenergized planning committee, Matt felt pumped to get together in the conference room, which he had found was his comfort zone. He would rather sit in a conference room chair than in the front seat of a vehicle as a number two going to run errands for the day. The simple errands were comfortable enough. The perfection of his one-arm clearing-the-desk move had become his go-to move when visiting new startups. Even after all the time he'd been with DMF, he still couldn't bring himself to wear a shoulder or ankle holster.

Matt was the first to arrive, while Liz and Amber were running late and hadn't changed from their workout at Pinky's when she arrived wearing a sweaty T-shirt and shorts. Matt smiled when they walked in together, laughing and seemingly at ease with each other. It made his life a whole lot easier to have them as friends and not rivals.

"Glad you could make it. Three weeks wasn't enough time off?" Matt laughed.

Amber leaned in and gave Matt a pat on his ass. "Calm yourself, sweetheart. I stopped and grabbed donuts. I'm hoping in the shower, but I'll be right down."

Liz opened the box to show Matt. "Your favorite, the double dipped chocolate with Captain Crunch sprinkles on top."

"Why didn't you say so? That's what I'm talking about."

———

The application invitations had gone out to the affiliated Henchmen's organizations, and the HTA leadership Team was waiting for the deadline to begin the review of each application. There was a steady stream of HTA applications coming in, and that brought a sense of accomplishment to Matt. For once, he was feeling like he was in the right place. Even though he was going to graduate as an actual HTA student with the first class, putting together the HTA was his baby. He sat back watching and listening to the group work and felt a sense of satisfaction that had eluded him up until these final stages of planning.

"Did you say the T-shirts and the other swag have been ordered? I know it's not the most important thing we need to get done, but it does need to get done," Liz said during their planning meeting.

"Yup, that has been done. Amber and I took care of the whole order," Matt said.

"Oh, I bet you did take care of the whole order. How's it going now that all of the *tension* between you two is gone?" Liz asked.

Matt blushed. "There is still tension, but it's not quite the same now. It's more like I'm in a constant state of anticipation about when I get to see her next."

Amber smiled and turned to Liz and said, "I told you. He's so sweet."

"Well, I don't know what to say about that. I'm happy for you, I guess?" Liz said, rolling her eyes. At Matt's frown, Liz added, "No, I mean it. I'm just getting used to the idea. It's been a long, strange start to the relationship, that's for sure."

"I couldn't agree more. We are both well aware of the conditions that were laid out for us. We plan on following the rules of not spending the night in each other's room, for now. And we will limit our time together in the House. And as you know, we are only doing drive-through dinner dates. It seems to be working for now."

Garrett stood in the doorway and said, "So it's true then, you guys are an official couple now. Took long enough. Congrats, man."

"You and Vanessa didn't waste any time. I think that's cool you guys are together. Do you miss her being gone now?" Matt asked.

Garrett slapped a large stack of files onto the desk. "Yeah, it's whatever when she's gone. It's all part of the job. I knew what I was getting into."

Matt's eyes widened at the stack. "Are those all applications?"

Garrett announced that this was just the stack of applications that came in over the weekend. He was responsible for the initial vetting, and if they passed his list of criteria, the applicants were moved to the next phase. Being moved to the next phase meant he would have the applications copied and bound into a small book. These were then distributed to the approval committee for their review. He had also created a scoring sheet for each committee member to attach to each binder. After all applications were received by the deadline set, they would meet again and go over which applicants had the highest scores.

The criteria to be approved for admittance to the HTA included things like length of service at their current organization, specialty skill set, leadership characteristics, an example of how they may have handled a particularly stressful situation, and of course their measurements, and a headshot. There would also be a Zoom call with each candidate to see how well they were able to communicate with other people. They all knew that this could be a particular challenge for many of the Henchmen. It wasn't necessarily a failure if they didn't have great interpersonal skills, but being able to follow social cues was an important criterion to receive a high score.

"These stacks are getting pretty huge. Are you sure you're turning some of them down?" Liz asked.

"Oh, you should see the garbage I have gotten rid of. Yes, I am only giving you the best of the best. It's only a few more days until the deadline closes everything off. I'll be putting a schedule together for each day. I'm hoping we can get them all evaluated in a week or so," Garrett said.

"A week? Holy shit, that's a lot of sitting. Be sure to give us breaks and lots of coffee and food," Matt said.

"I already let the kitchen know that they will need to be providing food to the conference room that week. I've got it covered, dude," Garrett said, giving a peace out sign as he left the room.

"He's such a weird guy. Well prepared, but a weird guy," Matt said.

"No weirder than anyone else, I guess," Liz said when there was a knock on the door.

Paul and Jonesy were waiting outside to be welcomed into the conference room. Their reports on the progress of the chatter on the dark web was always enjoyable for Matt to hear about. He was always happy to spend time with his friends from the good old days. He had seen them transform from goofy guys living in their parents' basements, with marginal jobs, to serious, hard-working, integral parts of the CM Team. They were absolutely dedicated to their roles with DMF, and they were like different people, all grown up and professional.

"I love the work you guys are doing. It is detailed with all the necessary information. Nice work, you two," Liz said. "I'm so glad I thought of bringing you both on!"

Paul and Jonesy both looked at each other, and Jonesy said, "Bro, it wasn't you? You didn't think of us first? That's pretty messed up."

"You know there were reasons for that. I wanted to make sure you both were safe first of all. Things were a little unstable when I first arrived. Thanks, Liz," Matt responded.

"They were right, he can't take any ball busting! We were just fucking with you," Jonesy laughed.

"Oh, funny. Were you talking to David H.? I bet it was him. Anyway, glad you guys are fitting in so well," Matt said.

"Thanks, we are happy here. We better get back to the message boards. But before we go, something a little strange happened that I wanted to pass along. It may be nothing, but where Four is concerned, well, you never know," Paul said.

"You have my attention, what is it?" Liz asked.

Looking at Matt and Amber, Paul said, "Well, the night of your date where the attempted kidnapping was, Four was acting really weird. Not just the usual irritating bullshit, but he was really wound up. He was pacing and talking to himself more than usual. Anyway, he kept looking at his watch, and right at 9:00 p.m., he left. Now, you know that he never leaves. I mean never. There are times we come into the workroom, and he's curled up in a ball on the floor, having never left and spent the night there."

Matt and Liz exchanged confused glances.

"You said 9:00 p.m.? Isn't that when the shit went down in the parking lot? That was the time to leave, right?" Liz asked.

"Wait a minute, you think Four had something to do with that?" Matt asked.

Liz spun her chair to face Matt, and said, "You have to admit, the quality of work was on par with what he would hire and pay for."

"What the fuck would he want to do with all of us?" Matt said.

"How was he when he came back into the room? Could you tell what kind of mood he was in? I know he's not the most emotionally intelligent guy on the planet," Liz said.

Paul and Jonesy looked at each other, and shrugged their shoulders, and both said in unison, "He didn't say a word."

"That little shit set the whole thing up. I'm going to go kick his fucking ass right now," Matt said, standing up quickly and pushing his chair into the wall.

CHAPTER 50
WHAT DID HE DO NOW?

"Not so fast, Sport. Remember, not being reactive is one of the main goals we're teaching at the HTA. We need to have a discussion about this, you can't just go in there with no plan. We need to get some intel gathered first. Cool your jets," Liz urged.

Matt stopped before he got to the door and slammed his hand on the wall. "I guess we don't even know how or if he's involved in this. Paul, how would someone go about finding out the history on Four's computer?" Matt asked.

"For fuck's sake, let's hope he was that arrogant to use the DMF server to hire Henchmen in a kidnapping plot against his own Team. But if it turns out that he did set this up, I'll bet he's going to be sorry," Paul said.

"We took the liberty of looking at what he's been working on. We figured you guys would want that information anyway. We didn't find anything on his DMF system, but we know he's got more set up in his room. We weren't comfortable going in there until we shared this with you," Jonesy said.

"That was smart of you. We need to make this happen without him knowing. I think this is a job for Amber," Liz said, looking at Amber, then at Matt.

Matt nodded encouragingly at Amber. He knew, unfortunately, when it came to Four, Amber was about the only person he seemed to listen to.

Jonsey filled everyone in on the latest possible Four scandal. Everyone knew that Four hated everyone and trusted no one. The only person Four hadn't continuously insulted was Amber. She was as close to a friend as he probably had. They decided that it would be Amber's job to keep him occupied while he was in the kitchen, hopefully even out of the House, but for sure not in the work room. They considered he may have some security software installed that would alert him to people poking around in his personal space.

"Even for me, this will be tricky. Of course, I'm up for it, but you're going to have to give me a minute to think about how to work this," Amber said.

"Is there anything you can bribe him with? I know he used to be a big fan of Starbucks. Could you offer him a Starbuck's trip or something? That may be too obvious though," Matt offered.

It was decided that Amber would get Four's favorite drink, a venti caramel Frappuccino, and dangle it in front of him. She would *accidently* sit next to him in the kitchen, then play dumb that she *forgot* how much Four loved those drinks.

"Look, I will really take one for the Team with this. I will even let him have a sip of my drink. Believe me, that's not something I ever thought I would do, but I will. It just will add to him really craving the Frappuccino," Amber said.

"So, what happens next? Are you going to make nicey nice with him and offer to take him to Starbucks the next time you go?" Matt asked.

Amber smiled back. "Yes, that will be the next move. Don't look at me that way, I'll be fine. I'm a big girl, Matt. When will you figure that out?"

"It would be helpful if you had him *accidentally* leave his phone here too. That way we can be sure there won't be any way to alert him when we find the spyware on his personal computer," Paul said.

"I'll help with that," Liz said. "Shouldn't be a problem. I'll tell him some crap about us needing to inventory it. I won't even try to be sneaky about it. He's rather frightened of me, so I don't think he will put up too much of a fight when I ask."

They were satisfied with the plan, but it wasn't going to be as timely as Matt would have liked. He knew that being patient and getting the best intel on Four was the ultimate goal, so he would bite his tongue and let Amber do her work. In a way, he loved to watch her work, and it made him proud that their relationship was more than just work buddies.

No one doubted that Amber would be able to work her magic with Four. He took the bait of agreeing to accompany Amber on her next trip to Starbucks. For the full effect, Amber had Skippy drive them to Starbucks. Matt and Liz trailed them in a discreet, tinted car. To complete the charade, they pulled two Henchmen, Tyler and Sal, to ride along for the protection factor. Everyone knew Four loved to get attention and to be made to feel like he was important.

Amber made sure that Four sat in the backseat with her. Skippy was instructed to go to a Starbucks that was nowhere near the House. The more time Paul and Jonesy had in his room on his system, the better. Liz was successful in getting the phone from Four, so they knew they had a clear shot and no alarms to alert him of someone working in his system. They knew that if they had at least twenty minutes, they would be able to find the data they needed to confirm Four was guilty of the crime.

Matt was getting tense while watching Amber and Four interact in the car ahead. "She's so good. Do you see that? She's even got him laughing. That's a first. He usually has a sour-puss face. God, I can't stand that she's that close to him, alone in a car."

Liz laughed. "What are you talking about? Do you think she isn't safe with him? Or is it that you think he will whisk her away from you with all his charm and swagger?"

Matt threw himself back in the seat. "I know, I know, I sound like an insecure middle schooler. It's not that at all. I just dislike him so much. I know she's only doing her job."

"Get over it, Sport. You're going to have to learn to leave the personal shit behind if this relationship is going to work. You will have to learn how to separate the two relationships."

"Yeah, I'll work on it. It's an unconventional relationship to begin with."

Matt and Liz kept their distance from Amber and Four, sitting near them but not so much that they could hear what the conversation was about. Whatever they were saying was making Four smile. Matt didn't want to watch, so he faced the opposite direction while Liz gave him a play by play.

Liz spit her straw out of her mouth. "I don't know how she can stand that stupid snort laugh he has going on. Oh no, this is too much. She just gave him the rest of her Frappuccino."

Matt shook his head. "I bet he looks like a puppy getting a treat."

Liz's face scrunched up, "Yuck. Oh, that's a big yuck. She stood to leave she bent down and placed a kiss on the top of his head, barf." Liz held onto Matt's arm. "Don't you dare get up and make a scene. It's work, remember."

Matt took some deep breaths until it was time to leave.

Four stood and strutted to the table where Matt and Liz were sitting with a smug expression on his face.

"How do you like them apples, Precious Prince? Amber had a date with a real man. Did you enjoy watching us? I don't remember you getting a kiss on your first date. I bet there won't be a kidnapping attempt with me. You see, no one likes you, and that's why they want you out of the House. Hope you aren't too heartbroken. Bye for now," Four said, sipping on the long green straw.

Liz put her hand on Matt's shoulder to keep him from standing. "Shut the fuck up, Four, before I let him get up and beat your ass," Liz said.

Four almost ran back to Amber. He interlocked their arms and walked to the door while Amber turned to Matt and mouthed, *I'm so sorry.*

CHAPTER 51

JOKE'S ON YOU

"See you boys later for our dinner and drinks," Liz said as Paul and Jonesy headed back to their work room. They had made it back just in time for Four to walk in and not suspect that they had just spent the last hour and a half playing around on his personal system.

Since dinner and drinks were not a typical night out at the House, food and drinks were brought to the conference room. The team gathered to hear what intel was found on Four's system. Fowler, Jimmie, and Garrett were there as well as the rest of the Team that were involved in the project to take Four down. The Team took food and eating very seriously, the only sounds were silverware clanking on plates.

As soon as the feeding frenzy slowed, Franco was the first to break the food induced silence. "So, how was your date? Did he ever stop talking about himself?" he asked Amber.

"Ugh, I could tell he was nervous at first, and he was rambling on and on about his fish and how much all that costs to take care of. Then it was as if he realized that he was talking too much about himself and strangely enough, he stopped. He just shut it all down. I didn't mind at all, so I began to slowly pry him back open, playing the helpless *girl* who just didn't fit in here. I even threw in a little bit about how frustrated I was with the level, or I should say lack of commitment Matt was giving me."

"It's fine, I will take one for the Team," Matt laughed.

"Don't get me wrong, he's still an awful little shit, but I actually saw a tiny bit of humanness in him. And that's all I'm saying," Amber said.

"Duly noted. Moving on, guys, give us an update on what you found in his computer," Fowler said, taking a sip of his red blend.

"We didn't find anything that either confirms or denies his involvement. We copied all of his chats and made packets for you to look at as well," Paul said while Jonesy handed out the information to the room. "To answer your question, yes, we think he is in contact with Leo, but we also think he's gotten played too. Maybe some catfishing going on. We think he was just venting on the chats to a random, but from what other information we gathered, we think it's been Leo all along."

"Back up, I know I'm old, but what the fuck does catfishing mean? I assume it has something to do with being scammed? I thought you said this guy was smart?" Fowler said.

"Four's smart, but socially, we all know he's not all together with it. I bet if someone is kind to him, and takes an interest in him, he would be all over that," Jimmie said.

"We think that's exactly what happened. So unintention-ally he was giving information about the gossip he'd heard about the DMV incident, and what we planned to do with Rossi," Paul continued. "We think the person he was chatting with pretended to be a girl. *She* spoke with more feminine phrases if you know what I mean, plus her handle is *Hrts&Flwrso6*."

"So, you're telling me he's been unaware he's been passing

some intel onto the asshole Leo? But that he hasn't gone out of his way to share things he shouldn't," Fowler clarified.

"We believe so. We did not find anything that tied him to the latest parking lot incident. The only reference to that was to make jokes about it. But the person he is talking to, *Hrts&Flwrs06*, asked way too many detailed questions. Things that he or she didn't need to know. You can see we have highlighted them in your packets," Paul said.

The Team paged through the packets to read the highlighted areas.

"This just looks like Leo, or whoever, was trying to get details on who the two Henchmen may have been," Franco said.

"This leads me to believe that they did work alone, that Leo was not the one to send them," Jimmie said.

"I agree. The only thing Four is guilty of is being lonely and trying to impress a girl online," Liz said.

"We did as much digging as we could in the short amount of time we had. But what we also did was install some spyware so we will be able to track the chats he has with *Hrts&Flwrs06*," Jonesy said.

"I like that, taking initiative. Glad to have you on our Team. You two can head out now. Thanks again," Fowler said.

"I will have to wait for another reason to kick the shit out of him," Matt said.

The discussion led to debating whether or not Four should be allowed to keep on chatting with Leo, or should he be called out for him feeding information to a random online acquaintance. Because of Paul and Jonesy's quick thinking and adding the spyware, it was decided that Four would be left to his guilty pleasure of chatting on the message boards, and possibly they could use this to their advantage down the line. Amber had already planned her next Starbucks trip with him, which would give them another chance to hop into his online history.

"He must think he's a real ladies' man now, taking Amber to Starbucks, and chatting with what's-her-name online. Maybe he will lighten up a bit. Or that may be just wishful thinking," Fowler said.

"I have faith in humanity, so my vote is yes, but I know I'm in the minority," Jimmie said.

"We still have Leo to deal with. I know that Vanessa is working her magic there, but what's up with him being so secretive? He could just ask us what we plan on doing with him. Why is he going through Four to get his information?" Fowler asked. "Can we get Vanessa to look into that? Have we gotten any updates from her?"

"I would assume that he wants more than Rossi information. He's trying to see what our plans are for him. I'm wondering if maybe we use Four to feed him crap intel. Just to see if we can pull him out of hiding. Vanessa is deep in there, really finding out what the climate is now as far as taking sides, finding out who is loyal to who, that kind of thing." Liz said.

"Let's get Paul and Jonesy to work on creating some fake 'gossip' for him to feed Leo about what we are planning to do with Rossi and with Leo. We just need to sit and let him take the bait," Franco said.

"Look who's catfishing now," Matt said.

CHAPTER 52
PATIENCE

THE ONE THING Matt lacked was patience. He was getting anxious with all the people milling about Pinky's, still suffering from a bit of PTSD himself, and wondering if any of them were the next team wanting to kidnap him. He just wanted the HTA to be up and running with its first class of Henchmen from the outside, Pinky's to empty out, and for him and Amber to have loads more alone time. Finding the right pace for all this transition wasn't what he wanted to deal with right now. He was becoming most impatient when it came to Amber spending her time entertaining Four. That was the hardest part for him. Reflecting back, Four was the OT, the reason Matt had lived in confinement for so long, the real reason he was at DMF to begin with. He knew that the way he got here was nothing he would have ever dreamed of and was glad for the direction his life took, but at the time, he felt more trapped and like he didn't have choices to make regarding his own life. Four could have had him killed if it hadn't been for Amber. He was most looking forward to the official start date of the newest class of the HTA. The affiliates had been narrowed down to thirty. They needed to meet to cut the number to eighteen for the first class. David H. had continued to do public appearances with Jace at his side to coach and encourage, and he had become quite the local celebrity. Despite David H. complaining about the spotlight being on him, he was actually embracing it and making a name for not only himself, but for the HTA.

The Team was having second thoughts about combining the affiliated and unaffiliated in the same classes. No one was able to predict how the two groups would mingle and get along. Most times in the Henchman world, the affiliates were seen as the upper class of Henchmen. Not that it was always the case, there were plenty of asshole affiliated Henchmen. The affiliates had been hand selected by the world's largest organizations and companies. The unaffiliated were the hardcore, sometimes sloppy and careless Henchmen who didn't play well with others. They had no ties to anyone or anywhere, loners. For most of them, they were too arrogant or just bad at their jobs to ever be tied to any particular organization. It would be a strange mix of personality types in the same room. Adding to the possibility of chaos, there may have been times when they were both on jobs, where their job was to kill the other.

The Top Five, William, Gabe, Skippy, David M., and Ricky, all had gone through the core classes taught mostly by Jimmie and Franco and were now ready to be instructors themselves.

The thought of sitting in a room for days deciding who would be accepted into the HTA's first official class did not sound like much fun for Matt, but it also served as a distraction for him. Actually, he was excited to see how the HTA was coming together. The details to get everything up and running was getting to be his full-time job. Matt didn't want to place more work on the kitchen staff at the House, so he hired out a catering company to provide the much-needed meals and snacks to the always-hungry Henchmen.

"Are we sure about the price? Does it seem to be a barrier

for them seeing the value?" Matt asked Garrett as they were getting ready to start the day of reviewing applications.

"Dude, I think it should be twice that. This first class is getting a fucking bargain if you ask me. I don't think we will keep it this low for very long. Do you realize how much money the training they get will save them in the long run? Not as many messy financial payouts and much less property damage."

"That's true. You are seeing the bigger picture, I guess. You know what else will save the money is the group insurance policy we are offering them. My friend Teddy from Tailgaters has all the plans set up and ready for them to be purchased. He said that after this gets rolling, he's going to open his own agency with all the business we will be sending his way," Matt said.

"Nice for him, but we are going to be adding to the DMF stash too. Kind of awesome if you ask me. The NFT hunt is going to start next week, right? Isn't that what I heard?" Garrett asked.

"Yes, they are timing it so that this first class will be just finishing up, and they will start after that, and the cycle continues," Matt said.

"Listen, you went through the HTA, what did you think of it? Was it worth your time? We all know you had a different background, but looking at it, what was the thing you remember the most about your classes?" Garrett asked.

"Honestly, I think what I liked the most about it was learning how to not be reactive when it's not necessary. I think I proved that I have good reaction time, but when I reacted, it was kill or be killed, not just to be sloppy and violent."

"Well, that's the main goal for the HTA. Perfect. I wonder how these new guys will take hearing they will have to take a yoga and meditation class. I'm hoping it isn't a completely foreign concept to them," Garrett said.

"Only time will tell. But I think those couple of classes are going to make the biggest impact on the way these modern-day Henchmen do business," Matt said.

The conference room began to fill with the reviewing Team comprised of the Top Five, Liz, Matt, and Garrett, who had made large packets that sat on the back table. Attached on the top of each file was a scoring sheet to be completed after each file was reviewed.

The coffee trolly was rolled into the conference room along with enough food to get them through until the lunch break. Before everyone took their seats, coffee was poured, and plates were filled. The review group settled in and waited for instructions. The Top Five had become a close-knit group in the past few weeks of training and even attending the first part of the HTA. They all walked with even more confidence and swagger than in the past. Even the shitty, negative comments from William had lessened. It was just in his personality to be a jerk, but he was also looked up to by the rest of the Team. The one aspect of training that hadn't been thought of was how to get the number twos up to speed. With the departure of the Top Five, their number twos had to be trained in a new position. The training was well received, with them appreciating a promotion when such a thing had never really been a possibility. Before, the only way to get promoted was when the number one retired or died.

"Welcome to the first ever review committee meeting. This is the first of many, and the first steps in changing the way modern day Henchmen do business. This is going to be really exciting," Liz said.

Garrett handed out the first round of packets around the table and gave instructions on what to look for, red flags, strengths, etc. Once they were done reviewing, they would score, then discuss with the group.

"You know what you are looking for in qualities of a Henchman, so take your time shifting through the packets," Garrett instructed the group.

———

The first-day vibes were way more upbeat and positive than they were the last few days. Being stuck in the room with the same people every day became tiresome. Throughout the week, each day the piles became smaller and smaller, and on the last day when the last packet was scored there was a collective sigh coming from the group. Some of them just got up and walked out, others cheered, others gave their neighbor a high five. "Thank Christ we're done with this bullshit. I wouldn't come back another day. My feedback is that there are too many days in a row. I'm fucking fried right now," William said.

"I hear that. We can get back to a normal schedule now. I'm glad I don't have to deal with the NFT hunt, I'm done being an administrator. Definitely not my gig," Ricky said.

"If we end up having to do this again, I'm not sitting in here all day, no offense, but I need to not sit in the same room day after day," William said.

"You guys are so grumpy! I was going to ask you to stay a while and work with us some more on the NFTs. Just kidding! You guys did great! I guess we will see who we end up with from the NFT search," Liz said.

"There won't be this type of vetting for them, no worries. We are going to hand them off to you as-is. You guys get to shape them into the Henchmen they will become," Matt said.

"I hope we don't end up with any as bad as you were!" William laughed.

CHAPTER 53
LET THE GAMES BEGIN

Four and Amber had continued to meet regularly either in the DMF kitchen or get Skippy to drive them to the Starbucks for a quick coffee and chat. Matt had given up on being over possessive of her time and knew that as soon as the HTA was up and running his schedule would allow for them to go on more of their own dates. For now, it was going to have to wait. Amber was at the point where Four started to talk about his parents, which no one could fathom raising him as a child. It was the perfect time for Paul and Jonesy to continue to monitor Four's personal computer as well. Amber and Matt had a long conversation about her continuing the coffee dates. Amber was quick to remind him that she and Four were having coffee, but Matt was getting way more than that since they were spending almost every night together. He'd even left a toothbrush in her room.

It took Paul and Jonesy a couple of weeks of tweaking after they found the perfect set of ex-DMF Henchmen to be the holders of the QR code both Europe and the United States. It was all coming together, the applications were approved for the new class, and the graduation certificate search was set. There was some confusion on a couple of the clues, but those had since been fine tuned. "I'm feeling good about this whole set up. Paul and I had a great time working with everyone to get the purple ticket NFT set up. I kind of want to go on the search too," Jonesy said looking up from his screen.

Four stood in the corner giving them dirty looks through squinty eyes. Matt tried to ignore him, but when Four's screen saver popped on the screen, he wasn't able to keep his mouth shut, despite Liz's urging. The screen saver was a picture of Amber. The pictures changed every couple of seconds, with each one a slide was a new picture of Amber. There were even a couple of both Four and her during one of their Starbucks dates.

Before Liz could interfere, Matt had his right hand on the throat of Four. It wasn't that he was squeezing tightly that was making Four squeal, it was the look in Matt's eyes.

"No one had ever seen me lose my shit, but there's always a first time," Matt said through a clenched jaw. The slideshow of Amber on Four's screen had sent him into a rage. "Dude, I think you crossed the line this time. I think he has every right to choke the life out of you," Liz said shaking her head at Four.

Matt had never been able to confront Four for the shitshow he had made of his life, the threats to his family and friends, all of it. The slideshow pushed him over the edge from his normally calm, chill personality. In his normal state of mind, he would have laughed at the absurd notion that Four and Amber would ever be a couple. Was this triggering him because he was also played by Amber? Had he ever really processed that with her?

Liz calmly watched as Four struggled to free Matt's hand from around his throat by trying to pull it off and aimlessly swinging at him. Paul and Jonesy sat in silence, not knowing what to do. All Matt saw was red and all he felt was rage. He'd killed people before, but with a gun, not with his bare hands.

"He's not worth it, Sport, let him go. I know why you're pissed, but let him go. This isn't the way to handle him," Liz said in a soft, calm voice.

Matt didn't acknowledge her. His eyes trained on Four, the grip getting tighter, until he heard Amber's voice. She gently placed her hand on his left shoulder, and said, "Matt honey, let's forget this for now, ok? How does that sound?"

It took Matt some time to realize what he was doing and to act on her request to let him go. It was as if he came back into his body. He took a deep breath in and removed his hand from Four's throat. Four dropped to his knees and began to cough and wheeze. Paul and Jonesy went over to see if he was ok and tried help him up.

Four crawled away from them and went to the corner of the room he sat in when he was feeling unsafe and said, "Back off! Leave me alone! That guy is a psycho. There was no reason for that, I guess you really are threatened by me taking your girl! Don't forget, I saw her first! I hired her to kill you!"

Matt shook with anger, his fists clenched and his jaw tight. He had enough sense left to realize he needed to get out of the room because there would be a breaking point, where nothing Liz or Amber could say would stop him from really hurting him. He turned to leave the room, as the others waited to see what his next move would be.

"You worthless piece of shit, go fuck yourself," Matt spat on his way out.

Liz followed him, putting her arm around him, and one hand on his chest. "You did good there, really good. I let you go just far enough. He knows you're serious now. Are you ok now? Shake it off."

Amber met up with Liz and Matt a few minutes later.

"Well, he totally deserved that. I think I calmed him down some. He's like a child. All you have to do is promise him something he likes, and he's fine. I told him we would go and buy a new fish."

Matt took a deep breath and averted his eyes from Amber. "I need some space, I can't talk with you right now," he said.

"Oh, I didn't realize you were that upset. Is it with me, or about me?" Amber asked. Confusion was all over her face.

Matt couldn't speak, so Liz said, "I think that's part of what he needs time to figure out."

"We can talk later then," Amber said, rubbing Matt's arm before she left.

"Thank you for saying that," Matt said to Liz. "I just need to cool off. I guess this is what happens when you stuff your emotions and don't deal with them. I didn't know I still needed some closure on the whole, Amber was hired by Four to kill me thing," Matt said. *Fuck, I thought I had moved past her kidnapping me and working with Four. This really fucking triggered me.*

"For what it's worth, I thoroughly enjoyed watching you scare the shit out of him. I really did get so much pleasure from it. And yeah, starting a relationship with someone who was hired to kill you and not talking about it, not the healthiest thing," Liz said.

"Live and learn, live and learn. I need a fucking drink. But before we do that, did the NFT hunt get started? I blacked out for a few minutes."

Liz nodded. "It's up and running. The CM Team is going to handle it from here. They have been trained and are taking shifts so anytime someone needs a new clue, they are there to give one. They are tracking any and all movements so they can keep the targets holding the NFT informed."

"Ok, that is fucking cool. I can't wait to see how it turns out.

Thank you for not letting me act even more out of control. That was a little embarrassing," Matt said.

"That's what friends are for. You better get your shit together and go talk to Amber before she runs off with Four," Liz said.

CHAPTER 54
THE FRESHMAN CLASS

THAT MORNING the affiliated Henchman began to arrive at the DMF House. The rest of the DMF Team were allowed to stay at their own homes instead of the House, which was tradition while they were working. The eighteen new HTA students were bunking two to a room, and sharing a bathroom, which to some felt like less-than-ideal accommodations. This group, now called Class One, were coming from some of the richest and most powerful businesspeople in the world. Despite the DMF House being first-class, having to share a room, much less a bathroom, was shocking to some. The move was strategic, using it as a way to bond, and to have a classmate close by to practice some of the new skills they would be learning with.

The new levels of testosterone were palpable, and it was making some of the new students on edge. They spent time sizing each other up and trying to mark their territory. Jimmie thought it best to have a House meeting to try and slow down some of the reactive responses to the new environment they were thrown into. The meeting was set to be held in the GCR, Global Conference Room, the largest meeting space in the House that was located on the other side of the House, across the atrium.

Walking with Liz to the GCR, Matt stopped and pointed to the place on the wall in the atrium where many months ago, when he was still trying to figure out his place in the House, David H. nearly broke both his arm and his nose. "I have come a long way since that day. Jesus, I never want to feel that out of place again," he said.

"I forgot about that. You were so lost!" Liz said. "I see you haven't had your talk with Amber yet. When are you planning on doing that, Sport?"

"Let me guess, you were in the Viewing Room last night? I thought I was done being spied on at this point. CCTV in a House should be illegal," he said.

"I was just messing with you. I saw her this morning at the coffee bar. She told me she would be patient for you to come to her when you are ready, no pressure. Your hallway is not a priority now with Class One here, silly," Liz said.

"Well, that's good to know. My shift in the Viewing room is coming up soon too. Hope it's entertaining." They stopped at the doorway to watch. All of Class One was already seated. None of them were seated next to each other, instead, they were scattered across the rows of chairs. "Jimmie won't let that go for too long," Matt said.

Matt was correct. As Jimmie called the meeting to order, Class One became attentive and respectful to Jimmie as he spoke. Matt overheard one of the students say, "I heard this guy is a badass. He doesn't look like much, but he knows all kinds of killer moves."

"His best move is the Death Stare, I'd say," Matt whispered to Liz. "Simple, but effective, and it works on me every time."

Jimmie started off by welcoming Class One to the HTA, while stressing the importance of the flagship class. He stressed the importance of them understanding their responsibility to carry what they learned into the world. Fowler was next on the agenda to speak. Matt noticed that he seemed preoccupied, or was it nerves? He wasn't sure. Fowler gave the same sort of speech, but in a more Fowler way, with a lot of fucks and other salty language that Jimmie tended not to use.

Garrett had made orientation packets for the Class and passed them out. It had been explained to them in their original acceptance letters that, for possible conflicts of interests, they would not be using their real names while attending the HTA. They were all simply given a number as a name, anywhere from one to eighteen. It was stressed that the numbers handed out came auto generated and had nothing to do with anything but that.

As expected, Jimmie had them all move up into the first two rows, not necessarily next to each other, but closer to the front of the room. The uncomfortable Henchmen looked around at each other before moving to a new seat. The sizing each other up felt like an MMA pre-fight stage show. As they settled in, Jimmie asked them all to take some deep breaths and went onto explain the importance of taking deep breaths, and that they would be learning more about that in their mindfulness and meditation classes. As he continued on, the room's vibe began to soften, even some laughter could be heard down the hall.

"He's quite talented when it comes to putting people at ease, isn't he?" Matt said as he and Liz continued to walk through the atrium.

"He wasn't always like that," Liz laughed.

———

The kitchen looked different the first day of classes. There were no suits to be seen, only Class One in their new HTA uniform of T-shirts and sweatpants. After meeting one-on-one with Jimmie, most of them had relaxed and seemed less defensive. The tables were filled with them talking and joking with each other. During the initial planning phases, it was mutually agreed upon there was no way they could use the number Four with anyone else, that number would be eliminated from all classes going forward.

"At least the food here is amazing. I'll give them that," said Ten, one of the Class One group.

Skippy had arranged to have them driven to the HTA each morning, making sure he scheduled extra drivers and that no one else checked out the Suburbans.

"I never went to summer camp, but I think this is what it must have been like," Sixteen said, piling into the Suburban.

Franco and David H. were at the HTA to greet and welcome the new students. Pinky was back to her regular gym duties and was assigned to help distract the more-than-usual crowds to not pay attention to the gigantic men filing into the classrooms. At least for the first few days, Amber had volunteered to be a Honeypot by working out in skimpy, inappropriate workout clothes while the students were arriving and leaving for the day. It was a raunchy thing to have her do, everyone agreed. But it did the trick. She was a distraction to the regular gym members to keep them from paying attention to the HTA students roaming the halls at Pinky's.

The students would be meeting three days a week with homework given to do on the other days. They were encouraged to come prepared to participate while in class. Jimmie had prepared them for this request in orientation by reminding them that this wasn't high school, acknowledging that many if not all of them may have had shitty experiences the last time they were in school. Matt was asked to speak during the first class. It became apparent most of the new HTA students knew something about his backstory, and how the HTA came to be.

Liz was there to go over their schedules and which specialty tracks they had been assigned to. When the class heard she was the boss's daughter, there was mumbling throughout the room. "Do you have something to say?" Liz asked the room.

"I do, I guess. Your reputation precedes you. All I have ever heard about you is that you are a badass, that you have no fear, that you are fucking great at your job, and that you earned the reputation. You didn't trade your father's name in for your success," Nine said.

"I've heard the same thing," Sixteen added.

"She is amazing. I can tell you a story about her from the first night I was here," Matt said. "I'll save that one to tell you over beers one night."

Pinky came to speak to the class to encourage them to use her gym after class.

Number Twelve raised his hand and asked her, "Don't I know you from somewhere? Didn't you used to work in Europe? I swear I did a couple of jobs with your Team."

Matt noticed for the first time, Pinky looked unsure of what to say. Her quick wit kicked in, and she answered, but not really answered, "I get that all the time! I must have a doppelganger out there is all I can think of!"

So Pinky could be rattled, interesting.

CHAPTER 55
A SURPRISE GUEST

THE START of week six at the HTA meant the core classes were complete, and they were now in the specialty tracks section. Most days, the class would stay and work out at Pinky's, which always put a smile on Pinky's face. If anything, Pinky was the ultimate hostess at heart. She loved to entertain them, and flirting was her specialty. Matt was back at his front desk duties, since he was only required to take the core classes, life was good for him. He and Amber had begun to pull back the layers of their relationship, and it was going as well as could be expected. There was a lot to sort through, but he was satisfied with the progress they were making.

Matt noticed that Benji, who was back on door duty, was intently looking into the parking lot from behind the tall plant. His hand was already on his holster when Matt walked over to him.

"Hey buddy, what's up? What are you looking at?"

Benji didn't respond at first, he was keenly focused on the three black SUVs that pulled up into the parking lot. "They have been sitting there for a few minutes. No one has gotten out yet. But I don't know who the fuck they are. Can you call for some backup? And the CUC, I have a gut feeling this could be bad news."

"Shit, yes, of course. I'm on it," Matt said, quickly pulling out his phone and sending nine-one-one texts to a group chat set up for just this type of emergency.

Class One was just finishing up their morning session, and some were making their way out to the gym floor for their mid-day work out, when Benji shouted to the group to go back into the HTA. Since the five rules of being a Henchman were taught the first day, they knew exactly what that meant. Rule number five was, *know your role, stay in your lane.* Matt noticed the group looked confused as it they weren't sure if they were being tested, or if some real shit was about to go down, but they left nonetheless.

Matt could now see why Benji called for them to go back into the classroom. Exiting the SUVs were twelve Henchmen, at least they were the size and suited as a traditional Henchmen would be. They were headed to Pinky's front door.

The army of men waited for another to join the front of the group. Matt blinked in shock. It was Four. Four was leading the group into the front doors of Pinky's, having to jog to keep up the fast pace and be the first one to throw open the doors.

"What in the fuck is he doing? Liz! Come here quick, get a load of this," Matt said.

Liz was already standing next to him. "I saw them on the security cameras. I have people headed here right now. Good move to have Class One back in the HTA, maybe they won't know we have extra men if needed."

Four got to the door and stopped, looking like he thought Benji or Matt would open it for him. When they didn't, the Henchman behind him shoved him out of the way.

All twelve Henchman and Four were now inside Pinky's looking ominous, all wearing dark sunglasses and not saying a word. Even Pinky looked anxious and not her cheerful self that ordinarily greeted new members as they arrive.

Matt watched Franco come to the window of the HTA, looking at the strange group through the window into Pinky's. They made eye contact, and Matt shook his head, indicating that Franco stay. He could be a much-needed element of surprise.

Liz was the first to speak. "Can we help with something? Are you fellas lost?"

The Henchman who was closest to her walked over, a little too close for anyone's comfort. Liz quickly put her hand up and said, "Hey, personal space, back up."

In a thick Italian accent, the man removed his sunglasses, and said, "Ah, you must be Liz, it is a pleasure to finally meet you. My name is Leo, and we are here to start classes at your HTA."

Liz crossed her arms. "Ok, so you are Leo, the same Leo that took over for Rossi, while he is indisposed."

"That is correct. You see, we all have been approved, accepted to be in your HTA," Leo said waving pieces of paper that looked like a printout version of the acceptance letter. "We want our spaces here as promised. We will be your second set of students to be trained. We know the first group is complete, so it is our turn. You know we have traveled a long way. It would be rude to make us wait any longer," Leo said.

"You little fuck," Matt shouted, looking at Four. "You filled out their applications with false names and information. I should have broken your fucking neck when I had the chance."

Four giggled. "You shouldn't have disrespected me. That's what you get. And come on guys, how dumb do you think I am? You had your stupid little friends come in and hack into my computer in my room, what a joke. You keep underestimating me, and now you're going to be destroyed because of your continued stupidness. I literally left that basic computer set up in my room for you to find. I have been working underground, stealth like. I have a whole other set up that no one even knows about. You are such jerks."

Benji reached for Matt, who was still trying to put all the pieces together.

"Mr. Four here has been very helpful to me. You see, I have offered him a lot of money to help me. He was very generous with the clues and other information," Leo said.

"What other information?" Liz asked.

"We heard some nasty little rumors about your father thinking it would be a good plan to take over what is now mine. You see, I don't like that. I have worked hard to have all of this. Segnor Rossi and I have come to an agreement about his retiring. At first, he wasn't certain that was the direction he wanted to go, but as you see, he's had a change of heart," Leo roared, pointing to his men standing behind him. "I think it's much better if I take what you have!"

"That's not going to happen, you smug asshole," Liz said.

"We will see about that," Leo said, and shouted to his Henchmen, "*Andate*Go!"

In an instant, guns were drawn. Not just the Italians', but everyone in sight had a weapon brandished. There were too many hands with itchy trigger fingers to know who took the first shot. Was it the Italian Henchmen? Or had Franco seen this coming and struck first? Matt saw Four run to the back hallway. Through a hail of gunfire, Matt chased Four to the now empty Classroom A.

"Now, you are mine, and I am going to kill you with my bare hands," Matt said, shutting the door behind him.

"You would be better off not doing that Precious Prince, my dad will come after you with vengeance!" Four shouted, cowering in the corner.

Matt kept coming toward him. "I don't care who your *dad* is, this is the end of you."

Four shrieked as Matt grabbed him by his shirt. He was ready to smash his face into the wall when he heard the door open.

"My son, there you are."

Matt's mouth fell open. "Rossi?"

CHAPTER 56
WHO'S YOUR DADDY?

"Papa!" shouted Four. "You have to save me. He's hell-bent on killing me! You have to protect me!"

Rossi rushed to his son and embraced him, stroking his cheek and whispering words Matt did not understand. Four stood sniveling and shaking.

Matt was simultaneously trying to process the scene playing out in front of him and listening to occasional gunfire from Pinky's main room. From what he could tell, most people from the HTA had taken cover, which left the Italians standing in the middle of the room. With a quick glance to the main room, he could see them standing in a circle with their backs to each other, Leo in the center cowering. Quickly switching focus to the shit show in front of him, he assessed his options. Again, wishing he would just get over himself and carry a weapon on him, he would have used it already without hesitation on both these two assholes. Physically, he knew he would be able to take them both, but, in all honesty, he had never taken someone's life with his bare hands.

Matt knew this was his mess to take care of. He trusted Franco's leadership and the training of the ten or so HTA Henchmen hidden out of sight from the chaos, plus he knew the CUC were on their way, or may even be here already. In an instant, he got the familiar tingle he would get right before making a solo tackle on the football field. Without hesitation, Matt took one step back and ran full speed right into the pair. His arms wrapped around Rossi, sending them both to the ground. Four squealed and ran to the far side of the room. Matt expertly pulled Rossi up to his feet, putting him in the powerful, well-known classic Henchman hold, arms twisted behind his back neck twisted in an unnatural position.

Before anyone spoke, the shots from the main room pulled their attention away from who had the upper hand in their personal skirmish. Matt was desperate to see what happened. Liz was out there, for God's sake. He thought about throwing Rossi back to Four to run out and see who was in control. Rossi was sobbing louder than any man should, but Matt dragged him closed to the door. The first person he saw was Liz. She was standing. *Thank God.* What surprised him the most was the fact that half of the Italian Henchmen lay dead, with the other half in zip-tie handcuffs, and there was no CUC Team in sight. The HTA Henchmen, along with Franco, had taken control without so much as a plan or warning about how to resolve this deadly situation.

As Matt turned back to Four, what he saw was familiar although not expected. Four was standing holding a handgun with both his hands pointing it at Matt. He was sweating, and his glasses kept sliding down his face, where he would quickly push them back up with his forearm.

Rossi shouted through his sobbing, "My brave son, I knew you would save us."

Matt tightened his grip on Rossi. "Shut the fuck up. You did see what happened out there, right? Your old pal Leo is sitting in his piss-stained pants in handcuffs, and your lousy team of Henchmen are either dead, or will be soon. Your pathetic son isn't saving you, you stupid old man."

Four wiped the sweat off his brow and spoke in a whiney, but sinister tone, "No one talks to my papa like that. I'm in control here now. You will do as I say, do you hear me?"

"Like I said to your old man, shut the fuck up. I've seen what poor aim you have. I'd be surprised it you even had the safety off the gun."

It happened in an instant. The safety was off, Four pulled the trigger, the gun was loaded, and Rossi went limp. Matt struggled to keep hold of his body, but knew it was a built-in shield if Four shot again. Which he did, over and over until the shells were spent. Matt felt the bullet tear into his bicep, he never felt pain that seared like that did. Rossi's body was riddled with bullets. Four stood shaking, dropping the gun to the floor. He was an even worse aim than the last time he shot at Matt. Having just shot his own father between the eyes and killed him, for once he was speechless.

Matt lost his grip on Rossi, and they both slid to the floor. Matt fumbled to push Rossi's dead body off him, bleeding heavily. He slipped in a puddle of blood trying to get up in time to pounce on Four.

"You fucker, you are a dead man," was all Matt said before his world went dark.

ALSO BY L.K. URBAN

The Henchman Training Academy 1: Evolution

Find out how Matt got involved with the Henchmen and began the evolution!

The Henchman Training Academy 2: Expansion

Rally behind Matt and the rest of the gang in this epic sequel.

NOTE TO THE READER

Dear reader,

Thank you for taking the time to read book 3 of The Henchman Training Academy series.

If you are wondering about how Fowler and Jimmie met, or wanting to know more about Matt, Liz, Amber, Franco, or anyone else, sign up for my monthly newsletter to receive more character backstories, and other adventures of the DMF Henchman Team. Visit LKUrbanAuthor.com to join the HTA.

It would mean a great deal if you could leave me a review on Amazon and Goodreads, and of course, spread the word.

Remember, listen to that quiet voice that is whispering to you. Follow it, see where it takes you, this is your truth, speaking to you. It is always there; we just don't hear it after a while.

Follow me @LKUrbanAuthor on Facebook, @LKUrbanAuthor on Instagram, and @LKUrban on TikTok for more content.

With love,

L.K.

ABOUT THE AUTHOR

L.K. Urban is a dreamer, writer, and adventurer.

She lives in beautiful Colorado Springs, Colorado, close to her four wonderful children.

Upon becoming an empty nester and entering into the pandemic of 2020, L.K. became one of many quarantine writers. Thanks to COVID, her first series, *The Henchman Training Academy*, was born and fulfilled her lifelong dream of becoming a published author.

In addition to being a creative, L.K. also holds a license as a Marriage and Family Therapist and is a working practitioner.

You can find her at:

LKUrbanAuthor.com

Or find her on social media.

facebook.com/LKUrbanAuthor

instagram.com/LKUrbanAuthor

tiktok.com/@LKUrban

www.ingramcontent.com/pod-product-compliance
Lightning Source LLC
Chambersburg PA
CBHW021223310726
48971CB00006B/1667